BULLET PROOF

K.M. MORONOVA

Published by Bloom Books, an imprint of Sourcebooks
1935 Brookdale RD, Naperville, IL 60563-2773
(630) 961-3900
sourcebooks.com

Cataloging-in-Publication data is on file with the Library of Congress.

The authorized representative in the EEA is Dorling Kindersley
Verlag GmbH. Arnulfstr. 124, 80636 Munich, Germany

Manufactured in the UK and distributed by
Dorling Kindersley Limited, London
001-360858-Apr/26
CPI 10 9 8 7 6 5 4 3 2 1

ALSO BY K.M. MORONOVA
FROM BLOOM BOOKS

DARK FORCES STANDALONES
Leave Me Behind
Bulletproof

DARK FORCES DUET
Your Knife, My Heart
My Blade, Your Back

For those who would entertain choosing
the dark path over the light.

PLAYLIST

Super Bass—Nicki Minaj

Thunderclouds (Lost Frequencies
    Remix)—LSD (feat. Sia,
    Diplo, & Labrinth)

Never Forget You (Price & Takis
    Remix)—Zara Larsson

Titanium—David Guetta (feat. Sia)

Perfectly Wrong—Shawn Mendes

orpheus—mgk

Automatic—The Lumineers

Poison—David Kushner

Softcore—The Neighbourhood

Dancing After Death—
  Matt Maeson

Innocence—Nathan Wagner

Love Is Going to Kill
    Us—David Kushner

CONTENT WARNING

This book is for an adult audience. The MMC is a bully and calls the FMC derogatory names.

Explicit language, gore, bullying, self-harm, mentally ill characters (explicit thoughts of mental illness and poor self-image), suicidal ideation, human experimentation, domestic abuse, attempted murder, murder, military operations (guns, violence, missions), ideation of the black market (underworld), and deeply flawed characters that entertain dark thoughts on life and death may be disturbing to some readers.

There are depictions of altering scars (self-harm) in this book. Do not do this at home.

Bane Falls is not a real town in Montana and is fictitious.

PROLOGUE

ROMAN

A promise can look like a lot of things.

It can be simple—a job, a reward—but a promise from the general of the Dark Forces looks a lot like freedom. One card that will set our villainous hearts on a path toward a normal life once more.

But that's the catch, isn't it? Because nothing is normal after your time in the Dark Forces.

"I'm getting too old for these games to continue dragging out like they are. I want the gatekeepers of the underworld hub in Bane Falls to be surveilled extensively for a year. They're the 'upstairs' organization called Sub-Rosa, and I want you to intricately weave yourselves into this corrupt little town. Befriend the contacts and gain their trust. I will update you with further orders as time progresses."

General Nolan moves slowly around his desk and organizes

his documents in a manila folder before he lifts those dark eyes at me. A devil's gaze.

He drawls on, "It's taken years for me to gain approval for a test squad like Icarus. You and your assigned team will be free to roam the town and set a perimeter around it. You'll get that taste of freedom you crave, Syxx. It might even be yours someday if you can prove yourself in this mission. Or you might see how ugly it really is out there and finally understand where your dark heart belongs."

I study the general carefully. His gray hair is disheveled today, which means he likely got some shit news from one of the other squads who flopped on a mission.

I know better than to ask what's above my rank. But why is he trying to put together Icarus now of all times? I've only been a lieutenant in the Dark Forces for two years and only two as a sergeant before this. When he first brought up the prospect of a test squad, he mentioned that I would need at least five years in a commanding role.

Something has him in a hurry.

But what?

I narrow my eyes at him and take a long sip from the bourbon he poured me. "You know, I don't like testing things, Nolan. I'm either doing this and ending my campaign with the Dark Forces, or I'm not doing it at all." My tone is flat. Why he thinks I'd want to stay here forever is beyond me.

I'm fucking tired too—we all are.

General Nolan looks at me with indifferent eyes, ones I've observed and replicated in my own expressions because if he's in charge, I want to do what he's doing. If I have to be down here, I might as well be in charge of the grunts. He got to the top somehow. I'd bet it's his seamless lies—little drops of poison that he trickles throughout his grand design.

Lies that weave hope for the weak.

But lies are fruitless. Eventually, your troops will starve and there won't be anyone left to lie to.

"I thought you'd say that." The general chuckles and unlatches the pistol from his waist. He lines it up with my forehead and walks toward me until the metal is burning my skin.

I crack a grin and shut my eyes as I take another careless sip of bourbon. "I can't be tempted with death, sir. You know that." *It probably wouldn't even kill me*, I muse with a chuckle.

Nolan is quiet for a few seconds before he laughs and pulls the gun back. "You don't even flinch. You never have." I blink up at him boredly. "Can you be tempted with vehicles and housing of your choice, then?"

My eyes widen, and I run my tongue over the bitterness the alcohol left behind on my teeth. "Now you're talking, general." I extend my hand, and we shake on it.

"There may be innocent casualties along the way. Anyone who isn't a part of the mission and gets too close or suspects anything gets terminated. This mission must be successful. I don't care how you do it, Lieutenant, I just want it done. Got it?"

Ah, so that's why he chose me.

He knows I have a knack for not giving a shit if randoms get in the way.

Even the pretty ones.

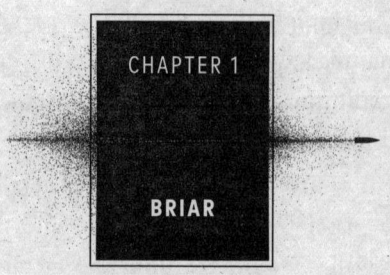

CHAPTER 1

BRIAR

My shoulder still burns where Callum impaled me with that knife. It's been three months since I've been on the run from him. Ninety days since my life took another fall into tragedy, only this time I've fallen into a hole I'm not crawling out of. Not unless I can outrun my past.

Thank God my estranged uncle's estate attorney called me when he did. The highlight of my shitty summer is being told that my last blood relative is dead.

Look, I'm not saying I'm happy about it, but it may have saved my life.

Ideally, I'd rather be in another country. I need to get as far away from Seattle as I can, and a small town in Montana isn't going to cut it for long. Although, it might be the perfect place to hide out during the late summer and fall months while I save up.

Who looks at small towns anyway? I doubt they have accurate records of literally anything. *Callum won't find me here.*

I squint at the old, worn-down sign that reads "Thornton Farm" and let out a sigh. It has to be pushing eleven p.m. already, it's fucking raining outside, *and* I just spent the last two hours lost in this godforsaken town. There's no cell service out here, and it's pitch-black outside. Every road and cornfield looks the same. I never thought I'd end up in the thick of farming town, but sometimes life takes you to strange places.

My fingertips drum against the steering wheel. If not for my fear of Callum discovering I'm still alive, I never would've agreed to this. I know it's an irrational fear, but what's that saying about it being a small world and Murphy's Law? If something can go wrong, it certainly will go wrong. It doesn't help that his work was in hacking into security systems and surveillance. I never knew exactly what it was he did, but I knew it involved finding people.

I'm a city girl, always have been and always will be. In fact, I've never set foot outside of Seattle. Why would I when the city has everything a girl could need? The thought never even crossed my mind to live out here in the countryside long-term, yet something deep inside my chest warms at the change in environment.

But I have a plan: Sell as much shit as I can. Get the money for a plane ticket. Leave and never look back. Then I won't have the looming fear of running into Callum.

No one would even know I'm gone…because there's no one left to look.

A small voice in my head nags that it will be worth the risk of staying in one place for at least a month or two, but I doubt I'll find anything of too much value in my uncle's things. This entire property is in shambles, at least that's what I can make out in the dark.

The attorney was clear: The entire property has to be cleaned up before I can sell it. I'm hoping this takes a few months at most, but from what I see in the dark, it might take much longer. I groan and press the palm of my hand to my forehead.

From the attorney's notes, it didn't sound like there were any animals, just crops, which is a fucking blessing. From what I know, there's a ranch hand that helped my uncle manage the property, so I'll get him to help as much as he can. I'm hoping he takes IOUs because there's no way I can pay him for labor until I sell the place.

My frown grows the farther down the driveway I get. The wooden fence posts are sagging in their centers from rot, the dirt road is overgrown with weeds and grass, and the house at the end of the driveway could literally be haunted. Its chipped paint and warped siding give it a foreboding look that screams *run*. Gray, long-worn deck planks don't add any charm either.

Is this where I'm going to be trapped for the foreseeable future? I groan and purse my lips.

I could kick myself for being so naïve. Why did I believe for a second that my uncle could be secretly rich? A farm shouldn't be this much work to fix. What the hell was he doing all this time? What did he even farm?

It doesn't matter. I sigh my frustration. I'm already here, and I can't change that. There's nowhere else for me to go, and I can't keep sleeping in my car or at motels. I'm already low on cash as it is. At least it's a free place to stay. Technically it's my place now. My nose wrinkles at the thought. I've never really had a home; this farm will be no different.

What's that?

Red taillights from another vehicle come into view as I pull up closer to the house. My brows arch and my stomach twists with uncertainty. Why is there a car parked out here in bum-fuck-nowhere at this time of night? The driveway alone is so long that I couldn't even see the lights until I was almost at the end.

I lock the doors to my Jeep and slow to a crawl as I gradually enter the round parking area by the front porch.

Just my luck... Is this person casing my uncle's house?

Mr. Holland, Uncle Thornton's estate attorney, warned me that there might be some interest from the townsfolk since it's such a small community, but I assumed if they were really that nosy, they would just come during the day and not so late at night.

The vehicle is a blacked-out Mercedes-Benz and is still running. There's no telling if the person is already outside of the car and scoping out the house or if they're sitting in the driver's seat. I drive slowly around it, reluctant to stop and put myself in danger. I've watched way too much true crime, and I'm not about to get myself killed by confronting whoever this person is.

I slide my phone out of my pocket and check to see if I have a signal. My hopes aren't high, since I've been without one for hours now. Who knew you'd need to worry about dead zones nowadays? I'm completely out of my element.

My phone's battery symbol is red, as it's been searching for a signal this entire time. *No bars. Great, I can't even call the local police.* That's lovely, now what?

The black SUV is ominous, idling as if someone is inside staring back at me. I consider running to the front door, but that seems like a terrible idea for several reasons.

I know I saw a diner a few miles back, and it looked like it was open. Maybe I should go to the restaurant and grab a midnight breakfast while I wait for the car to leave. They should have a pay phone there that I can use to call the police if my phone still can't get bars.

Well, I guess that's if this small town even has a police station. Uncle Thornton's farm must be pretty far out of the community because the only thing I've seen so far is the diner and farmland. The few lights off in the distance are comforting, though. There must be some sort of civilization out here.

As I make my way around the Benz, the driver turns their high beams on, and my heart falls out of my chest. *Holy shit there really is someone in there watching me.* I take that as a warning from them that I should leave and put my foot on the gas, speeding down the road leading up to the property.

I hold my breath a few times after I'm out of the long drive, as I take uncertain turns down roads that all look identical. Then I let out a relieved breath when I find the diner several miles out. A small, nervous smile curls my lips as I pass under the sign—thank God it's a twenty-four hour diner, which is a little surprising since the town is so small, but I'll take it.

I'm in no position to question any mercies thrown my way.

I'm still jittery from the farm and the car casing it by the time I park. I quickly look around my car to make sure that the Benz didn't follow me before I get out. I exit the car and trot into the diner.

There are empty bright-red booths and round stools with iron legs at the countertop. It's a ghost town in here. My keys jingle as I take a seat at the bar.

Vacant restaurants at night like this used to really freak me out, but I've been through so much that it takes a lot to rattle me. Certainly not a quiet diner.

The person casing the farm will realize it's a shithole soon and leave, I tell myself.

"Hello?" I call out gently for a staff member since no one has come to greet me yet. I fish out my phone to see if they have Wi-Fi here since I can make phone calls if connected to the internet.

Crap. Of course they don't.

A waitress in a nineties-looking diner uniform comes out from the swinging door. She sets down an empty mug and lifts a pot of coffee. She doesn't ask me if I want any, but she raises her brow, indicating that she's offering.

My legs bounce anxiously as I take her in. She doesn't look like the friendly type, judging by her frown and narrowed eyes that study me as thoroughly as I do her. She's a gorgeous brunette; I'll give her that. If it wasn't so late and I wasn't so tired, I might've tried having a conversation with her. Maybe another night.

"Do you guys have a phone I can use?" I ask as I nod toward the coffee cup for her to fill it.

She doesn't reply right away; she chews her gum and stares at me with an uninterested expression. "Yeah, we've got one of those," she mutters slowly as she fills up the mug with black coffee. I half expect her to ask me if I want cream, but she turns on her heel before I can even ask.

How pleasant.

I slip off the barstool to look around for the phone. This diner is bigger than I expected. It has an entire other section that wraps around the side. As soon as I make it around the other end, I hear laughter spilling into the building as a group of people come in through the front door.

So there *are* people who live in this town. The sound of people chatting soothes my nerves a little. It's weird, but this place just gives me a bad feeling. Like when you enter a building

11

and you feel eyes on you—that's how this entire town feels. Like I'm being watched. A shudder runs down my spine.

I make a note to not watch any horror movies for the foreseeable future, even though they're my favorite.

I continue to look for the phone and find it in the back. A stretch of black and white tiles leads up to a vintage red phone booth. It almost feels like I've gone back in time. These old diners have always been a favorite of mine for that reason. They hold so much charm. My dad used to take me to them when I was younger, and we'd order pancakes every single time. I smile to myself at the almost fuzzy memory.

I miss him. I wonder what he would think if he could see me now. Flipping my life upside down at twenty-five because of an asshole ex and running to the first escape option that pops up… It's not what I ever planned for my life to look like, but I never had much of a running start. Dad died when I was eight; Mom, when I turned thirteen. I can't remember what they looked like, or even where my childhood took place. Just the warm memories of comfort while they were still alive.

My family is cursed to die out. It's a fate that has slowly unfolded. Maybe it's why I never really tried to make anything of myself or pursue my passions. I always sort of thought death was coming for me next.

And it did. Callum saw to that, and now I have severe trust issues.

My old therapist said I should try to look at the positives instead of all the bad things in my life. He always wore a sharp black suit and tapped his fingers on the table. *At least I'm not dead.* I grin grimly to myself.

I pick up the phone and dial the police. The phone rings once, then goes straight to voice mail. "You've got to be fucking kidding me." I curse as I set the phone back down on the ringer harder than necessary.

Of course, this town doesn't have a full-service police station, but they have a twenty-four-hour diner, which makes *total* sense. I guess waiting for that car to leave before heading back is my only option. I check my phone for the time. *Midnight.* Maybe a few hours will be enough time. I can sip on coffee and eat for that long.

The ten-hour drive here already took it out of me. The last thing I want to do is camp at this diner and wait, but I don't really see any other option right now.

I stop in the bathroom and freshen up. After washing my hands, I reluctantly look at myself in the mirror. My ombre ashy-brown-to-blond hair is a tangled mess, and my eyes have dark circles around them.

Sleep wouldn't be so hard if I didn't have night terrors about what Callum did that night. I shut my eyes and fist my hands at my sides. *No.* If anyone can escape that memory, it's me. *I've got this.* I firm my resolve and look back at the mirror, redoing my ponytail and tying my hoodie strings so it doesn't look so disorderly. I don't need any more judgmental looks from the freaking waitress.

I walk back out to the main dining area and spot four men sitting at a booth in the corner. They're loud and rowdy and look like they could be in a biker gang. They're wearing all black: slick sport jackets, jeans, and combat boots. Each of them has a muscular build and trouble written all over their foreheads. By the way they're dressed and lounging, I'd guess that they are only a handful of years older than me at most.

I quickly avert my gaze before I get too interested in them. The last thing I need is to make eye contact with one and have my time here filled with whatever drama they're sure to bring. Guys like them always have bad things they drag around. And if there's one thing I don't need, it's bad guys with baggage. Seems to be my weakness.

I head back to the bar for my cup of coffee, but just as I'm sitting down, one shouts over at me, "Hey, cutie!"

My cheeks turn red, but I don't look their way. Ignoring horny idiots is usually the best way to avoid their harassment.

Hurry up, waitress. Come back out here so I can order food—to go, so I can head back to my car and eat in private. My leg starts bouncing again.

I shut my eyes and take a sip of the hot black coffee; choking it down would be an understatement—it's so bitter that it makes me grimace.

The next thing I know, an arm wraps around my shoulders, and the smell of cheap beer coils around me. A shiver goes up my spine, and I fist my hands against the countertop instinctively. Who the fuck walks up and touches a stranger like that?

"Didn't you hear me?" a smooth voice murmurs against my ear.

I flinch in his hold and shrink into myself. "Oh no, sorry, I didn't. Can I help you?" I lie sweetly. It's better that they think I'm some sweet lost girl. It always is. Then they don't see the pocketknife I have in my bag coming.

The man chuckles and lets go of my shoulder. I take the moment to swivel in my chair and look at him. I wish I hadn't—I should've just gone straight for a slap across his face.

He's stupid hot—tall, muscular, and he has a charming smile that promises he's broken way too many hearts. His chest-nut-brown hair is styled and swept to the side, giving him a sharp look.

14

"Is it just you here? Why don't you come sit with us?"

"Oh no, that's okay, I'm getting my food to go." My fingers tap anxiously on the counter.

His eyes narrow at my hand, and his grin grows with amusement. "They don't do takeout. New to town?" He looks me over again with a little more interest.

Fuck, of course they don't do takeout.

"Come on, we don't bite." He turns up the charm. I cast a look back at his group of friends, all of them are staring at us. Two of them are grinning and one has an annoyed furrow to his brow.

I guess it would be really awkward to sit here and eat after he's come over. Plus, they're all pretty cute. With the shitty day I've been having, I could use a distraction.

"Okay." I sigh with resignation. His expression lights up instantly.

Honestly, what's the worst thing that could happen? They are just some good-looking guys. *Bad ones*, I think, but still. Maybe I can get some useful information on this town and what there is to do around here. I'll definitely need something to kill time besides cleaning up the farm.

I grab my cup of coffee and walk toward their table. He wraps his arm around my lower back and guides me to where he was seated.

I offer an awkward smile and sit down. The men are all sprawled out, not too concerned about me joining them, but they do have a glimmer of interest in their eyes. The man I sit next to has his arm set above the back of the booth. I don't have any choice but to scoot as close as I can because the one that asked me over here sits down next to me, boxing me in.

Welp, this was probably a mistake.

"What's a prissy little thing like you doing out here in the middle of the night?" the man across from me asks. He's a little taller than the rest, and he has tattoos that crawl up his neck and end at his jawline. God, I've always had a thing for the tattooed ones. They can handle pain, and something broken in me really likes that.

Prissy? I've been called worse.

I consider lying and telling them I'm out here just for fun or to be with family, but if I run into them later, it might be a hard lie to keep up with. I don't have the bandwidth for that right now.

"There was someone casing the house I'm supposed to be staying at. I didn't feel like being axe murdered, so I left. I don't have any cell service out here, so I came to this diner hoping to use a pay phone." My words trail off as I think about how stupid it is that their police station is closed right now.

"Let me guess, you were going to try to call the police but realized they close at eight p.m. around here." The guy next to me chuckles.

"Eight p.m.?" I emphasize, genuinely flabbergasted. Is that even legal? My opinion of this place keeps declining.

"Yep, Sheriff Murray doesn't work very late. How long did you say you were in town for?" the guy who came up and grabbed me asks with a flirty tone.

I firm my lips and rub the edge of my shirt as the wheels in my head churn. I'm not sure I should mention how long I'll be here.

The hot blondie in the corner across from me seems to catch on to my uncomfortable expression. "I'm John. What's your name?" He offers a charming grin that soothes my suspicion a bit.

Callum won't find me here. He thinks I'm dead, and there's no security cameras in small towns like there are in the city. I calm my thoughts. But a little lie won't hurt to help me stay hidden, right? "My name is Briar," I say sheepishly, keeping up with the sweet girl facade. It's not like it's a complete lie. I've been going by Briar for months now. Chloe Thornton is dead—she died a long time ago.

"That's a pretty name," John says with that cheeky smile I'm already fawning over. His eyes are a deep blue that could sweep me off my feet. He's the one that would break my heart out of them all.

"I'm Gale. That's Taylor and Bensen." Taylor is the one who keeps calling me cutie, and he grants me another smile when I look at him. Gale shifts in his seat across from me. He's the only one who looks a little uncomfortable with me sitting with them.

John speaks up again, setting his elbows on the table and resting his chin on his knuckles. "You look like the type of girl who likes to have a little fun." He bites his lower lip suggestively. He's the most attractive of the bunch, but he's definitely out for a fling. My thighs warm, and I shuffle my feet.

A little trouble might be the only thing that gets me through my time in Bane Falls.

"Uh, yeah, I guess. Except normally I'm in the city partying, not out here in the countryside. What do you guys even do for fun? Tip cows?" My tone is full of sarcasm, but I'm genuinely curious what the heck they do out here.

"Oh, a city girl, huh?" Taylor says as he nudges me from my left side. I laugh awkwardly. "Do you actually think we tip cows?"

I crack a grin at him and shrug. "It's my best bet."

"Well, a late dinner is usually fun enough around here. You can hang out with us for the rest of the night while you wait for the car to leave your place if you want," Bensen says as he drops his arm from the booth and lets it land on my shoulders. His hand is as warm as his grin. He has the softest brown eyes and short brown hair.

I clutch my mug and take a long sip before looking back up at them. "I might actually take you up on that."

The waitress comes back out of the swinging doors that lead to the kitchen and approaches us with four more mugs. She gives me another once-over and scrunches her brows. "You guys know her?" Her voice is cold and distant, like she wants me out of her diner right this second.

Taylor smiles and shrugs. "She's our new *friend* visiting from the city." He caresses his finger against my knee. My thighs rub together before I can consciously stop it. He notices and lets a small chuckle slip.

Come on, Briar, you don't need strangers stirring things up for you in town already.

The waitress—Lana, her name tag indicates—narrows her eyes at him as she hands out their mugs, slowly filling them with coffee before dropping a menu. Her eyes linger the longest on John. "Just don't cause any problems for me tonight, okay?" she mutters stiffly before heading back to the kitchen. Well, that validates my suspicion of them being menaces.

"She's friendly," I whisper, letting my gaze shift toward the menu across the table. My stomach growls, and everyone looks at me before they share a laugh.

"Yeah, she's usually not this grumpy," Gale says as he slides the menu toward me. I take it and flip through. It's all breakfast, so I settle on pancakes. The nostalgia of them makes me feel a bit more at home. "She's usually not on the night shift—her coworker normally is."

"Yeah, she's not keen on tourists either," Bensen adds.

My attention flicks to John, who's looking toward the counter where Lana is cleaning with a washcloth. *They must be seeing one another.* I internally pout. One thing I definitely don't need right out of the gates is drama. John is off the table if I want to be able to eat here often. It's close to the farm, so it might be a regular spot if the food is decent.

Benson takes the menu from me and hands it to John. "So do you have family out here or something?" Bensen asks as he sips on his coffee. The bitter scent is comforting. I let my guard down a little; these men don't seem like they're crooked. At least not in my definition of the word.

Crooked is Callum.

"Yeah. Well, at least I did. He passed away recently, so I'm just here to take care of his estate." I stare down at the mug between my hands and take in the silence that's shared around me.

Everyone is always so quiet when death is mentioned. I get it, but at the same time, I don't. I've been around it my entire life and at some point, you become desensitized to it all. I feel like I'm always watching how others react and trying to blend in by matching my expressions to theirs. "We didn't really know one another, so…" I add gracelessly.

I'm no stranger to being labeled bad or weird for feeling nothing about having no family. It's all I've ever known.

"I'm sorry, Briar. That sucks." Taylor's voice is low. Another beat of silence.

John clears his throat. "What are you ordering? Want to chill with us after this, until morning? We have a pretty sweet hangout on the outskirts of town."

I force a smile at him. "I'd rather not get murdered on my first night here."

Gale laughs and presses his hand to his chest. "Ouch. You think we're like that, huh?" He shoots me a grin that sends butterflies through my stomach. Winning over the cold one is always a good start.

"You can never be too careful," I say with flushed cheeks. They know how attractive they are. If I had cell service and could send a picture of their IDs to a friend, then I'd be more comfortable, but it's best to play it safe for tonight.

"Smart girl," Taylor coos and signals to Lana that we're ready to order. "But we have Wi-Fi at our place, you know, if you need to check in with someone."

My eyes light up. "Yeah, I really need to check my emails, actually." Mr. Holland probably already sent me over some disclosures to sign, and I promised him that I'd check in once I arrived in town. Given that I don't have cell service and that I doubt my uncle has Wi-Fi, this might be my only chance this week to check in.

John scowls. "*Emails?* Oh God, you care more about your work than checking in with family?"

My expression falters. *Great, here comes the awkward conversation already.* Might as well just rip off the Band-Aid. "I don't have any family left… They're all dead."

They stiffen and share a collective grim look.

"Fuck, sorry." John rubs the back of his neck and gives me an apologetic frown.

I shake my head. "You couldn't have known. I've always been sort of on my own anyway." My attempt at a cheerful smile must be shit because they only look more down about it.

The waitress comes back at the perfect time, disrupting the negative vibe that curtained around us, and we all order. I decide to forgo the pancakes, like I used to order with my dad, and order waffles instead.

Sitting with the group of guys makes me forget for a short time that my life sucks.

Gale and Taylor share stories about their motorcycles and the maintenance they've been doing on them over the summer. It sounds like they all work at the same autobody shop in town.

"I've never been on one before," I admit as I bite into my waffles.

Taylor stifles a laugh. "Did you think any of us actually thought that a girl like you would've?"

I shoot Taylor a glare, and Gale gives me a daring lift of his brow. "It's true, Briar. You look like you belong in a little bookshop with a cup of tea."

"And what's wrong with that?" I shove another bite of waffles into my mouth. They share a chuckle and tease me more about it. Sure, so I'm not some badass girl who rides motorcycles, but it's not like I couldn't try. I flatten my lips in annoyance.

John and Bensen are the car guys of the group. It makes me smile hearing how they all share an obsession with vehicles, specifically fast ones. I've always found the roar of an engine to be another level of sexy. The rumbling that you feel as your foot presses that pedal to the ground is euphoric.

"All right, so you'll ride with me, and you can crash at our place until morning if you want?" John winks at me. It makes my heart flutter, but I quickly cap the feeling and dare a look over at Lana. She's furiously sweeping the booths at the other end of the diner, but John wasn't trying to be quiet by any means, so I'm sure she overheard. Maybe they aren't an item and just randomly hookup sometimes.

21

"Sounds good to me," I chirp, excited about where the night is headed. I check my phone and see it's already pushing two a.m. Lana took our payment an hour ago and has given us death glares at least four times now.

Bensen grabs my side and tickles me. *God, I love the ones that open up quickly to tickling.* "Are you sure you don't want to ride with me instead, Briar?"

I'm laughing and leaning into Bensen's arms when the bell hanging over the door dings. All four men seize up, and the atmosphere changes swiftly.

"Fuck," Taylor whispers, giving me a hesitant look like I shouldn't be here.

"What?" I ask, sitting up straight.

"Just be quiet. Let us do the talking," John says quickly. Their uncomfortable expressions and demeanors send some red flags up.

My eyes track toward the front door, landing on a male dressed head to toe in black motorcycle gear. He has a helmet clutched in his right hand and a fabric mask over his head, revealing only his bright hazel eyes.

But it's evident that he is very pissed off.

And staring directly at *me*.

Who is he? I haven't even seen his face yet, but I know he's the one I hope chases me this fall. Shit, masks are one of my kinks.

He storms over to our booth, slamming his helmet on the table so hard that it shakes a few forks off plates. He reaches up and tears his mask off, revealing a sharp jaw, straight nose, and gorgeous cheekbones. His black hair is matted down, and he has a wild look in his eyes. I swallow roughly.

"What the fuck are you guys doing?" he snaps. His voice is lovely, dark, and smooth like someone who's always in complete control. He's absolutely terrifying. I fidget and fist my hands in my lap.

Taylor stammers, "Oh. Hey, Roman. We just came here to have a meal and ran into Briar." He makes it sound like I'm not a complete stranger that he hassled into joining them.

Roman narrows his eyes like he's never seen something he loathes more than me. I make eye contact with him and flinch at the hostility I find in his gaze. What's his fucking deal? I've never met this man in my entire life, and he wants to be a dickhead?

"Leave," he says sternly, splaying both of his hands against the table and leaning closer toward me. I've never seen a scowl as sharp as his. This guy has red danger tape wrapped all over him. I shrink into myself and unconsciously scoot closer to Bensen.

Gale lets out an irritated breath. "Oh, come on, Roman. That's not fair. She hasn't done anything wrong."

Roman jerks his head in Gale's direction. "I'll deal with you later. I don't want to hear another word out of your goddamn mouth. Out of any of your mouths." They all go quiet, and Taylor slowly slides from the booth to let me out.

I hesitantly shift out of my seat, hardening my courage as I stare up at Roman.

By God, this man is ridiculously gorgeous. He has a red tattoo or scar, I can't tell which it is, of the Roman numeral VI on his left cheek just under the outer corner of his eye. A long scar cuts across his forehead and almost looks like barbwire, and he has a decent-sized scar over the edge of his lips. *Jesus, what has he been through?* The look of disdain is still written all over his face as he growls at me, "Get back in your shitty car and leave Bane Falls."

Shitty car? I've worked my ass off just to put gas into the damn thing. *The absolute audacity of this man.* I take it all back. He's not hot at all.

"Excuse me? Leave *town*? Who the fuck are you to tell me what to do? I'm here for at least a few months, so get used to seeing my face, *Roman*," I retort, crossing my arms and leveling him with a scowl.

He smirks at me with cruel amusement. The muscles in Bensen's jaw flex with unease.

"A few months?" Roman barks out a manic laugh. "No, you're going back to whatever city you came from, right now."

The nerve he has thinking he can tell me what to do sends rage through my veins. "You don't own the goddamn town, asshole," I shout, storming past him toward the diner door. I'm sure the car that was casing my uncle's farm is gone by now, so I'm going to head back and forget any of this even happened. It's way too late to deal with some hot, tattooed psychopath. What's that saying? Nothing good happens after midnight?

A gasp tears out of my lungs as someone grabs my hoodie and yanks me back, practically choking me.

Roman spins me around and lowers to my level, saying with a gravelly tone, "If you know what's best for you, you'll leave tonight."

Tears prickle my eyes and I have to fight to get the words out. "I can't just leave. I have nowhere else to go." I hate that I cry when I'm frustrated. It always makes me feel so stupid. It literally feels like there's a rock in my throat that I can't choke down.

He offers me a look that conveys he couldn't care less about my living arrangements. "Well, that's too fucking bad. I don't need your slutty ass lingering around my guys," he says scathingly.

Wow. Okay, king of the dickheads.

Roman drags me by my arm to the front door and pushes me down the three steps. I barely catch my footing and stumble a few times on the pavement before whirling and glaring at him.

He's shooting one right back at me. "I'd better see you turn left on the highway on your way out of town."

I don't know if it's the coffee, how tired I am, or how much I hate this rude fucking prick, but I give him a smug grin as I flip him off. "I'm not leaving town, you hillbilly fuck." My cheeks are on fire, and my voice cracks, but I've never been more sure of my words and how I want them to land like a bullet through his thick skull.

My eyes flick to the window of the diner briefly, where the four guys are still sitting at the booth. All of them are pressed against the glass with mortified looks. My heart beats erratically, and I quickly glance back at Roman.

He cracks his knuckles and tilts his head like he's fighting back the urge to hurt me. He's not laughing at my insult, not finding it amusing in the slightest. In all honesty, it scares me a little. He's a terrifying man. "It's not negotiable. Don't make me *scare* you away."

I scoff. *Oh, he wants to play this kind of game, does he?*

Callum tried to murder me—I'm fucking impenetrable now. "Dude, I've met men way scarier than you. Take it from me, you're fucking *nothing*."

Roman's eyes widen like he's offended I don't think he's the biggest, baddest ghoul in this ghost town.

I turn my back to him without another word and stride toward my car. The moment I open the door he throws his hands down against the metal, slamming it shut and pinning me against the window with a hand on each side of me. My heart races, and adrenaline pumps through my veins.

A darkness falls over his eyes, and he gives me a sinister grin. "No, you haven't. Not even in your darkest of nightmares have you met a man like me." He has my chest pinned against the car with his torso burning heat into my back. Each word he says is hot against my ear, making chills crawl up my arms.

Who the fuck is this guy? I grit my teeth and fight back the urge to scream for help. *No*, I chide myself. If I could survive Callum that night, I can survive Roman.

I learned never to rely on others by the time I was ten. No one is coming to save me. No one ever is.

"Look, I'm just going to go back to my place, take a bath, and go to bed. I'm not causing any trouble, and I don't even want to be here, so can you please just leave me alone? Your friends were nice. I don't know what's wrong with you, but I'm not going to do what you want just because you think you have a huge dick you can swing around." He's lucky I don't say much more.

He lets out a long breath that skates across my neck. "You're really going to make me have to do this, aren't you?" The warm evening air does nothing to stave off the cold edge of his voice.

"Make you do what? I'm not making you do anything. Can you just fuck off?" I snap back, shoving my ass into his crotch so he has to take a few steps back.

He laughs and snatches the car keys from my hand. A rush of anger bursts into my veins, and my heart pounds loudly in my ears. "What are you doing? Give those back!" I shout, patting my pockets for my phone, only to realize he took it too. Not that it would have helped, with no service, but I still need it.

The diner door swings open, and all four of the men run out. Taylor's the first to speak up. "Come on, leave her alone. She's not doing anything, and it's my fault—I convinced her to sit with us." His voice is filled with concern. Which doesn't make me feel any better about my situation.

John tries to take the keys from Roman, but the asshole shoves him back hard. "This is on all of you. Whatever happens

26

to her is your fault. I told you that no one I don't approve of comes near us, especially after last time." Roman's voice is threaded with cold malice. Their expressions fall, and they look almost guilty.

Whatever happens to me is on them? What the hell is that supposed to mean?

The four of them keep their mouths shut and give me dreadful looks. Roman is about to turn back around, but I don't wait. I take off running.

"Goddamn it, stay here and make sure the waitress doesn't do anything stupid," Roman shouts as he chases after me.

I slip a few times on the gravelly outskirts of the parking lot but quickly make it into a field of dry grass. It's not very wide, and I can see what looks like a patch of someone's land on the other side. Roman's footsteps are gaining on me, making each breath hitch in my lungs.

The field leads up to a wooden fence. I easily hop the three-foot structure, thank God I kept up with track in college before I dropped out, and find myself in an old cemetery. My throat is on fire, and it's hard to see clearly. It's too dark with all the trees looming and blocking out the moonlight.

I try to cut across the graveyard as fast as I can, but trip over a small broken headstone. My hands and knees take the brunt of the fall, shooting pain through my palms and legs. I don't have time to stand back up before Roman comes down on top of me. A cry is torn from my throat as he pins my wrists against the damp grass and mud.

I stare up into those soulless eyes, knowing that whatever he's about to do, there will be no stopping him. He doesn't care, not about me, not about himself, not about anything. You don't have to know someone intimately to know that they harbor demons.

If I hadn't already survived the worst night of my life with Callum, maybe I'd be paralyzed with fear, but a dark part of me wants to give in. Let him finish me off like leftovers—something wicked about the rush of adrenaline makes me excited.

Roman's eyes narrow when my arms go limp and I slow my breathing, willing him with my eyes to do his worst.

"You're so pathetic," he growls, dipping down and stroking his tongue up the side of my neck. Chills race up my spine, and a sinking feeling twists in my gut. He puts more weight on my secured wrists and pushes them farther into the ground. The scent of earth and wet grass fills my senses, instantly taking me back to the night Callum tried to murder me.

It's odd how something as small as a familiar smell can trigger you. It pulls you right back into a moment in time that still lives in the darkest part of your soul, trapped in the grave of your memories where only terrible people still stir occasionally. Raw terror pools in my chest. "Why did you do this to me?" I cry, forgetting Roman is the one pressing me into the mud.

I thought I was past that trauma, but clearly I'm not. It still haunts me. All I see is Callum and the same terrible lack of a soul behind those eyes.

I blink a few times and realize it's Roman staring down at me, not Callum. Roman lifts a brow, seemingly trying to understand what's going on in my head. His scent falls over me like mist on a cold morning, washing away the smell of being buried alive.

He loosens his grip on my wrists, and the moment he does I reach for him, wrapping my arms around his neck and holding on to him as if he helped me out of the loose dirt that night. Roman goes deathly still, holding us up with his palms pressed into the earth.

This cruel, beautiful man smells like engine oil and

teakwood. Someone who showers often but constantly has their hands on engines. It's a lovely smell. It's better than death. It's the most wonderful scent I've ever met.

After a second of clarity, I realize I'm embracing someone who just chased me down in a cemetery.

I gasp and release him quickly. Roman remains still, but his cold eyes are locked with mine. "Oh, now you want to be the sweet girl throwing hugs? The problem is, I don't think you'll leave unless I make you. Isn't that right?"

I swallow my pride. I don't know what to say to him. "I'll leave, I promise. I'll leave town as soon as I've taken care of my uncle's estate."

The face of the devil himself grins widely at me—it doesn't come close to reaching his eyes. "No, baby, you're leaving tonight."

He sits up, my wrists pinned now with his thighs on each side of me. He unlatches his belt and pulls it from his pants…to tie me up, I fucking hope. Because It'd be better than the other idea floating in my head.

Oh my God. What the fuck is going on in Bane Falls?

CHAPTER 2

BRIAR

What are you doing?" I ask, fear evident in my voice. My hands are trembling at my sides, and I try to shake myself from his hold to no avail.

Roman rolls his eyes dramatically, like I'm an ingrate for thinking he'd dare touch me. "Showing you what nightmares are really made of," he says scathingly as he shifts off me enough to flip me over onto my stomach.

Dirt gets in my mouth as he shoves my head down before binding my wrists together with his belt. It's thick leather, almost like it was made specifically for this purpose of binding a person. I didn't pin him as a murderer, but holy shit, if the shoe fits.

A sound halfway between a choke and a cry breaks from my throat as Roman forces me to stand back up. His scent moves through me again. It wouldn't be a stretch to assume he works at the same shop that the other guys do.

I swear to God if I get out of this alive, I'm torching that place to the ground for what they're letting him do to me. Didn't their mommies teach them not to fuck with someone who has nothing left to lose?

A gasp slips past my lips as he spins me to face him. In the dim light, it's hard to discern much of his features other than his empty eyes. They send chills through my entire nervous system. There's no doubt in my mind that he's killed people before. People don't just have this calm, depraved aura about them unless they've seen the lights go out in another's eyes.

He doesn't bother saying anything to me. Instead, he gives me a once-over, taking in the mud-stained clothing I'm drenched in before turning me to face the darkness of the graveyard. He wraps his hand around my bound wrists and shoves me toward the farthest headstones. I stumble and break the contact with his hand.

The moment I'm free I think about trying to run back to the diner but decide that it's likely what he wants me to do. He must get off on feeling powerful and making people scared shitless. So, I don't give into it.

Roman laughs, a vicious and unrelenting sound that makes me tense up. His arm is hooked around my waist, securing me to his side. "You really aren't afraid of me, are you?"

"No," I say sternly, trying to push away the memories the scent of the graveyard brings me and stay grounded in the now.

He considers me for a moment. "But you're afraid of *someone*."

My silence is answer enough for him.

He scoffs. "You are one of the dumbest girls I've ever met. A whore. You were going to fuck at least two of them tonight, weren't you?" His voice is gravelly and buries into my core. Fury rears back into my throat.

"Why? Are you jealous that they catch women's eyes because they aren't all fucked up like you?"

He works his jaw and grips the collar of my hoodie, pulling me in close and whispering over my lips, "Jealous? Of them sharing a girl as artless as you?"

Artless? That's a punch to the fucking face. I don't respond to that. If he wants to call me whore, I'll show up for it.

I just start moaning as loud as I can to shock him, and it works like a charm. It's like a natural reflex for everyone to panic when they aren't expecting someone to moan. His hand comes down hard over my mouth.

Perfect. My teeth sink into his fingers.

"*Ow*, what the fuck!" he curses and throws me to the ground. "Now I'm really going to bury you, you fucking brat." He seethes. My laughter is unfiltered and surprises him as he reaches down and drags me by my arms. My pants are wet around my knees, and I'm sure I'm bleeding in at least ten different spots.

None of this is funny. But I can't stop giggling, and I can tell it's pissing him off to no end.

He tosses me up against an old tombstone and pulls something from under his jacket. I squint to make it out. *A knife?* My pulse jumps. *It's a huge fucking knife.* The blade must be at least seven inches long. That gets me to stop laughing.

Shadows fall over his eyes, firming his resolve. Roman closes the distance between us and grips my jaw firmly, pressing that military-grade-looking knife against my throat.

My heart all but stops. I haven't felt this alive in months. Almost as if I've been numb to the world and I'm only now coming back to life. I hate how much I've changed since I've been on the run. Feeling exhilarated with a stranger and his threats—the adrenaline is addicting, the rush of every breath we share makes my thighs warm.

Sometimes I wonder if my body knows the difference between fear and lust. My heart beats to a rhythm it doesn't seem to know. Roman is something entirely new.

"Last chance. Get the fuck out of this town," he whispers. Our eyes are locked, and neither of us blink. He adds a little bit of pressure on my throat, and something warm streams down my neck, pooling in my collarbone.

Horror must flash through my gaze because he gets a satisfied glimmer in his eyes before he cuts his belt from my wrists and pushes me back toward the diner. He tosses my keys and phone at me.

"If I see you again, you'll never be found."

His threat is filled with malice. I lift my fingers to my neck and pull them back, finding blood smeared on my hand. I glance down at it, the red makes my vision blur and anxiety race through me. *Fuck.* I can't handle seeing blood. Not after Callum.

My eyes meet Roman's, and I find nothing there but a wild, dangerous creature.

"Too late, I've already been buried. I'm already a lost girl," I say ominously and flip him off. His expression twists with thought. There's an air of interest that blooms over his features.

I don't wait for him to warn me again. I run as fast as I can back to my car. Rage-filled tears falling and crashing on the ground. My clothes are stiff from the mud, and I smell like worms and earth.

The four guys aren't here anymore, and their vehicles are gone.

They seriously left me with that psychopath? I furiously blink away the last of my tears. Assholes. I'll make sure they know who the fuck they are messing with. I'm anything but a pushover, and I'm not going to let some boy gang scare me out of town.

I fumble with my keys before successfully unlocking my car. I get in as fast as I can and drive away in the direction Roman told me to go. I know he's watching from somewhere in the shadows, so I don't risk it.

A mile down the road, I spot the four men with their hands in their pockets, leaning on the hood of a blacked-out Mustang. I don't know what I was expecting, but it wasn't for them to just be standing idly by and leaving my fate to their fucked-up leader or whatever the hell he is to them.

Is it even worth staying? I question my own motives. I decide to keep driving out of town in case they follow me for a bit.

It takes about thirty minutes before I pass the sign on the interstate that points toward the town, Bane Falls, and almost immediately, I get my phone service back. Relief floods me as messages start popping up on my phone, including voicemails and missed calls. Strange, I never get messages anymore. Not since I cut what few friends I had left out of my life when I changed my name and went into hiding.

I quickly check the messages, glancing down at my phone as it charges, seeing that I missed a call from Mr. Holland. I go to the voicemails and click on the last of the five voicemails he left me. *Shit, did something happen?* I bite my thumbnail.

Mr. Holland's voice is filled with excitement, which slightly lifts the dread that's lodged into my chest thanks to that ass-face.

"Hello, Miss Thornton. It's Mr. Holland. I thought I'd give you a phone call to let you know that I found a record for an item of high value that should be at your uncle's estate. This might be of interest to you, and I thought you might like to know what to look for. It's a black flash drive that's worth more than the entire property. You're

34

looking at a minimum of at least two hundred thousand dollars'
worth in that alone. I know your situation is…rocky. So I wish you
luck in finding it as well as getting the estate put back together to sell.
Give me a call when you can."

I slam on the brakes and stare down at my phone.

Did I hear him right? Why would my uncle have something
that valuable on his crappy farm? And what information is on
that flash drive that's so damn important? It sounds like he
might've been into some bad shit. It occurs to me that I never
asked Mr. Holland how my uncle died.

Was the farm a facade? That would explain why he didn't
have any animals.

My heart pounds in my chest, and I drum my fingers on
the steering wheel. That much money would be life-changing. I
could escape everything and start over somewhere far, far away
from here like I wanted.

Callum's face flashes through my mind, and a shudder rolls
down my back. I clench my fists and grab my phone, punching
in an alternate route to the farm that will avoid any roads near
the diner. I save the route so that when the signal dies, I'll still
have it.

That psycho-dick won't actually hurt me, I reassure myself.
But just to be on the safe side, I turn my headlights off and drive
slowly down the alternate route. And for once I'm thankful that
this country town seems to be completely abandoned.

I can handle a few months of hazing from a group of jerks
for a life pass.

I hope.

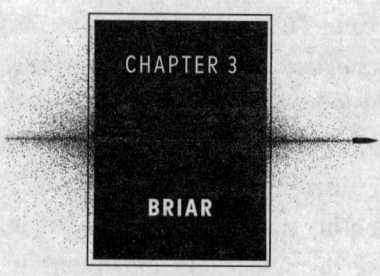

CHAPTER 3

BRIAR

slept like absolute crap. One eye open and constantly waking up all night until the sun rose around eight a.m. Less than three hours of sleep should be enough for my first day here since I don't plan on leaving the house for anything.

Roman may not scare me as much as he wishes he did, but this creaky house put the fear of God into me. Either there are rats in the walls or the wind is enough to blow this place to the ground.

Ugh. Whatever. I stumble half asleep through the crowded hallways to the kitchen. God, my uncle was a hoarder. There's not a room in this old house that isn't packed with black containers and cardboard boxes. The only room semi-organized is the one with his computer.

I scowl at the pantry that's filled to the brim with empty boxes and not a scrap of food. Just like that, my hopes of finding coffee deflate. If I don't have my caffeine fix in the morning, you can consider me a grump for the rest of the day.

A sharp knock comes from the back door as I'm wallowing about the lack of coffee. My entire body stiffens, and my breath catches in my lungs as I glance over my shoulder.

The back door is a flimsy white chipped-paint wood, one with a window cut out. I damn near have a heart attack when my eyes connect with a stranger's.

He's wearing well-worn work clothing that fits the ranch hand vibe: a plaid unbuttoned shirt and a baseball cap that's moth-eaten along some of the sleeves. He has a scruffy beard that's just a little longer than a five o'clock shadow and a jawline that is practically sculpted from marble.

A surprised expression must etch into my face because the stranger grins, lifting both of his hands innocently and saying loud enough for me to hear through the glass, "I'm Grahm, the ranch hand. Did Mr. Holland tell you about me?"

I nod absently and walk over to the door. "Did he tell you my name?" I ask, furrowing my brows. I don't trust him just because he knows about Mr. Holland and the fact that my uncle had an employee. Anyone in Bane Falls could know that.

Grahm nods, keeping those cool, summer-green eyes on me. "Chloe, right?" he replies. Unlike the guys last night, Grahm actually sounds like he's from here. He has a subtle accent. One that instantly distinguishes him as a cowboy. Not southern, just a northwestern cowboy living out in the plains of Montana.

I frown at hearing my real name, but only Mr. Holland knew it so Grahm must be legit. I sigh and give him an apologetic smile. "Yes, please come in." I unlock the door and let Grahm in. "I changed my name to Briar, though. So please don't repeat the other name."

He takes in my sour tone and just when I think he's going

to be curious enough to ask about it, he just pats my shoulder roughly. I blink up at him, waking up more with the hard pats.

"Rough night, *Briar*?" He winks at me with the emphasis he puts on my name. I crack a smile and nod.

"You have no idea."

Grahm looks around the trashed kitchen and then back down at me. "Want some coffee? I could use a cup before we dive into the Thornton Farm conversation." He rubs the back of his neck and has a forlorn look on his face. I wonder if he was close to my uncle. This must be hard for him. It makes me feel out of place because I'm not sad about his death. I didn't know him very well and only met him a handful of times.

"I'd love some coffee." I motion my hand to the pajamas I have on. "Let me get changed first. I'll meet you out front in five." He nods and heads back outside.

I throw on my only other pair of jeans—the ones not caked in mud from last night—and slip into a tank top before heading out the door. Grahm is leaning up against his truck, an old cherry-red pickup. It's in pristine condition. I'm impressed and a little hopeful for what he can help get done around the farm.

"Hop on in." Grahm smiles and crosses to the driver's side.

I get in and melt into the passenger seat. I'm so tired and worn down from the night prior, and I hadn't thought of the bruises that are showing before I put this tank top on. My wrists definitely reveal that I've been restrained, and my elbows are scraped up and bruised too. *That pretty-faced asshole*, I fume thinking about Roman.

If Grahm notices them, he doesn't bring them up. Thank God.

He's quiet for a few minutes as we get on the road heading into town before he speaks up. "Did you find your way into town all right?"

I hate small talk, but I relent. "Yeah, as much as a twenty-five-year-old with no phone service or a map can navigate." Grahm casts me a sidelong glance, grinning and running his hand over his scruffy beard.

"Shoot, I should've told that attorney that I'd meet you at the fork in the interstate. Lots of out-of-towners lose service coming in and get lost. Glad to see you made it, though."

Yeah, that would've saved my entire crappy night if he'd met me there to guide me back. I wouldn't have been lost for hours and likely would've deterred the guy casing the farm. Which reminds me. "There was someone at the farm when I pulled in last night, actually. It really freaked me out. Is that common around here?"

Grahm lets out an irritated huff. "Not usually, but as of late there's been an uptick in reports of people snooping through abandoned properties. Unfortunately, Sheriff Murray doesn't have anything to go on and nothing's been stolen or broken into, so he's not taking it as a high-level concern."

I glower. This sheriff sounds like the worst guy for the job. "Not surprising, considering he closes the station at eight p.m.," I grumble and cross my arms around my ribs.

"How'd you know that? Did you have to go to the station last night?" Worry flares across Grahm's face. At least he is a normal human being who reacts the way people should.

I lift a shoulder and firm my lips at what unfolded last night. "No, but I tried calling from that twenty-four-hour diner out by the farm."

Grahm hits the brakes, and I damn near fly out of my seat. I brace my hands on the dash and give him a wild look.

"What the hell!"

His face is serious. "You went to the Rose Diner? Are you

39

okay?" His eyes drag over me with new enlightenment behind them. My elbows are freshly bruised and scraped up, and so are my hands. I don't even want him to look at my wrists. It's evident *something* happened out there.

"I was trying to use the pay phone, and that's when I found out the police suck ass in this town. But then this little biker gang roped me into sitting with them and—" Grahm's mortified expression brings me to a halt.

"*They* did this to you?" His tone is half-furious and half-mortified.

My brows pinch together. "No. Not them. Their little ringleader, Roman." I don't keep the disdain out of my voice.

Grahm's hand goes straight over his face, and he drags it down like he's just been dealt a shitty hand in a game of cards. "You need to steer clear of them. They're bad news, Briar. Not *knock you up* bad news, but *people have gone missing in our town since they arrived* bad news." His voice is stern and genuine enough that I nod in agreement.

It's clear that Grahm only wants the best for me while I'm here. *Although I think they are also* knock you up *bad news too*. Amusement spreads across my lips.

"I'm not kidding. If you see them, you run the other way. Got it?"

I lean back in the uncomfortable seat and nod. "What's their deal anyway?"

Grahm takes a steadying breath and puts the truck back into Drive. The town is finally coming into view over the horizon of hayfields. "They don't cause any trouble during the day, but it's a different story at night. And no one can prove shit, so they've never been met with the law. I tend to keep my nose out of the townies' drama, but I know they keep a tight crew and only mess around with those who Roman approves of. I'm guessing Roman didn't approve of you."

I roll my eyes and stare out the window at the cows and horses in the distance. "Fucking cult."

Grahm chuckles. "Exactly. Something ain't right with them. You stick to the farm and town, don't go out at night unless you're with someone." I lift a brow at him. I appreciate the concern and advice, but he's starting to sound a little controlling.

"So, about the farm…" I change the subject.

We both order coffee at the Cow Bean Café and sit in the dining area while we discuss what the future of the farm holds. The café is endearing, small and quiet with a handful of regulars I'm guessing by the way they chat casually with the lady at the register. The atmosphere is nice too. This is a great alternative to the diner. Which is a bummer because I really did like its food. Not so much the service. I purse my lips as I recall Lana's rude glares willing me to leave the moment I sat down.

I tell him that I have no intentions of staying long-term. I just want to get the property cleaned up to sell. I consider telling him about the flash drive but decide it might not be a good idea until I get to know him more.

Grahm is a nice guy and agrees to my offer of paying him after the sale of the property. By the time we're wrapping up our conversation, it's already almost noon.

"Can we start tomorrow? I'm pretty exhausted from the long night," I say sheepishly as I place my cup at the edge of the table where the waitress can pick it up.

Grahm stretches his arms over his head and leans back in the chair across from me. His knees bump into mine gently, and my eyes catch on the abs that peek out from his rising shirt. He catches me looking, and my cheeks warm instantly. "You should come out to the party tonight. It'll be good for you to meet the townsfolk and loosen up from yesterday. Not everyone in Bane Falls is a jerk, you know."

I consider his words. Normally I would be quick to decline the invite, but I could really use some alcohol and a little bit of fun. If Grahm's going, then it might be worth attending. He's giving flirting energy that I'm eagerly returning.

"I might actually take you up on that." I grin, trying to hide the flush of heat that races across my cheeks.

He licks his lips, and the motion draws my attention there. "I can drive. I'll be at your farm at nine."

My eyes narrow playfully. "Didn't you just tell me never to go out at night?"

"Unless you're with someone," he clarifies with that smooth voice, and he casts a wink my way. "I've got you, Thornton."

"Hey, that's not fair. I don't even know your last name," I tease with my nose wrinkled playfully.

"Grahm Sutherland." He sets down a twenty to cover the bill. I open my mouth to protest, but he shushes me.

"*Sutherland*," I mock, and he snorts.

"Coffee was my idea. Besides, you can pay me back after we sell the farm." He tips his baseball hat at the waitress.

"Have a nice day, Grahm!" she chirps as we exit. Unlike the hostess from last night, this one gives me a bright smile that I return easily. Okay, at least the daytime people here are much better than the night crowd.

Grahm tells me about a few of the shops as he drives through Main Street on his way to dropping me back off at the farm. We share a few laughs, and by the time we're pulling into my driveway, I'm giddy and looking forward to seeing him again.

"See you tonight, Thornton." He dips his head in that sexy

42

way he did with the waitress, but he holds my gaze for a few seconds longer.

"Nine sharp, Sutherland. Unless you want to prove to me that there are more assholes in Bane Falls," I shout as I walk backward toward the house.

He gives me one of those smiles that can knock you over, the kind that meets his eyes and makes me want to go buy a pair of overalls to fit his farm-town vibe.

"If I ain't fifteen minutes early, I'm late." His accent brings a grin to my lips. He doesn't wait for me to respond before he peels out of the driveway, kicking up dirt as he waves out his window. I catch his bright smile in the driver's side mirror, and he watches me beam one right back at him.

Holy shit. Okay.

I'm going to forget everything crappy that happened yesterday. I deserve to have a little fun tonight.

The entire afternoon flies by. Because honestly? This work is cut out for me. My uncle was a terrible hoarder, and I'm the opposite of that.

The farmhouse is crowded with boxes and useless things that seem to only have a purpose of adding clutter. The pantry of empty boxes was just the beginning of the absolute mess I have on my hands. It takes some serious elbow grease, but I'm able to clear the main part of the house before five p.m. I fill all four garbage bins out back and throw the larger trash into a burn pile in the dirt field.

Maybe I can have a bonfire. That's what the country people do, isn't it? I've watched it in a few movies, but I'll have to have Grahm help me. I've never used anything but gas fireplaces.

My cheeks warm thinking about his easy smile. There are plenty of things he can *help* with if I was reading his body language right. I don't mind the ones that are flirty right off the bat. The guys last night had such promise if not for their weird loyalty to Roman—pity.

I take a deep breath and purse my lips with frustration. There's still no sign of that flash drive anywhere. No sign of anything worth a penny. My hopes were set a little too high, thinking it'd be easy to find.

My stomach growls, and I reluctantly go back to the horror-show kitchen that I just cleaned out. I still need to mop and sweep, but it's better than it was. I'm just relieved there weren't any rat droppings. *Probably because there's nothing to eat.*

I bite my nails as I stare at the empty shelves. I should probably stock up on food; otherwise I won't be eating at all tonight. I have enough cash to get me through the end of fall and part of winter as long as I don't splurge. That means lots of pasta and ramen. Wine, of course, is a must.

I can't even remember what a hamburger or pizza tastes like. It's been a long time since I've forked over money for something like that.

When Mr. Holland said that I'd be going to a farm, I imagined one with crops and animals to tend to. Fresh eggs, milk, and vegetables. I guess that was a little too hopeful. But I certainly did not expect this wasteland of nothing. What was my uncle even doing out here? He owned, like, fifty acres but didn't bother tending to it at all. It's weird. How did he make a living out here? There're hardly any signs of life. I find it hard to believe he stayed in this house at all.

From what I remember, my dad used to say that his brother was secretive and lived on the go. It was impossible to get in touch with him unless he reached out first. Which only adds to my stack of questions. What could he have possibly been doing all these years? Did he steal highly classified information? I bite my nails, considering if I'll check what's on the flash drive when I find it.

My stomach growls.

Regardless of the answers to my questions, one thing remains: I need to go grocery shopping.

It's almost seven p.m. by the time I'm peeking outside the blinds to make sure the coast is clear. The Benz that was casing the farm last night might come back, so I check every window I can before slipping out the back door and locking it. Not that it'd keep anything out with how flimsy it is, but it gives me a little peace of mind.

I quickly get in my car and check my makeup. I did a thin line of liner around my eyes and some mascara, nothing too flashy since I'm not trying to attract too much unwanted attention.

My worn-down blue hat pairs perfectly with my boyfriend-cut jeans and a tucked-in, oversized white T-shirt. It's the closest thing to the *townie* vibe that I have. I'm hoping it helps me blend in with the locals.

My ombre ashy curls are exquisite today. It's weird, I haven't felt this good in such a long time. I remind myself not to get too attached to anyone here. Including Grahm. And as far as I know, I'm certainly not welcome.

I tug down my baseball cap more to hide my face, just in case I run into those guys again. *I'll be in and out. I'm not talking to anyone unless I have to*, I drill into myself.

It's only seven thirty by the time I get to Main Street, but the streetlights are already on and many of the small shops are dark with their closed signs on the doors.

This is a different part of town than Grahm took me to this morning, but I recognize it. I drove through here at three a.m.

last night on my alternate route to avoid the assholes. It was a ghost town at that hour, but now there are plenty of people still out and about. Families walking around and groups of teens and adults heading toward the small restaurants and bars.

A few of them glance at my car with curious looks but don't pay too much attention to me. I let out a breath of relief. It's actually a pretty cute town when you see it during the day.

There're definitely more people living here than I originally thought too. It likely just doesn't have a night crowd, I'm guessing. Or they stick to the bars and not random-ass diners in the middle of nowhere. I give it more thought. Or maybe they go to whatever party I'm attending tonight. That could be it.

The grocery store isn't hard to find. It's at the end of town and has a moderate-sized parking lot filled with cars. I drive through the rows to make sure I don't see any of the motorcycles or vehicles I saw at the diner last night.

Satisfied, I park and head inside.

I grab ten boxes of pasta, sauce, a few bags of rice, more coffee than an average person needs, and a carton of ramen. The only thing I've ever actually cooked is spaghetti, and I'm very aware at how judgy people are of a young woman who can't cook. Imagine them casting me looks at the food in my cart while I'm glaring at a package of cookies and debating whether or not I can afford them.

Familiar voices come from the row next to mine. Deep laughter and teasing followed by a woman's faint chuckle.

The guys from the diner.

My eyes widen, and I quickly toss the cookies back onto the shelf and beeline it for the checkout line. *Fuck, of course they're here, of all places.* I try not to look too suspicious, but the cashier is already giving me a curious lift of her brow.

I messily stack my items on the counter, a little annoyed that there isn't a self-checkout here.

"Hey, you're a new face around here," the cashier says cheerfully.

I flinch and look up at her. I'm taken aback for a second; she's the prettiest blond I've ever seen. Her hair is styled perfectly, curls that shimmer effortlessly. She's rocking the hell out of that black store apron too. Her lips kick up into a sweet grin.

"What brings you out here?" She swipes a few items slowly, clearly trying to drag it out so we can talk. If not for the guys from the diner, I'd love to chat and make a new friend. But I simply don't have that luxury right now.

"Family," I mutter, keeping it short and sweet.

Her brows pinch and a devious smile forms across her lips. "I'll need to see your ID." She nods down at the wine.

I fish out my wallet and hand her my ID.

She looks at my age and my name, then flicks me a bright-eyed smile. "Briar. That's a pretty name. Barely legal, I see." She giggles, and it confuses me.

I awkwardly grin, casting a weary glance over my shoulder to make sure the guys haven't spotted me yet. "Barely?" I chuckle. "I'm four years over the drinking age."

She entertains me with an amused smile. "Twenty-five is still really young. I've got six years on you, sweetie." She passes my ID back to me casually, only holding it with her index and middle fingers. "My name is Hailey."

I shove the card back into my wallet. She's so kind that I can't help but relax my shoulders and spare some chitchat with her. "Nice to meet you, Hailey. Have you lived here long? By the way, your hair is gorgeous." Complimenting another woman is the apex of being a girls' girl.

She giggles again, and I wonder how a person like her is stuck here in Bane Falls. "Yep, I was born and raised here. But for a small town, it's actually pretty busy. And thank you! I was just about to say the same to you." She winks as she bags the rice.

"Pretty busy?" I try not to grin. "This is easily the smallest town I've ever been in."

Hailey laughs. "Trust me, there are towns around here much smaller than Bane Falls. And yeah, every summer we get a few big concerts that use our amphitheater. Being out in the middle of nowhere has its perks. It's a great place for music festivals. It brings a ton of people through here. But we also have some of the most insane parties out in the mountains. How long did you say you're staying again?"

Is this the same party that Grahm's taking me to?

"Hopefully just for a few months," I say sheepishly. It's clear I'm stuck for at least that long no matter what. Even if I find that flash drive, I need to sell the farm.

Her smile falters as she scans the last item. "Yeah, I figured. No one stays that long if they aren't from here or come here for work." She pauses for a few moments before an idea clearly hits her and lights up her expression. "Do you like races and beer?"

"Races? Like car races?" I half laugh.

"Yeah, they're not official or anything, but it's a lot of fun to do on the weekends around here. It's the party to go to in Bane Falls. You should come out tonight!" It's nice meeting another friendly person. It makes me sure that last night was just a fluke with the wrong crowd.

"I'm actually going to it already, I think, so it sounds like I'll see you there. How does everyone keep contact out here without any service though?" It's been a humbling day without a connection to the real world, and I'm annoyed by how off-putting it's been not having access to my socials.

The corners of her lips pinch together like she's confused before realization strikes. "You don't have phone service out here?" Her voice is filled with amusement.

"No," I say shyly. "I forgot to ask my ranch hand this morning. Any help is appreciated." I laugh and rub the back of my neck.

"That's probably because you're from the city and you have a carrier that doesn't have service over here in a small town like this. Oh! That reminds me, you said you're here for family, right? I know everyone in town. Who are you related to?" she asks, seeming genuinely interested.

I cast another look over my shoulder to make sure they haven't worked their way through the store yet. "I'm staying out at my late uncle's farm, Arnold Thornton. You know, the one past all those cornfields."

She gives me a hesitant look. "Oh… I'm so sorry for your loss. Arnold was a quiet guy, but he was kind. You're staying out there all by yourself?"

I shrug. "Yeah, it's not so bad, a little too eerie out there at night for me, though. It's so quiet."

Her expression turns concerned for a second before she slides a bag of groceries across the counter to me. "I'll be at the party a little after nine tonight." She changes the subject back to the party, scribbling down her phone number on the back of the receipt and passing it to me. "I'm sure you'll figure out your cell service eventually. Just stop by the tech shop on Main Street. Shoot me a text when you get service, 'kay? But I'll see you tonight, I'm sure!"

I offer a grin. "Thanks, Hailey." I wrap my arms around the paper bags and scoop them off the counter.

Deep laughs snatch my attention.

Shit. Hailey was so easy to talk to that I let it drag out too long. I flick a worried look over my shoulder and spot Bensen's dark hair. Hailey opens her mouth to say something else, but I'm already racing out the door.

"See you around, Briar!" Hailey calls out, an innocent smile tugging at the corners of her lips.

Oh crap.

I look at the group of men and catch eyes with John. His arm is wrapped around a brunette woman's shoulder. Gale has his hands shoved in his shorts' pockets. While Taylor and Bensen look like they're ready to run after me.

John's eyes widen, and his jaw clenches. The girl gives me a once-over and furrows her brows when John lets go of her.

I bolt, nearly dropping the precious groceries I can barely afford as I race across the parking lot. I start my car with trembling hands and speed down the road. I glance in the rearview mirror and spot Gale and Taylor running out of the store to see where I went.

Goddamn it. They're going to tell Roman I didn't leave town.

My leg bounces the entire drive back to the house, a thought gnawing at my stomach the whole time.

The diner guys like fast cars and motorcycles. They're definitely going to be at the party tonight.

CHAPTER 5

ROMAN

The guys have been acting weird since getting back from the store. It's obvious they're keeping something from me. As the lieutenant of the Icarus Squad, I know each of them inside and out. I have to. It's my fucking job.

"Whatever you guys are hiding from me, it can wait until after phase one of our mission," I say with an air of annoyance as I slam down the box of trackers for tonight's operation. We're going in with minimal firepower tonight, since there will be a heavy civilian presence.

After the first few parties, we learned that we really didn't need more than our knives and handguns. Sub-Rosa hasn't quite put it together yet that we're here and trying to infiltrate their gate in Bane Falls.

Gale drags his hand down his jaw—his telltale sign of being uncomfortable. John shifts in his seat and stands, changing the subject before I look too far into their little secret. "Lieutenant,

I still think it's too soon to approach Sub-Rosa members. They might just be the small fish we've identified in the organization. We need to be one hundred percent sure that the eagle has landed before we blow our cover."

Taylor rubs the back of his head and nods. "Yeah, I mean, they very well might shut down the whole thing before the end of summer if we aren't careful. Then there goes our entire two years of being stationed out here, wasting our time and fucking efforts."

I glower at them. "You mean I've been wasting *my* time. You guys haven't been doing anything except hooking up with the locals like fucking hounds. And no one said anything about blowing our cover. I told you, this is an insertion to see if they bark when we prod. The general hasn't given his orders yet on what he wants us to do once we locate their gate." My fists clench at my sides.

It's *my* neck on the line with this entire mission. The Dark Forces aren't for the weak. They are for the fucking deranged criminals that somehow make it out of the Under Trials boot camp.

And of course, I get completely fucked with the short stick. After all my time served in the secret forces and working to prove myself worthy of being a sergeant, then a lieutenant, I get dished the role of being on an outpost squad.

Icarus is a test squad for long-term, integrated missions off base. From what I gathered during my time in the Dark Forces, only the seasoned squads get to go out on these missions and have that taste of freedom that we're all chasing. I stare out past the auto shop's garage door and narrow my eyes at our fake life filled with things I've only ever dreamed of having. Being out here in Bane Falls has been like a fresh start, but every dream has a price that must be paid.

These are things we might be able to keep if we can successfully pull off this mission. Our time here has paid off. The locals trust us now, and the Sub-Rosa men have been slipping up with their security, so we have a good idea of who's running the entry points into the underworld.

The Icarus Squad. I wrinkle my nose at the name. When General Nolan pulled me from a particularly heinous mission I'd just returned from and said he had a vision for something new, I never could've imagined it would be this. Turns out he's been putting secret squads together for some time. It makes my stomach turn, wondering how many of us, disposables as he put it, are out there. Would we even know when our time is up? Our only source of communication to home base is through Nolan.

And of all the superior officers, I trust him the least. The crooked chain of command is General Nolan and Captain Bridger at the top—men who made it clear they have no problem getting rid of squads that don't perform well.

I've delivered on every single one of his orders. Because that's what I fucking do, I get shit done so that my squad gets to see another day. But I didn't expect him to change the direction of our mission so suddenly yesterday.

A bead of sweat rolls down my temple as I think about the ruthless general. I don't trust anyone. We've all learned the hard way at some point in our lives not to trust entirely. Unfortunately, it's my Achilles' heel. You have to trust your squadmates one hundred percent when you're in the field. And that ship sailed a long time ago for me.

Even now. I don't know if I can trust Icarus without a shadow of a doubt. Not after what I endured to get into the Dark Forces.

A flash of Dalton's face flickers through my mind. Opening

old wounds in my heart that I thought had long since iced over. I don't feel things the way I'm supposed to anymore. I never entirely did, to be frank. But after losing Dalton in the Under Trials because I trusted… No. I shake my head to ward off the memories. I'll never forget how shitty that felt and how the last of my humanity slipped away with him.

How I let down my only friend and had to become a vile man for it.

Bensen taps on his beer can, and the sound draws me from my thoughts.

John smirks and tosses a black fabric mask to Gale. "At least they have friendly people out here to hook up with. I grew up in the city, and no one will even bother smiling at you there. Everyone is too dissociated and miserable. I can't help that I want to get to know some of the locals," John comments, pulling his own mask up too.

I blink, dumbfounded that I spaced out for a second. The stress of keeping this mission on track and giving Nolan what he demands has been weighing on me. The guys don't know that if we don't provide results tonight, proving that we're getting closer to uncovering the black-market, aka "underworld," gate here, our time is up.

We'll be terminated.

Nolan's voice was so sharp last night, I can still hear it: *"I've received word that there's a little package being delivered to the Thornton Farm tonight. It's your ticket into the underworld, Syxx. Do not fuck this up."*

He didn't say it was a fucking young woman.

He knew I would've spoken up about it if he disclosed over the phone that the "package" was a person. I'm heartless, but unnecessary deaths are starting to seep into my dreams.

This is his way of shoving it down my throat. *I scared her away, though.* The general can't be upset if the package never arrived in Bane Falls, now can he?

She surprised me with her attitude. It's been a long time since I've met a wild one like her, and yet when she went slack and stared up at me like she wanted to see the worst of me... I shake my head, dismissing the girl's pretty face from my mind, and put on my mask.

She's gone. That's all that matters.

We have to be more discreet out here since a group of special ops soldiers would stick out like a sore thumb. So we play the small-town bad-boy group angle. And as stupid as it sounds, it works. A little too well, actually. I mean, the townsfolk are gullible to begin with, but they are the perfect cover for anything. I can see why Sub-Rosa chose this place as their base. Everything they do is hidden under hay bales and stalks of corn.

And crowded parties in the goddamn hills.

Since we're pretty muscular, it fits that we all work at the auto shop and stay here. No one suspects a thing.

Taylor was an engineer in his past life before he turned to a life of crime a few years after he graduated. So luckily for us, he was able to be assigned to our squad and makes pretty cool shit for us that blends in with the norm.

I grin at the motorcycle helmets that are bulletproof and fully equipped with speakers. According to Bensen, if we can't rock out to our favorite songs when we either kill or be killed, then he doesn't see a point. I get it, but at the same time, it's incredibly distracting.

Nolan doesn't give a shit about us, so I don't see the point in not letting my men enjoy their time as much as they can, while they can. The design of the helmet is flawless, slick, and we go unnoticed—passed off as some rowdy assholes that like to drive around fast and cause trouble.

Our pants and jackets have concealed pockets for our weapons too. Likewise, our vehicles are equipped with hidden compartments.

Tonight they're all riding out on the crotch rockets, so they don't look weird stepping out of cars with their helmets on. I always take the Mercedes to the parties, though, and tonight is no exception. I haven't missed a race since we arrived, and if I skip out, it will stand out. We don't have any room for doubt or error—not after building the townspeople's trust this far.

Taylor grins at me and stares down at his hand as he twirls a wrench. "You know, that girl last night was actually really sweet. You didn't have to be so mean to her and scare her off. She wasn't going to stick around for long anyway," he says with a flat tone, but his eyes are filled with amusement. Taylor's always a little too curious for his own good.

"Yeah, what was your deal with her? You haven't done that to anyone else we bring around." John sounds more annoyed than the rest. He seemed to be really awed by her compared to the others.

I don't want to tell them about Thornton's Farm and her being a package mentioned by the general. Not yet.

Nolan said that the man who owned that farm and died recently was a sleeper agent—a soldier who lived a normal life undercover until he was called upon for duty. He had knowledge of something so important that Nolan won't even trust me with it. I guess he's been burned by those he trusts before too.

I question whether Nolan had Arnold killed or if Sub-Rosa got to him first. Who sent his niece to clean the property? It weighs heavily on my mind, that girl and her stupid fearless eyes.

I haven't had to pull my KA-BAR on someone to spook them in a long, *long* time.

Does she know what her uncle did? Nolan wouldn't be tracing her if she didn't. Great, that means she's likely in danger no matter where she goes.

As for Arnold, his cover must've been blown. I don't know how else a guy capable of being a one-man squad just up and dies. Arnold Thornton was rumored to be quite the monster in his time in the Dark Forces. It's been almost twelve years since his time in the trials, though. Who'd have guessed this is where he ended up?

And his niece too.

She didn't see me earlier that night, thanks to my blacked-out windows, but I saw her clear as day. A woman so thoughtlessly striking and aloof that my cold heart shifted a bit inside my chest. I don't like her. Not one bit.

Innocent, beautiful things cannot be trusted.

I knew she was the package instantly. I also knew that she wasn't some trained agent or soldier either. She looked horrified that I was waiting there in the dead of night.

I concluded that the only person who would go out to Thornton's Farm, unassigned, would be a family member—his death was a pretty big deal in Bane Falls. He knew a lot of the locals and had integrated himself well.

Arnold never spoke with us. I wonder if Nolan even told him we were here. I certainly didn't know about him until the general explained that he failed his mission.

But what does that hopeless girl have to do with this? Why is Nolan pushing her into our world?

I firm my lips and glance at the clock. It's already almost nine. We need to hurry up if we want to be at the peak time for the party.

If it were anyone else in that diner, I wouldn't have had to be so vile. But I was pissed off that she was the thing Nolan sent my way.

It was for the best that she left and stayed out of this shit. The last thing we need is some brave, bratty girl getting in our way. Whatever it is that Nolan intended me to use her for, I'm sure we can find another way.

"You know how I feel about new girls at that diner. Only Sub-Rosa goons go there that late at night. She could've been setting you up. For all we know, she's working with them and they're on to us," I snap back at him, aware of how paranoid I sound. "I think you men have been getting a little too cozy in this life. Do you need to be reminded how high the stakes are out here?"

They all dip their heads and furrow their brows.

There used to be six of us.

The county coroner deemed that it was a suicide, but we all know it wasn't. Leon was our close comrade, the youngest of us at twenty-two. He was missing for a few days; even General Nolan couldn't track him down because his chip had been removed. Two days later, his body was found in the field behind the diner. The shotgun barrel was still in his mouth.

We don't know who he was tailing or how they found out he was looking into them. But it's clear to me that he put his trust in the wrong person in town, someone who convinced him to sneak out late and meet them alone. Nothing came of it in terms of our hideout being uncovered, so I'm certain our soldier didn't talk, but his loss was heavy on us nonetheless.

If he had just told me he was meeting someone, I would've tailed him and could've protected him.

"No way. She was so girly and innocent. She's from the

city, just like she said. I'm certain of it." Taylor's voice is flat and vexed. God, it's annoying how much they seem to like her.

I'll have to tell them about Nolan's part with her eventually. But it'll have to wait until after tonight.

"She sounds like the perfect weapon to fool anything with a dick." My tone is sharp as I pop a piece of gum in my mouth and flip through the playlists on my phone.

We're lucky we are allowed to have cell service, something that General Nolan only permitted because I convinced him that we'd be weirdos and stand out from the civilians without it. The phones are all chipped, and the Dark Forces IT team constantly checks our messages for security. It was made clear that if we tried to form plans to escape our mission or go MIA, we'd be terminated on the spot.

I primarily use mine for music; I don't text. I'm especially not going to hand out my number to any of the women in town trying to get in my pants.

"Last time I checked, you have one of those too, Syxx," John mumbles sarcastically and the others laugh. They're lucky they can't see the vexed expression beneath my mask.

I turn on the song "Mask Off" by Future, then give the squad a middle finger. They laugh and follow me over to the vehicles, strapping on their helmets and drowning out their rowdy chatter. I get in my Benz and check it to make sure it's prepped for the race.

Tonight's the night we make headway on this mission.

That girl is out of the way.

All I have the capacity for right now is finding this goddamn gate to the underworld.

CHAPTER 6

BRIAR

rue to his word, Grahm shows up fifteen minutes early. A bubbly feeling rises in my chest when he leans over and pushes the passenger door open. He's wearing a gray hoodie and light-wash jeans that match his baseball hat, looking as handsome as he did this morning.

"Come on, we don't want to miss the races, Thornton." He smirks and winks at me. I take a deep breath and shake sense into myself. *Stop staring at him like you've never seen a country boy before.*

I hop up into his truck and have to tamp down my excitement. I have no idea what to expect. It's surprising enough that this town has something like this.

I consider telling him about my little run-in with the guys at the grocery store but decide against it. I'm just going to stick close to Grahm and ignore that entire group if I see them.

"You look good, Thornton. I thought you were stunning this

morning, but fuck, those jeans are working for you. I would've told you earlier, but we weren't going to a party together yet," he says smoothly with one hand on his steering wheel and the other perched on the door. My cheeks warm with his comment.

"Thanks." I grin. "These are the only ones that fit me well. My only other pair are covered in mud," I admit sheepishly.

"Do you need more? We have some pretty good shops in town. Although I think they might be a little too townie for you city folk." His tone is full of sarcasm.

I give him a wry grin. "Anything to help me blend in, honestly."

He chuckles at my comment, but I'm not even kidding. No one wants to stick out like a sore thumb, especially when the last thing I need is to be noticeable.

We stay on the highway for ten minutes before Grahm pulls off onto a dirt road that's heading toward the mountains. It's thickly forested and the moon won't rise until at least midnight, so visibility is practically zero. If it weren't for the line of taillights ahead of us, I would be concerned about being in a car with a practical stranger driving toward the woods.

"*Wow.* Who knew there could be traffic on fire trails. Are *all* of these people really heading to the same place?" I ask as I roll the window down and pop my head out to see further ahead. The first thing that hits me is the fresh pine air and the cool, late-summer breeze.

My lungs fill with the euphoric scent, and chills spread up my arms. Music plays in the distance, "Super Bass" by Nicki Minaj. It must be *loud* because I can feel the vibrations rumbling in my sternum from here.

"Oh my God, this looks like fun. Is this legal?" I laugh, and the elation must show on my expression because Grahm leans against his arm, elbow perched on his door, grinning at me.

"Murray doesn't give a shit what we do out here as long as it's all adults. Think you can keep up with us out here tonight, Thornton?" he teases. His eyes linger around my breasts for a moment before flicking back up to my eyes. I lick my lips and can't for the life of me wipe this giddy grin from my face. I haven't felt this way in such a long time.

"I guess we'll find out, Sutherland."

For a foolish moment, I forget about all my problems. All ninety-nine of them, including those assholes. Tonight, I'm just going to forget about my past. Start anew.

We luck out on parking and get a spot in the field closest to the main area. A huge bonfire is already roaring. The music is so loud it feels like I'm at a concert.

"I guess we don't have to worry about wild animals with the music being this loud!" I shout even though I'm standing right beside Grahm.

He laughs and bends down to my level. "Nope! Let's grab some drinks. Follow me." He threads his fingers with mine and guides me through the crowd.

Everyone is singing along to the music, beers and canned margaritas in their hands as they sway to the beat. My shoulders are already moving of their own volition.

I spot Hailey by the coolers almost immediately. Her hair is pulled up into a high ponytail and it still meets her mid-back. My jaw drops. Talk about a freaking queen. I let go of Grahm's hand and make my way over to her.

"Briar, wait," Grahm whisper shouts, but I'm already walking up to Hailey so I ignore him.

"Hey! Is there a canned sangria in there somewhere?" I don't have to yell now that we're a bit farther away from the speakers. Hailey lights up and gives me a big hug.

"Briar! I'm so glad you're here!" she says with a slight slur. "Yes, oh my God, here, this one is the best." She hands me a Moscow mule.

I'm not picky about drinks and I don't mind this one, so I just laugh and nod at her. "Thank you."

"Who are you here with?" Hailey lifts a suggestive brow at me. "You look ravishing, so I want to know who the lucky guy—" Her words fall as her eyes lift to meet Grahm's.

There's an awkward beat that passes through them, and I feel it like a gut punch. Grahm's frown is half shocked and half pissed. My brows pull together, and I look back at Hailey. Her high spirits have been severed, and a dead-eyed stare has set in.

"Be careful with him, Briar." She locks eyes with me before turning abruptly and stalking away.

"What is she talking about?" I snap my attention to Grahm. He runs his hand through his hair and lets out a long sigh. His pupils are blown wide, and he looks furious.

"We used to date, and she didn't take the breakup so great." He sounds genuine, but there's something about her warning that makes me think it's more than that. Girls don't warn each other for nothing. Something happened that wasn't okay, and it sends the red flags up.

"Okay," I say slowly, wrapping my arms around myself uncomfortably.

"*Fuck.* Hang tight. I'll go get her to explain. I can't stand you looking at me like that, Thornton. And I want to have a good night." He gives me a pleading grin before setting his beer can down on a stump to chase after Hailey. I watch him disappear into the dark trees before I turn my attention back to the party.

I don't want to just stand here and wait with my thoughts, so I decide to venture out into the crowd. I'm swallowed whole by the music and the swarm of the bodies around me instantly. I'm glad I didn't bring a sweater because it's hot with all the people dancing and bumping into one another. Not to mention the bonfire blazing in the center only twenty feet away.

There's something so invigorating about being in a new town where no one knows you. It's like a new lease on life. No one knows your past, and you don't have any baggage or drama attached to your name. In my case, it's a dead family and murderous ex. But still. I can be whoever I want to be now.

I smile at a few guys who keep stealing looks my way.

I move my hips and sip on my drink. The light buzz starts to sift in after a few minutes, and a group of people have moved in around me, dancing with their hands in the air and having a careless, fun night. It's easy to get swept into, and I enjoy every second of it. It's like a nightclub in the fucking forest.

After a few songs, I cast a glance back in the direction where Grahm went after Hailey. He should've been back by now, right? I don't see either of them back by the coolers. *Weird.* I frown and start to maneuver around people and head in that direction.

A hand snags around my wrist and pulls me back against a hard chest. I stiffen and look over my shoulder, meeting John's sultry eyes.

"Hey, Briar, thought I saw you at the store today. *Weird, though.* I could've swore that Roman told you to get out of our town." His grip on my wrist is tight, but everything about his tone and facial expressions are disarming. Playful rather than threatening.

I turn to face him, giving him a scowl. "Funny, I thought I saw you too. Are you incapable of keeping your hands off women?" I reply sweetly.

His smile fades and his eyes darken. "Briar, you should

leave before Roman sees you out here. We did you a courtesy not saying anything to him, but you need to get fucking lost somewhere else." He starts pulling me toward the parking lot.

I tear my arm from his grip, garnering a few bystanders' attention. "I came here with someone, and I'm not going anywhere. What's the difference between me and the woman you were with earlier today? I don't see her being dragged out of town."

His expression is unreadable, and his jaw is flexed.

"Fine." He takes a wide step back and lifts his hands in surrender. "But don't expect me to help you later, Briar."

I give him a fake smile. "Gee thanks. I'll keep that in mind."

John's returning grin is filled with amusement. "Someone has spunk. I hope you keep it. I hate seeing the girls that lose it." He pats my head as he walks by and moves into the crowd. I lose sight of him in a mere second and can only assume that he's off to find his little posse of douchebags.

Great. Well, I didn't last long before getting spotted. I'd better find Grahm. I finish off my mule before passing the coolers and moving into the dark shadows that the forest creates.

"Grahm?" I say moderately loud. The music is still bumping, so there's a good chance he didn't hear me. I narrow my eyes and try to see better but can only make out some figures in the trees. There are a handful of groups standing around and talking while they sip their drinks. A few couples are pressed up against trees and making out.

Where the hell did he go? My eyes skirt over another couple before I pause and look back at them. It's Hailey and Grahm. It's too dark to see what they're doing, but he's leaned up against her, and their faces are close enough for me to draw conclusions.

The blood leaves my face, and my throat knots up. I know

we just met, but I had hopes that *I'd* be kissing him tonight. *Damn it.*

Good for them for working things out, I guess. I shake my head and smile. They are both nice people, so it makes sense that they'd be magnets to each other. The kind of guys that I'm always drawn to aren't as friendly as him.

My feet are sluggish as I move back up toward the bonfire— that drink hit me harder than I thought it would. When did I become such a lightweight? I stagger a few more steps before looking up. My gaze catches on someone standing perfectly in the center between two trees and blocking my way back to the party.

His jacket is familiar, with the cargo pockets and a hoodie slung over his head. *No.* I could never forget that arrogant lopsided stance, like he doesn't care about anything. The jacket is the exact same one I saw him wearing last night too.

Thank fucking God Roman's looking the other way.

I take the opportunity to quickly turn back around and maneuver my way through the forest back toward Grahm and Hailey. They've moved somewhere else, but I spot his hoodie and hat hanging on a branch near where I last saw them.

There's not much of an option since I don't feel like dying out here tonight. So I quickly head over and snag Grahm's hoodie. It's enormous and drops down to my knees. *So much for dancing and having fun*, I fume as I pull his baseball cap over my head.

It smells like Grahm, and I get another stomach twist at the turn of events. He could've at least told me not to wait up instead of leaving me there to look like an idiot. I glare into the dark trees and huff. I don't feel bad for taking his things. He owes me this at least.

I turn to try to find another path up to the party but am

met with a broad chest and the lovely scent of teakwood and motor oil.

Fuck, it's Roman.

"Oh, sorry," I say sheepishly, making sure to keep my head down and try to get by him. He grunts and steps aside. *He didn't recognize me!* I get a few steps up before I hear him following me.

"Hey, have you seen a couple of dumbasses around here? Bensen and Gale, if you are familiar with them." His voice is cold, but he's not being a complete jerk. His calm, maybe mildly annoyed, tone is one I could listen to for hours.

I shake my head. Not sure if he would remember my voice if I spoke more than a few words. I swallow my concern. "I saw John up at the bonfire not long ago. The rest can't be far since they seem to only do things tied together or not at all," I retort. I can't help but include the snide comment. My steps are even, and I try to remain calm so I don't give myself away.

He's quiet for a few moments, then huffs. "I'm so fucking tired of keeping track of them. They have no idea how much I protect them from." He sounds pretty stressed out.

I tilt my head in his direction, making sure to keep the hood down so he doesn't see my face. His hands are shoved into his coat pockets, and he's lingering a little too close for comfort. Who does he assume I am right now? A friend? Who in their right mind would be his friend? *Shit, this is bad.*

"Mm-hmm," I mumble, hoping he'll fuck off and I can try to catch a ride to town at least. I knew I shouldn't have come to this stupid party; it was marked to end badly from the start.

Roman takes a few wider steps as we reach the top of the slope and reenter the party. He walks at my side and grabs the sleeve of the hoodie with his thumb and forefinger. It's such a soft gesture from him that it gives me pause, and I hold my breath.

We both stop walking at the same time. I lift my head enough so that I see his nose and lips, careful not to go any higher and risk him catching my eyes. It's still relatively dark, but the bonfire gives enough light that I see his face clearly.

He has so many scars—so many, that it sinks into my chest and wrenches my imagination about what could've possibly led to them. Some look like tattoos, but there's no doubt in my mind that they are all scars. Some are jagged and others are carefully designed. Crafted by him, I suspect.

He looks out toward the dancing bodies, and I steal a glance at his face again. The scar across his forehead I saw last night is the worst, like barbwire was drug across it at one point in his life. One cuts through his top lip and connects to the bottom. Then there's his neck, and it almost looks like a mural of fire is wrapped around it.

I tip my head back down to the safe level and stare at his hand, still carefully holding my sleeve as if I'm an anchor. I softly clear my throat. "Um. Do you want a drink?" I ask, hoping I can slip away with the excuse.

He grunts. "Let's get you one. The race starts soon, so I'll have mine after."

Motherfucker. I keep burying myself in a deeper hole. If he finds out I'm not this girl he thinks I am, I'm *fucked*.

He doesn't let go as we make our way toward a different part of the party. I glance back several times, hoping I'll see Grahm and he'll save me. But there's no sign of him, and I'm left to whatever fate I've been dealt tonight.

I can't help but notice how weary Roman's eyes are as he grabs a drink from the cooler and tosses it at me. I make sure to duck my head more before he looks up. "You know…you look pretty tired. Do you get enough sleep?"

He stills before lighting a cigarette and inhaling deeply. "Says the girl looking like she just crawled out from under an oil spill."

My brows quirk and I glance down at the hoodie. It's covered in dark red and black stains. These were *not* on Grahm when he chased after Hailey. What the hell happened?

The blood from my face drains and my breathing grows heavy. She said he was dangerous… Did he hurt her?

"Chill out. It just looks like oil," Roman says nonchalantly. Is that him confirming it's blood? *I have to act casual or he might suspect something*, I remind myself.

Roman is quiet as I sip on the sangria he grabbed for me. It was the one I wanted in the first place, so I don't complain as I drink it and follow him down a dirt road toward the back side of the mountain.

The entire party seems to be heading this way. I keep my eyes peeled for his little cult somewhere in the crowd and hope that once they are all reunited like little puppies I can make a break for it. I really don't like pretending to be someone. In my defense, I wasn't trying to. He just happened to assume.

"Looks like they are just going to be watching from the stands. All right, you're with me then," he grumbles, offering his hand for my empty can. I set it on his palm and he tosses it into a garbage can before he approaches a blacked-out Mercedes. It looks like it's had aftermarket work done to make it look more… *aggressive* is the word I'd use.

It looks familiar, but I'm too panicked to think much on it.

My stomach churns when Roman turns the car on and looks straight at me as if I'm supposed to get in.

"Are you feeling okay?" he asks with a frown starting to pull at the corner of his lips. I turned my head a little late—I think he saw my face.

The jig is up. I shake my head instinctively and turn around to bolt. He's far enough away that I have a chance of losing him in the crowd.

"Wait," Roman shouts. His voice is quickly drowned out by the music from above and from the chattering people who are pouring into the racetrack and stands.

My heart races, and I don't dare look back. There's no fucking way I'm getting into a car, let alone be in a *race*, with that psychopath.

"Hey, you stole my hoodie!" Grahm's voice rings through the air, and I've never wanted to die more than I do in this moment. My head snaps up, and I meet Grahm's eyes. He's with a man I haven't met yet. The man looks right at me just as surprise shoots across Grahm's features before he stupidly shouts, "Briar?"

To say my legs turn into stone would be an understatement. I cast a mortified look over my shoulder and find Roman standing just a few feet behind me. His expression is unreadable, but his eyes trace over my face, and I watch as the muscles in his jaw feather with fury.

Roman looks past me and stares at Grahm as he says with a deathly cold tone, "*Sutherland*. Why am I not surprised you're clinging to the new girl in town?"

Grahm's mouth is parted, and his lips twitch like he wants to say something but can't find the words. Roman sets his arm over my shoulders, sending a shudder up my spine. My brows pinch together as I'm helplessly pulled away by Roman. Grahm just watches; he doesn't intervene like I thought he would.

What did Roman mean by that? It sounds like they know each other a lot more than Grahm led me to believe. I have to bite my lower lip to keep my mouth shut. The last thing I want is to make this situation worse.

He drags me all the way back to his car, where someone my height and wearing the same hoodie is standing and waiting. I don't get to see their face before I'm shoved into the passenger seat and the door is slammed in my face, but I'm betting that's who he mistook me for.

I wrap my arms around myself, trembling, as I wait for him to get in on the other side. He says a few words to the person he thought I was, and they head toward the stands, where people are waiting for the race to begin.

Roman throws his door open and plops down, cursing under his breath as he starts the engine back up.

I try to open the door but it doesn't budge, and I can't find the lock. How the fuck do auto shop guys in the middle of nowhere get their hands on a car like this?

I try to make myself as small as I can, digging my nails into my leg to punish myself for being so stupid and allowing this to happen.

The silence of waiting for him to say something is worse than his blow-up last night. I'm leaned up as far as I can get against the door and watching him carefully.

He ruffles his hair with a frustrated breath, then shoots me a dirty look. "You're in serious trouble, you little brat. Did I not scare you enough last night?" His eyes shift lower to my waist, and I hold back a scream as he leans over and grabs the seat belt. His scent drenches over me and a small, scared whimper escapes my lips as he clips the belt into place.

Roman's face is a mere few inches from mine when he looks up at me, grinning despicably. "You think I'd bother touching someone as worthless as you?"

Okay, ouch.

He drops the e-brake and shifts his car into Drive, pulling us forward up to the line where the other cars are currently revving their engines. "You better hold on to something if you don't want to smack your head. Although I wouldn't be upset if you did, conniving brat."

My hand quickly snakes around the door handle. "Who did you think I was? It's not like I wanted to be dragged into a car with Satan's right ass cheek."

Roman rolls his eyes and flexes his jaw. "Believe it or not, we usually have a trusted co-rider in the car during our races. Mine happens to be a meek young woman who doesn't whore around with my squad."

"Dude, you have some severe mommy issues, don't you?" I snap at him and instantly regret it when he glowers at me.

He takes one look at my stiffened state and sighs before shoving his helmet on. *I don't get one of those?* I want to shake him and force him to let me out of the car, but the flag girl is already walking out onto the runway and getting ready to wave it.

"If you try distracting me in anyway, I won't hesitate to hurt you. My mission doesn't include dancing around a dumb bitch," Roman warns.

As if I thought I loathed him last night.

I fucking hate his guts.

I hold on to the designated handles for dear life as the flag girl waves the red cloth around and brings it toward the ground in one fell swoop. *Wait, he said mission… What the fuck is that supposed to mean—*

Roman throws the stick into first gear and floors the gas pedal.

The song "Thunderclouds" by LSD comes blaring out of his speakers, it's a remix that I don't recognize, so my eyes flick down to the dash screen and it reads "Lost Frequencies Remix." The cabin of the vehicle is soundproof and the speakers are top-of-the-line, so I can barely hear anything other than the music pulsing through my veins and the furious roar of the engine. The bass is so intense it vibrates my thighs and forces a mewl from my lips.

Thank God he can't hear any of the embarrassing sounds I'm making. Not with how fucking loud it is in here and definitely not through that helmet he's wearing. The G-force from the initial takeoff has my stomach in knots, and I can barely force my eyes up to the windshield to see the road.

I instantly wish I hadn't. We're going at least 100 mph on a dirt road, and a huge turn is coming up. Only one other car is head-to-head with Roman, and he's not letting up on the gas at all.

I duck my head and scream as Roman rotates the wheel quickly all the way and the car starts drifting. Even above the music and my bloody-murder screaming, I can hear Roman fucking laughing at me. Honestly, I couldn't care less if he's laughing. I'm trying not to vomit up the two drinks I just had.

He straightens the wheel, and the car snaps back into full throttle. I look up, thinking the worst is over. That's when the car head-to-head with us slams into the driver's side. My head jerks and smacks against the passenger window.

The last thing I hear is that godforsaken asshole laughing before everything goes black.

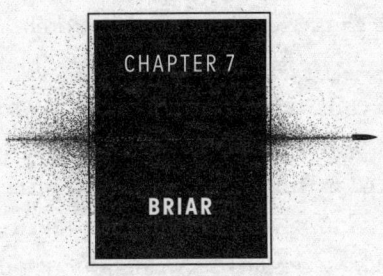

CHAPTER 7

BRIAR

A familiar voice stirs my mind back into the present. *God, my head is killing me.*

I groan and try to move to sit up, only to realize someone's holding me. We aren't moving. I'm in someone's lap. I try to think coherently, but the throbbing headache is making me disoriented.

"Briar, are you okay?" A fuzzy voice echoes through my head.

"Fuck, you're such an asshole."

"Why didn't you give her the helmet?" Another voice, clearer this time.

Three separate males are bickering at the person holding me. They are recognizable, but I can't focus on anything right now. All I know is that my head hurts really bad and I'm extraordinarily tired.

I groan again and bury my face in the crook of the person's

arm. Some part of me guesses that it's Roman holding me, but his bitchy exhale as a reply to the others confirms it.

Where are we? How did the race end?

Roman sets his other hand gently on my shoulder. I flinch and draw myself closer to his chest. He pauses before setting his hand down on my head instead, brushing hair away from the side of my head that hurts. His fingertips skate over the tender skin, their coldness sending a shudder through my bones.

"I told her to hang on," Roman mutters with zero empathy.

"What do we do, Syxx? There's no way Grahm fucking Sutherland isn't a gatekeeper. We confirmed it. What the hell is he doing with her?" John's voice is threaded with concern, although it doesn't sound like it's for me.

Roman's last name is Syxx? My mind snags on that information for some reason more than the other concerning things they're saying. I blame my pounding headache.

"Hmm. Yeah, I agree. Which means she's undoubtedly involved in some part of their plans. She might even be one of them for all we know." Roman's grip on me tightens.

One of who? What are they talking about? I try to sit up again. This time, I'm able to prop myself up with my arm. I'm met with Roman's intense stare, unreadable as always—and stupidly handsome beyond all reason.

"Ow." I wince as pressure shoots through my brain, and I press my palm to the side of my head.

John is at my side in a second. "Briar, are you okay? Let me drive you to the next town over. There's a hospital—"

Bensen cuts him off firmly. "No, I can patch her up at her farm. She's likely concussed. Let's head over there, and I'll get her taken care of." They all share an uncomfortable look. Well, all of them except Roman. His eyes are still firmly planted on my face, observing me like he's waiting for me to bite him or spread wings—or shit gold.

There's no way in hell that I'm letting them go to my farm. I shake my head and try to stand, stumbling and about to hit my knees before Roman snakes an arm around my waist and pulls me back into his lap. *God damn it.*

"Everyone, head back to bas"—he clears his throat—"the shop. I need to take care of our little problem here." The group gives him disapproving glares.

"She's hurt. At least give her the night before you—" Taylor cuts himself off and grits his teeth. "Fuck. Just take her home tonight. We'll figure this out tomorrow, okay?"

Bensen and Gale nod. John folds his arms. "I still think you should take her to the hospital in Bascliff. Her head is still bleeding a bit." John's voice is pained.

Bleeding? I lift my hand and dab my temple with my sleeve. A red smudge is left behind on the gray fabric. *Not that it matters with the stains already there.* A worried itch pulls in the back of my head. *Where is Hailey?* What the hell, how much can go wrong in one freaking night?

Roman sighs. "Fine, I'll take her to the fucking farm on one of your motorcycles. But stay up until I get back. We need to discuss what happened tonight. Keep an eye on Sutherland until he leaves."

John grabs my hand and squeezes it before saying, "I'll drive her, and you can follow behind. Look what happens when she's left with you."

Roman gives John a death glare. "I won't tell you again, *Bishop.*"

John's mouth firms, and he swallows whatever it is he wanted to say before giving me one last troubled look before moving aside. Roman stands with me in his arms and doesn't wait for John or the others to acknowledge us leaving as he carries me away. There's some grumbling behind us before the others head back to the party to do… I don't know what.

What the fuck are they doing? Are they undercover cops or something? They're acting so strange. Is this what small-town cults do?

It's much darker than it was earlier, and I can't see the light from the bonfire anymore. "What time is it? Where did everyone go?" My voice is hoarse, and I'm just realizing how dry my mouth is.

"You were out for over an hour. The party is on the other hillside. We couldn't exactly let everyone see my injured passenger after the race, now could we?" Roman says with an unapologetic tilt to his heavyset frown.

I grunt at him and shut my eyes. "I'm going to the police in the morning, asshole. You guys are going to be in deep shit."

Roman cackles, the vibrations from his laughter roll through me. I glare up at him. It's hard to distinguish his features clearly in the dark, but I catch the locks of hair that fall over his brow and the slight amusement that flickers across his gaze.

"I'm going to pretend I didn't hear you say that. Because if I *did* hear you say it, I'd have to cut your pretty little tongue out." Roman's voice is flat and humorless.

"What are you guys mixed up in? Whatever it is, I swear I'm not a part of it. I'm literally just trying to get my uncle's estate ready to sell, that's it." I'm not sure how much me rambling will help my case, but I have to try, don't I?

He glances over his shoulder to gauge how far back the other guys are before he sets his attention on my pissed-off expression. "I know you are a part of it. You were practically delivered to me tied in pretty bows, Squirt. You really fucked up with Grahm, by the way."

"Delivered to you?" I deadpan. "Don't fucking call me Squirt." I push against his chest, but he doesn't even seem to notice. *I can't handle his fucking arrogance.*

He studies every reaction I give. "Hmm. You really had no idea." His statement is more of a mumbling to himself than it is for me. He blatantly ignores my comment too.

"No idea of what?" I wriggle in his arms, and he's forced to stop and let me down. I stumble a little but am able to remain standing this time. "Grahm is the ranch hand that helped my uncle. I kind of need him for his work around the farm. I can't get all the repairs done myself, and I don't have the money to hire anyone. It's not like I know Grahm personally."

He looks at me like he's trying to decide if I'm telling the truth or not. We walk slowly, and I can hear someone catching up to us from behind.

Our bickering falls silent until the person passes and heads toward their vehicle in the parking lot up ahead.

The quiet tension between me and Roman is worse than the bickering, so I stir the pot. "Your last name is Syxx?"

He side-eyes me. "Something like that."

My sarcastic side wins over my sensible one. Probably because I'm concussed. "Roman Syxx sounds like a super made-up name. I mean you literally have a Roman *numeral* six on your face."

We step into the parking area, where it's much brighter with the bonfire in view now and the solar tea lights throughout the tree boughs.

Roman ignores me, but I don't miss the way that his hands curl tightly at his sides like he's about to burst. It's good to know that I at least get on his nerves without him losing control.

Maybe he's more level-headed than I pinned him for. It's his eyes that give away his calm yet pissed-off mood. Callum's eyes were void of anything human the night he buried me. You can tell a lot through someone's eyes.

We stop in front of a motorcycle, a crotch rocket, to be specific. I give Roman a contorted expression. Half *What the fuck?* and *I'm not getting on that.*

"You'll be fine. Just hold on to me."

"Can't you just drive us back in the Mercedes?" I'd hate to get back into that car, but it beats this death trap a million to one.

He shakes his head. "No can do. I lost it in the race thanks to you."

I glower. "What?"

His expression doesn't lift in the slightest. "Those are the rules. Don't worry though, I'll steal it back. Here, put this on," he says so nonchalantly as he hands me a helmet.

"Oh, so there *was* a second helmet," I say scathingly. "How often do you lose? And for the record, I'm really not surprised you're into grand theft auto."

"I can toss the helmet in the woods if you want to keep complaining about it." He mounts the bike and starts the engine. "This would be a first, again, thanks to you."

I hesitate to put the helmet on, worried that it will put pressure on my throbbing temple. I gently brush my fingertips over the side of my head to test how tender it is and wince at the pain. Roman glances over and notices my pause.

He lets out a big sigh and throws his head back, turning off the bike. "If we get caught and I have to beat some dude up, it's your fault." He takes the helmet from my hands and sets it back on his bike along with his.

This night has been such crap that I don't even care what he's doing, I just want to be back at the farm and in bed.

Roman selects an SUV and tries the door. Of course, small-town folk always leave their doors unlocked, so it opens. *Now he's making me participate in auto theft too?* I cross my arms and shiver as a cold breeze moves through me. He finds keys under the visor and starts up the car.

He motions for me to get in.

"You're so corrupt," I mumble as I climb in, wincing at the pain that jolts across my head.

"And don't forget it."

He drives in silence, and after the first few minutes I quickly start dozing off only to have someone shake me awake roughly by my shoulder.

"You can't sleep, Briar." His voice is sharp but somehow fuzzy. I groan and hold my head. It's hard to keep my eyes open, but after Roman gets tired of shaking me every few minutes, he just turns the radio up really loud.

It's the longest drive of my life.

Once we get to the farm and park, Roman is quick to get out and usher me toward the house. Jesus, he's acting like we're being followed. Paranoid much?

He grabs the sleeve of my hoodie like he did at the party, but this time he's not as gentle with it. He guides me to the door and looks at me expectantly. "Either you unlock it and we act like normal people, or I kick it down and we can continue on with our eventful night."

I'm two seconds from punching him in the dick, I swear to God.

I relent and grab the key from my jeans pocket. "I don't

think you know how to act like a normal person," I state plainly as I unlock the door and push past him. Roman grunts and shuts the door behind us, flipping the lock as if we might be expecting visitors. With how he's acting, I'm starting to think we are.

He moves to the windows and shuts all the blinds in the kitchen and living room. "Sit," he orders, pointing at the sofa I spent all morning cleaning off.

I'm tired and my head is pounding, so I do as he says and plop down. He stares down at me for a few seconds before he disappears into the kitchen. A handful of minutes later he returns with a wet towel, bandage wrap, and an ice pack.

I put on my best annoyed expression and avoid eye contact as he sits down beside me. He doesn't speak as he inspects my head wound, and I'm glad for it. If I have to hear him say anything else, I think I might lose my temper again.

Roman gently pats the towel over the cut. I flinch and fist my hands on my legs. Despite my best efforts, a small pained whimper escapes my lips.

He hesitates, lowering his hand out of view enough that our eyes catch. My pulse leaps—I didn't realize his face was so close to mine. There's something in the way that he analyzes my features that makes me nervous. I can't tell if it's in a good way or a bad one. I only know that he gives me the same adrenaline rush that his erratic racing did.

Dangerous.

But not in the same way Callum was. No, Roman is a new definition of the word.

"Why did you let me think you were someone else tonight?" he asks coldly, holding eye contact with me and not letting a single thought reflect in his gaze. *He should be a fucking FBI agent for his poker face alone.*

I break and turn my head away. He's so intimidating that I can't look him in the eyes and talk. Roman grabs my chin, not roughly but firmly, and forces me to face him again.

"Why?" he asks slowly.

I swallow my pride. "Oh, I don't know, maybe because you threatened me last night and I didn't want you to literally kill me." Tears bubble up in my eyes, and I have to furiously blink them away because I'll be damned if I let him think I'm anything but angry. "I was just trying to get by you, but you thought I was your co-rider or whatever the hell she is. And I have no clue what your little cult is doing illegally, okay? It's been a shitty forty-eight hours, and I just want to go to bed and never see your face again."

I firm my trembling lips and shut my eyes. He's just staring down at me with the emptiest expression, like he has no empathetic bone in his body.

"Cult?" he sounds genuinely perplexed at my label for them.

"That's right."

Roman holds on to my chin for a few more seconds before letting go. I let my head lower and gaze at the floor, remaining still as he finishes cleaning and tending to the wound.

"Did you know your uncle?" He doesn't sound as irritated anymore, more analytical and thoughtful. Curious, even. I dare to look at him and find that he looks more relaxed now. Does that mean he believes me?

God, I hope so.

"I met him a few times. We weren't close by any means, but he was the only living relative I had left. I'm here because of the estate attorney." I delicately reach up to touch the bandage work that Roman did.

He grabs my wrist, drawing a gasp from me.

"Leave it. You smacked your head pretty bad, and I think Bensen is right, you have a concussion." Roman's brow quirks a bit, with guilt I dare say.

"I'm fine." I jerk my arm out of his hold and rub his touch from my skin. "You can go now."

"What was the estate attorney's name?" he presses me, ignoring the rest.

"Mr. Holland. Again. You can *leave*."

Roman flexes his jaw but doesn't move; he only watches me ever so carefully. "You're not fine. I'm going to stay here to make sure you don't sleep for at least a few hours." He doesn't sound one bit sorry either.

I narrow my eyes at him and give him a fake smile. "*Great.* Well, I'm hungry, so I'm going to make something to eat." I get up and head to the kitchen. There's not much in here, but I'm so glad I went to the grocery store today.

Roman follows me and takes a seat at the counter. He looks around the room and furrows his brows. "How well do you know Mr. Holland?" He obviously is still digging for details, and he seems oddly interested in the estate attorney.

I turn the stove on and set a pot of water on it to cook noodles. At least Roman doesn't give enough of a shit about anything to notice how pathetic my food situation is. I turn and lean back against the counter to look at him.

"Not at all. I was surprised he even knew how to contact me." *Considering I've been on the run and changed my name and number.* How *did* Mr. Holland find me? The thought never occurred to me, and now that I think about it, it's rather unsettling. I shake my head—I'm sure there's a reasonable answer, but no matter how long I think on it, I can't remember having that conversation with Mr. Holland. My head throbs again.

Roman firms his lips like the entire idea of me even existing stumps him. He reaches into his pocket and pulls out a cigarette. He doesn't bother asking if he can smoke it in the house, and I don't care enough to stop him.

A huge plume of smoke rolls from his lips as he exhales. I watch and hate how sexy he is. He's the complete asshole version of what I would want in a guy. But Roman Syxx is like *broken* broken. Some people fall under the shadows too deeply and they never come back out the same.

Funny, I wonder if he sees the same thing in me.

Callum killed every part of Chloe Thornton. I wouldn't even recognize that girl. I'm just Briar. The girl no one gives a shit about, and that's how I like it. The more someone cares about you, the more danger you're always in.

I learned the hard way.

"I know it was you casing this house last night." I break the silence. My arms are crossed over my chest, and the water is boiling in the pot beside me. Now that I'm not panicking, I remember where I saw the Mercedes. It's the same one from last night.

Roman takes another deep pull from his cigarette before grinning. "And?" he says as he exhales effortlessly.

"What could you possibly want from this dump?" My mind goes straight to the flash drive, but how would Roman know about it? It sounded like even Mr. Holland didn't know until he found the paperwork.

He leans up on his forearms before standing and walking over next to me. I stiffen but don't budge. Roman grabs a handful of pasta and snaps it in half before throwing it in. He puts in way more than I can eat.

"I'm going to assume you don't want to actually know." His tone is a warning.

"That's too much." I frown as he adds another handful of noodles to the pot.

"I'm having some too." His eyes flick to mine. I'm shocked for a split second before glowering. Great, now he's eating my food too.

He's not wrong, though. I don't really want to know... especially if they are mixed up in some shady shit. Was my uncle tied up in all of this too? I never asked Mr. Holland how he died, but now I'm considering asking.

The noodles cook as Roman texts, I'm assuming his friends. I'm grateful for his questions to be staved off by something else. When the noodles are done, I grab the one sauce jar, I have, and to my surprise, Roman doesn't say anything about it, nor does he give me shit for having the cheapest, most bland brand. He pours half the bottle in the pot and looks to me for forks.

Okay, I guess I'm just casually eating with a dickhead tonight, concussed and wishing to forget everything that has anything to do with Bane Falls.

"Listen. I don't trust anyone, so don't take it personally. I don't think you are a danger to my squad, but I won't let even the slightest chance slip by. Got it? The only reason your tongue hasn't been cut out is because I am a good judge of character, and you are the most plain Jane, helpless girl I've ever met." Roman's words punch me in the gut before he takes a huge bite of spaghetti.

I'm happy I get to keep my tongue, though I doubt he'd actually cut it out. *Tough guy.* He's secretly soft somewhere in there behind all those threats.

"What's the story there? Is it why you're so messed up?" I gesture to his face with my hand. He has to know that I'm referring to all the self-inflicted scars.

His eyes widen, and he cracks a smirk. "Messed up? *Me?* This is called control, Squirt."

I watch him take another big bite, and my appetite is already fading. I grab a small forkful and twirl it on my plate a few times.

"How so? And why are you calling me Squirt—I feel like you're wanting me to ask, so I'm asking," I press him. It's weird that he smiles at insults and nothing else. God, he would've been a hell of a case study in college.

Roman licks his lips and pulls down his hoodie enough so that I can see his neck. My stomach turns as I take in what looks like brand marks of fire that wrap around his throat.

"Control in how I process whatever I want, how I want," he says like a shell of a man. His eyes are empty and loathing for everything. It's actually kind of sad, because I thought I was the most pitiful thing in the world. Yet here is Roman Syxx.

The mess of all messes.

I choke back the urge to ask him if he's okay. Clearly he isn't.

"I'm calling you Squirt because you look like you'd be a squirter." He's full of amusement as I choke on a sip of water.

I definitely thought he was going to say because I'm short, *not* because I'm a squirter. "Care to elaborate?" I say smoothly, forcing myself to take a bite of food.

"Yeah, when a woman comes, sometimes she—"

"Oh my God, not that!" My cheeks flush, and I can't stand that devious smile that tugs at his lips.

He watches me for a few seconds before taking a breath and giving me a distant look as he gets serious. "You wouldn't get it. How could you? Look at how unmarred and foolish you are to everything around you." His voice turns more vexed. Like he's envious of my shit, simple life. Or at least of what it looks like on the surface.

If he knew of the bad things that hid under my bed, he would swallow those words like poison. Two can poke this fucking bear.

"Hmm. Sounds like you're using self-punishment to justify whatever it is you and your *squad* do, right? You're defeated, and you cope by hurting yourself in ways you can't forget." I give him the same emotionless expression that he's been giving me this entire time to see how he likes it.

The vein in his forehead protrudes, and he clenches his jaw. "I'd be *very* careful how you use that sly tongue of yours. I'm not opposed to cutting it out still."

I don't let the fear reach my eyes, even though my heart is pounding out of my chest. "That's the third time you've said that, Roman. If you're done playing house now, you can leave."

I lift the empty pot and take it to the sink. Before I can move, Roman's hands come down on either side of me. His hot breath coasts across the shell of my ear. I become acutely aware of every place his body is touching mine and take a deep breath.

"If you are lying about anything, you better tell me now. I won't be willing to clear the air later, Briar." His hard chest against my back sends chills up my spine.

A knot grows in my throat. *My real name is Chloe.* I want to tell him. But if he's keeping all these secrets, my name shouldn't be a problem. Especially since I'm in hiding.

I shake my head. "Does that mean you'll leave me alone and I get to stay?"

He's motionless. "For now. You're involved in this, so you don't really have the luxury of leaving anymore."

"Involved in what exactly? And I get to keep my tongue?" Unnecessary to add, but I can't help but push his buttons.

He shifts away and unblocks me. I turn to face him. His dark hair is messy, a few locks hanging over his brows. His features are sharp yet so soft in the crappy kitchen lighting. He's dangerously lovely. A dark ocean that would drown me in a second if I dared to wade in too deep.

His gaze softens a fraction. "For now." A slight, mocking grin that may or may not reset my headache.

I watch the stolen SUV idle two hundred feet down my driveway for an hour after he supposedly "left."

Is he watching me?

A terrible feeling coils in my chest. I don't think it's just a cult.

CHAPTER 8

ROMAN

stop the car halfway down the driveway and throw it in Park. My phone lights up with the hundredth text from the squad giving me updates on the movements of Grahm and a few other Sub-Rosa men we've been tracking.

Hopper: Normal activity at the bonfire. Sutherland hasn't raised any alarms regarding Thornton that I'm aware of.

Bishop: Movement identified in the field leading up to the farm. Keep sharp to the right.

Viper: I'm with Zeus. We trailed the two men to the laundromat. Can confirm that this is where they've been passing information for a few nights now, but I never see them go inside. We were able to get a tag on one of their bags before they left the party, so we'll have more data soon.

I take note of John's intel and glance up to the right side of the driveway. It's pitch-black out there, and I don't have any of my night gear, but it's not a problem.

I shoot a text back with a thumbs-up before unsheathing my combat knife and stepping outside the car. The air is brisk—the scent of snapped grass and dust fills the night.

There's not much I enjoy more than blowing off some steam. I pat the side pocket on my left leg to make sure my pliers are there. I need them more often than I don't.

I pull my hood over my head and slowly wade through the tall grass. It doesn't take long before I see the footsteps in the dry dirt. Looks like my little friend is out here waiting for Briar to go to bed so he can either cut her throat or kidnap her.

My curiosity is piqued. Why did Nolan tell me she was a precious package? And why does Sub-Rosa give a shit about her? It has to be for the same reason.

She has intel, and it must be valuable.

Rustling off to my left brings me to a halt. I readjust the grip on my knife so that I can take the person out quickly. Tall grass sways, and that's when I spot the top of a baseball hat. Whoever it is, they are dressed in all black and even have a mask covering half of their face.

I crouch and observe them for a few minutes to see if he'll pull out his phone to take pictures of his target or go through his texts. I'd prefer to have it unlocked before I start the interrogation.

He does exactly what I predict, pulling out his cell and

zooming in to the room that Briar likely uses as her bedroom, since it's the only one with the lights on.

There's not much time for him to react, other than a short gasp before my blade is pressed tightly against his throat. He's confident and fast, drawing his handgun quickly and aiming it at my head.

I anticipated the move and wedge my finger beneath the trigger and handle so he can't pull it. A wicked grin spreads across my lips and I push the sharp edge of my blade farther into his neck. He lets out a sharp grunt and drops his weapon.

"Who've I got here? I doubt it's Sutherland. Is it Hogan? Or maybe it's Lane." I kick his gun five feet away from us so he doesn't try to go after it when he realizes I'm not here to let captured rats go free.

His muscles seize up, and his breath hitches. "Sutherland...? How do you know who we are?" His voice sounds like Hogan's.

I pause and consider his confused tone when I brought up Sutherland. Is Grahm not a part of Sub-Rosa? We were thorough. There's no way that he's not. I make a mental note to come back to that with the squad later. Grahm is involved somehow, but maybe he doesn't get his hands dirty.

"Oh, I know many things about Sub-Rosa, Hogan. What I don't know is why you're out here tracking down this girl." I lean in closer and tilt his head up with the knife so he's looking at her window again. "What does she have to do with the underworld? Why are you here?"

He tries to look back to see my face. It earns him a bash across the head with my pliers. "Ow, fuck!"

"I'm already in a really shitty mood, so can we get to the part where you just tell me?" I tap the side of his jaw with the pliers while increasing the pressure on the knife.

"Okay, okay. She apparently has the code to a flash drive that our boss wants. It's the same one he had…you know, Arnold, killed over." He sounds like he didn't agree with Arnold's death, but I wouldn't doubt that he was the one who scouted his schedule the entire time just to figure it out in the first place. That's what these fuckers do. They're patient, if anything.

Was Arnold involved in Sub-Rosa? What the fuck did Nolan have him doing out here, and why was it never brought to my attention that a sleeper agent was out here?

I think on that for a moment. How would Briar even come across this code? Are they assuming, or do they have intel?

"You're sure she knows this code? Who was your source?" I dig the tip of the knife into his Adam's apple.

He makes a choked sound and scrambles for words. "No, I'm not sure at all. We're just doing what we're told, and right now it's to keep her under surveillance."

My brow furrows. Maybe they aren't trying to kill her, but she's piqued someone's interest just like she did Nolan's. "What's on this flash drive anyway?"

He shakes his head. "I don't know. But apparently, she has the code to unlock the secured data on it. Fuck man, she might not even know that she knows it."

Briar definitely has no clue about a code or a flash drive. She's so innocent it makes me sick.

"Okay, and who would've given her this code?"

He shrugs. "I don't know, man, maybe Arnold. This girl says he's her uncle, right? It would make sense. I don't know anything else though, I swear."

"Great." I shove him forward and pretend to let him go. I lose any joy in killing when I already have them helpless and pissing their pants. It's only fair that they have a little bit of hope before I devour it.

Hogan shifts on his feet and quickly grabs his pistol, aiming it at my head and pulling the trigger. It clicks a few times before he realizes that I flipped the safety on.

I grin. "Nice meeting you, Hogan."

My KA-BAR is lodged in his neck before he can even shout.

CHAPTER 9

BRIAR

There are coyotes out here, or bears…possibly raccoons. All I know is I'm sick of picking up trash off the ground every goddamn morning for the past week now.

Sweat drips off my forehead as I grab the last balled-up piece of paper and stuff it into a new, unripped garbage bag. I'm adding padlocks and chains to my shopping list today. No more nuisances.

Speaking of nuisances. I scowl as I spot Grahm's truck pulling up to the front of the house.

He's stopped by every single day since last Saturday night. Every other time he's come over, I've been safely hidden away in the upstairs bedroom, but of course he catches me outside today. *Shit.*

I try to make a beeline for the back door, but he's already running around the corner of the house, breathing heavily and with worry in his eyes. "Briar? Oh my God, I've been so fucking worried about you!" He tries to come up and hug me, but I take a step back and give him an uncertain once-over. Between Hailey's warning, his bloody hoodie, and what Roman told me, I don't trust him one bit.

Every time I've swung by the grocery store this week, Hailey has either been on her break or taking a sick day. Her coworkers seem to be covering for her, and it's fucking weird. I just need to make sure that she's all right.

Grahm looks like he's lost sleep. He's not the flirty farm boy from last week. He has a few cuts on his left cheek that would suggest that he's been in a fistfight.

"I'm fine," I say under my breath.

He takes in my posture and moves back a little to give me space. "I'm so sorry about the party last weekend. I lost track of time, and by the time I finished talking to Hailey, I couldn't find you. I shouldn't have left you alone. Did Roman hurt you?"

Grahm sounds like he's been worrying about me, but I honestly don't know who to trust anymore. Not after the stunt he pulled.

His eyes catch on the bruising around my temple, and he visibly pales. "I'm going to fucking kill him!" Grahm shouts and starts stomping back to his pickup.

I panic and run out in front of him with my hands raised to calm him. "It wasn't him. I'm fine, honestly. I just got lost and tripped and smacked my head." I hate how well I lie. I hate that I know each one will come back and reap what they sow even more. But it works. He lets his muscles relax, and his expression softens.

"Briar, I feel terrible. It's my fault."

It totally is. I firm my lips.

"The last I saw of you, you were getting in that fucker's car for the race. I about drove to Murray's house and made him get his sheriff's uniform on to find you that night." He lets out a breath of relief.

Then why didn't you? I arch a brow. "Oh?"

"I mean, I drove by after the party and saw your lights on, so I figured you were okay. And when you ignored me, I thought you just needed some space." I give him a pointed look. "Listen, I'm not good at this kind of thing. But are we okay? I still want to help with the farm and make up for my behavior." He gives me a hopeful smile. Damn his sparkling eyes. It also helps that he did actually show up every day, even when I ignored him. It shows that he's at least devoted to helping me sell the farm.

But what about Hailey?

"Your hoodie was covered in…oil or something dark. What exactly happened between you and Hailey?" I have no proof that he did anything at all. So I don't want to jump to conclusions.

"I didn't want to say anything, but we sort of hooked up. I took my hoodie off and some asshole must have dropped it in the dirt or something. Who cares if it's stained? I'm just glad you're okay." His answer seems honest enough and he has guilt in his eyes, admitting to hooking up with Hailey, which is what I originally suspected.

I cross my arms and roll my eyes. "Fine. But I'm still pissed at you."

His eyes light up.

"And you owe me answers," I tack on, lifting a judgy, untrusting brow at him.

Grahm laughs and rubs his beard. "I'd expect nothing less. Thanks, Briar. Should we head to town and grab some coffee while you interrogate me? It's on me."

I chuckle and let my shoulders relax. "I could really use it."

The café is as pleasant as it was the first time. The atmosphere is warm and smells like coffee beans and vanilla. The tables are empty, except for one person in the far front by the windows, who is typing furiously on their laptop.

"I think you owe me an explanation," I mumble as I blow the steam from my latte. The weather has been gradually getting colder, which I absolutely love. Today is one of the last warm days of summer. Thank God for having phone service again. It was the first thing I did Sunday morning after the party last week. Granted, it's a prepay plan, but it's better than nothing.

I still need to stop by the grocery store and thank Hailey for telling me where to go for it. And even though Grahm said his hoodie was stained by someone else, I'm still concerned and would feel better once I see her for myself. I left the hoodie in the basement on top of the washing machine. Even having it in my house makes me feel anxious because what if he's lying and it is blood?

Grahm nods reluctantly and runs his hand down the side of his neck. "I was going to talk to Hailey and… Well, one thing led to another. We used to date, and I just wanted to know what she meant by telling you to be careful with me… Obviously that conversation went in a different direction. By the time I remembered you were waiting for me, I couldn't find my hoodie and then I found you with Roman."

I narrow my judgmental eyes at him. "Good to hear that I was an afterthought."

He winces. "Fuck. No, you're not. Again, I'm sorry."

I sigh and take a sip from my coffee. "It's okay. I've had worse things happen." There's a beat of silence as we both take another drink. "Can I ask you something?" I say in a serious tone.

Grahm looks at me thoughtfully, like he knows what I'm going to ask.

"What do you do besides help out at my uncle's farm?" I try to keep the skepticism out of my tone, but it bleeds through.

He leans back in his chair and tilts his head with a slight grin. "Briar, don't go poking your nose where it don't belong." His accent is light and disarming, even though that sure as fuck sounds like a warning if I've ever heard one.

I set down my cup and stare at him for a beat, trying to decide whether or not it's a good idea to straight up ask him. "Are you into, you know, some bad things for work?"

Grahm leans forward and is about to say something when the front door swings open and two men walk in.

"Hey, Briar!" Taylor lifts his hand in greeting and seems all too jovial after the last time I saw him a week ago. My blood runs cold. Why did he and Gale come in and walk straight over to our table? How did they know I was even here?

My eyes instantly flick to Grahm. His jaw is set, and he takes a casual, long sip from his coffee. Although I've never seen a dark gaze replace kindness so quickly in someone's eyes before. The air is electric with tension. Not like where you don't know who's going to punch who first, but with the fake grins that have sinister undertones kind of tension.

Gale eyes him carefully before muttering to me, "Come on, Briar. We're already late because you weren't at the farm."

My brows instantly quirk. "Go where? I'm not going anywhere with you."

Taylor drops his smile and shares a look with Gale.

Grahm slowly stands and crosses his arms. "Is there a problem?" he says in a calm, yet dangerous tone.

Gale, who's only a smidge shorter than Grahm, sets his hand

on the ranch hand's shoulder and squeezes. "There will be if you try to do anything stupid, Sutherland."

"Fucking shitheads," Grahm curses, glaring at them as the two look at me expectantly.

"Either we walk out together or we carry you out, cutie." Taylor smiles like a lunatic, and I unfortunately know he's not joking.

"It's fine, Grahm. I'll talk to you later. My phone is working now, so I'll text you when I get home. Is your number still the same as the one my uncle had pinned on his fridge?"

Grahm nods, still looking pissed off and like he might try to stop them from taking me.

I snag my drink and am glad that I got it in a to-go cup instead of a mug. Taylor grunts as he hooks his arm over my shoulders and guides me outside. Roman's Benz is parked out front, and even though I can't see through the blacked-out windows, I know he's in there. It's annoying seeing the same car that was parked out front that first night and now I'm being forced into it.

I can't believe he already got it back after losing. What did he do? Pull someone's teeth out? I shudder as the very realistic image of him doing that runs through my head. *It's messed up that I can picture him doing it.*

"What's this about?" I snap and tear away from Taylor's arm. He chuckles and ruffles my hair. I bump into Gale as I try to get out of Taylor's reach and realize that there's something strapped to his waist that feels a lot like a pistol.

Is he carrying a gun? My eyes widen, and my stomach churns. I hold on to my coffee cup a little tighter as we approach the car.

"Not much. We just want to have some fun with our new friend in town. There's no harm in that, now is there?" Taylor says with too much optimism. After a week of bliss, I thought I was in the clear and that they had forgotten about me. Obviously, I was much too hopeful.

The door swings open, and John extends his hand to help me into the car. My eyes go past his hand and straight to his waist, where I notice he also has a pistol holstered there. My heart races as I take his hand and am placed on his lap.

Taylor takes one side and Gale takes the other. Bensen turns around from the passenger seat and shoots me a big grin. "Long time no see, Briar."

I give him a tight smile. "Not long enough."

John laughs and threads his arms around my waist. The weight of his hands around my stomach makes my cheeks warm.

Roman is sitting in the driver's seat and doesn't turn to look at me. My eyes shift to the rearview mirror, and it's there that I meet his heavy gaze. Those eyes are as cold as they've been since we met. He doesn't say anything as he looks away and focuses on driving.

My stomach flips as John sets his chin on my shoulder. "I hope you like swimming," he mumbles.

I mean I *can* swim; I wouldn't say I enjoy it. Not this late in the season. "You're taking me swimming? I don't have a swimsuit," I say cautiously.

God, I know they are up to something awful. I just don't know what that awful thing is yet. They wouldn't just take me out somewhere fun for no reason. And regardless of how friendly the rest of them are, Roman's doom-and-gloom expression is enough to set the forecast.

"We're all adults, Briar. Just wear your bra and underwear. It's the same shit." Gale sounds like he's not enthused about where his day is going either.

"Don't worry. No one's going to hurt you, okay? How's your head?" John asks softly.

Jesus Christ, I didn't think anyone was going to hurt me, but now I have doubts. I swallow thickly.

I want to tell him that I've had headaches every single day that have made working on cleaning up the farm impossible, but I just settle with "Fine."

Roman reaches to the center console and turns the volume up until our voices are drowned out by music. He clearly doesn't want to hear anyone talk. God, he's such a douchebag.

After a few minutes of music playing and being on the highway heading toward the mountains, my muscles relax a bit more, and I allow myself to lean into John's warm chest. He's at least the kindest of the group and I trust him the most out of all of them. His blond hair smells like the ocean, hints of bergamot and salted evening waves.

His chest is warm and his breaths are steady. One arm is securely fastened around my waist while he gently brushes his fingertips through my hair. It's been such a long time since anyone has held me like this. Since I've allowed it. I didn't really have much of a choice in the matter, but it's nice, and I find my eyes being lulled into closing as I let myself enjoy the fleeting moment.

I hate how easily I can feel his chiseled abs through his shirt. My lewd mind focuses on what his body would feel like pressed up against mine in bed. The thoughts make my thighs warm, and I can't help but wriggle a bit in his hold.

John chuckles and slips his hand beneath my shirt, teasing my stomach with soft, languid motions. "You're so beautiful, Briar," he whispers against my shoulder and presses a kiss there. I let out a small whimper before turning to look at him.

I'm literally surrounded by four other guys who could catch on to what he's doing any second. For some reason it only makes my core heat up more and my excitement grow.

John glances up at me, staring at me with gorgeous blue eyes that look right through me. My mind goes completely blank, and I barely register that his eyes dip down to my lips before he steals a kiss.

I breathe in, shocked and instantly melting into his arms. The kiss lasts maybe a tenth of a second, maybe longer, but when he pulls back, his brows knit a little, and he looks up at me and murmurs, "Wow."

There are no words. No thoughts. Only a whimper when he kisses me again and moves his hand farther up my shirt and palms my breast over my bra. *Holy shit, this is so hot.*

I forget where we are and that there's even other men in the car for a moment. It's hard to remember anything when John's erection is growing beneath my ass.

All of the sudden the music cuts out and Roman shouts, "Bishop, get your fucking tongue out of her mouth before I cut it off!"

We simultaneously jolt, and my eyes shoot straight to the rearview mirror. Roman's glare is next to none. He could strike fear into a fucking bear with it.

"Damn it. Don't stop. I caught on to what was happening too late." Bensen laughs and gives us a sarcastic smile.

I cover my face with both of my hands, and a hot flush races across my cheeks. "Oh my God."

John chuckles, and it's such a smooth, calming sound. "Sorry, Briar, I couldn't help it."

Taylor and Gale are quiet. When I look at them, both of their faces are beet red and they're sitting at weird angles.

How embarrassing. I want to hide, but I can't go anywhere.

My gaze reluctantly finds Roman's again, and he pointedly looks away. But upon closer inspection… *No.* Are his cheeks flushed? A small smile grows across my lips.

Not so tough, are you?

The drive only lasts another ten or fifteen minutes before Roman pulls over into a dirt parking lot. So many of the parking lots are dirt or gravel in Bane Falls, it's ridiculous. I would've bought a pair of boots if I'd known how dusty and muddy everything got out here. I make a mental note to stop at the boutique on Main Street that Grahm told me about.

The guys exit the vehicle, and John lets me slide off his lap before he moves. I had a creek or river in mind, but I didn't expect them to take me to a lake—a big one too; I didn't even know there was one out in this area. The mountains are tall on either side of it, with snow already at their peaks. A hidden gem, one the rest of the world hasn't quite discovered—and perhaps never should.

Roman nods at his guys and they make their way down to the beach side without us. A trail is present, and it looks like it wraps around the entire lake. I've given up being afraid that they're going to kill me. They're clearly all talk and no bite. And I doubt John would fondle someone he's about to murder.

Whatever game they're playing, I'm tired of playing it.

Roman shoves his hands into his jeans pockets. It's much warmer today than it's been; summer is truly leaving with a big send-off. So instead of his jacket, Roman's wearing a black biker vest with patches on it. His arms are bare, and I can only assume he's shirtless under the vest. All the scars above his collar line extend no mercy to his arms. They are covered in jagged marks, some designed, some not.

Masochist. Yet I can't drag my eyes away. I want to memorize each one and know what they mean. I want to know why someone like him has such deep wounds that he refuses to let go of. What could be so twisted in that head of his that he has to do this to himself?

Nope. Let's not think about Roman shirtless and humanize him when he clearly wants to be an asshole instead. I force the thoughts away.

"I caught a little snake outside your house last week," Roman mutters as he places his hand behind my back and nudges me to walk with him. We make our way down toward the other guys.

"One, what the hell were you doing waiting outside my house after you said you left? And two, what snake?" My voice is threaded with concern. I'm not stupid. I know he's not actually talking about a reptile. He's talking about a person. A bad one.

He sucks in his lower lip and bites it. I hate how I bite my own in response. "One, I'm trying to keep your ungrateful ass alive for some fucking reason. Two, the snake I'm about to show you. You seem to think that your situation isn't very real. You live in a delusional place in your mind, don't you? Where bad things don't happen to people like you."

I stop dead in my tracks, kicking up sand with the abruptness of it. Roman takes a few more steps before he stops and turns to look at me, lifting a brow.

I fist my hands at my sides and take a deep breath. "You think bad things don't happen to everyone? You think you're the only person that bad things happen to? Wake the fuck up. Terrible things happen to people every day. And you have no idea what I've been through. There's no way in fuck you can tell by the way I *look*."

Roman's eyes widen, but I'm not done.

"I know dangerous shit is going down here in Bane Falls, okay? I'm not this clueless, stupid person you pin me for. Have you ever stopped to think that maybe the reason I'm not crying and running off like a helpless little girl is because I've been through worse? I've been left for dead by someone much crueler than you. Sorry, Roman. You're nothing. *Nothing*."

His lips part, and he looks like he's trying to think of something to say, but I don't wait to find out what it is. I walk ahead without him, making quick work getting down to the beach where the others are waiting. Around the corner of the bay is a dock and a simple fisherman's boat tied off at the pier.

John runs his hand through his perfect blond strands before glancing back at Roman, who has reset his expression back to being completely unreadable as usual. Jesus, does that man even feel things?

He's the one who doesn't have a sense of reality. I cross my arms, pissed off and annoyed that they dragged me out here on one of the last nice days of summer. I was going to sunbathe in the backyard and enjoy some of the wine I splurged on.

"All right, let's go." Gale tilts his head toward the boat. I firm my trembling lips. *They won't hurt me. Even if they have guns.*

Taylor hops into the boat first and helps me in before the rest of them get on as well. We look like a normal group of people going out for a fishing trip. Either that or eager young adults heading to the opposite shore for a fucking gang bang.

"Why couldn't you bring any of your other girlfriends?" I pipe up, feeling a little unsettled.

John and Gale look away. It's Taylor who replies, "Because today is about you, sweet little Briar." His smile is innocent enough, but I don't like how ominous it sounds.

Bensen steers the boat using the motor in the back. The men

seem particularly focused on the shores on both sides. They don't let their guards down, and it starts to give me the feeling that we aren't alone out here. The water sprays up at the edges of the boat and prickles me with cold drops. If I close my eyes, it feels like I'm back on the coast, the moisture in the air on my skin giving me a sense of nostalgia.

When we're about mid-lake, Roman lifts his left hand and Bensen cuts the engine. I look up at them, but no one is paying attention to me except the king asshole himself.

"Why did we stop?" I ask. Dread seeps into my chest at how quiet they're being. God, this really couldn't be any creepier.

Roman offers me his hand. I take it and stand on uneasy legs as he nods over the edge of the boat. I hesitate. I mean, is it really that irrational to think that he might toss me overboard?

I swallow my fear and my grip on his hand tightens as I lean over the edge, looking down as he is.

An abrupt gasp tears out of my lungs.

There's a dead man three feet under the surface.

It's out of sight unless you knew exactly where he was. His eyes are open and staring up at me. His mouth gaping as if he's trapped mid-scream. His neck has a two-inch puncture wound that has long since stopped bleeding. A large chain is wrapped around his torso and legs, leading down as far as I can see.

I cover my mouth with my hand and try not to gag.

"Recognize him?" Roman's voice is low in a whisper, drawing chills across my neck.

He's the man I saw Grahm speaking with at the party. I know he saw me watching them because he looked right at me. He was at the farm last week? The blood drains from my face, and I feel like I'm going to be sick.

"I'll take that as a yes." Roman pulls me away from the edge as I start to feel lightheaded. His hand is still tightly clasped with mine. It feels like an anchor, even if it's to a horrendous man.

"Why?" I manage to mutter.

"Why did I kill him? Or why was he at your farm?" Roman asks indifferently. John breaks his focus from the shoreline and spares me a quick, concerned look.

I glance down at Roman's side and spot the very combat knife he probably used. Another wave of nausea runs through me. He literally had that at my neck the first night we met. "Both, I guess."

"I confirmed that you're a target for them. He didn't seem sure whether or not his little club was going to kill you or kidnap you, but either way, I'm not one for letting innocent women die…sometimes. Anyway, I needed you to see that this is real so that you won't fight me on this next part." He must be lying. I refuse to believe that Roman would do *anything* in the name of someone being innocent. He fucking terrorizes me every time I see him.

Wait, *next part*? I frown. There's more?

"We'll be staying at the farm to protect you."

I burst out laughing, and all the men stiffen. Maybe it's my reaction to seeing a dead body and the shock is making me manic, but I can't help it. Roman's gaze doesn't falter, but I swear to God I see the vein in his forehead protrude with ire.

"I don't need you to stay at the farm. Jesus Christ, I'll just leave. There's a fucking dead guy in the water! The last thing I want is a bunch of psycho fucks 'keeping me safe' at the farm," I shout, throwing my hands into the air.

Roman's hand is over my mouth in a heartbeat. The men are dead silent. "Bensen, get us moving toward the far bank. Gale, sink the snake," Roman says smoothly as he stares deep into my soul. "This man was going to kidnap you or kill you, Briar, because of all things, he was led to think that you're important. Which means so do I. You're not leaving Bane Falls."

"First you wanted me to leave and now you want me to stay? Which is it, asshole?" I shove Roman and he grabs both of my wrists.

"Push me again and I'll have to restrain you. You like that though, don't you?" he says mockingly. "It's whichever I say, Squirt. You all but belong to me—you just haven't accepted it yet." He tucks his hand into my pocket and tosses my phone into the lake.

That hits me like a brick, and I stare up at him in horror. It's stupid that a phone means that much to me. But it just shut off all my communication to the world. And I *just* paid for the prepaid plan too. *Least of my worries right now honestly.*

"Ah, there it is." He brushes a strand of hair behind my ear. "Reality settling in sucks, doesn't it?"

Gale pulls the big chains from the bottom of the boat and tosses them into the water, coiling them around the dead man a few times, and then the corpse sinks into the dark water as if he was never there.

Bensen moves in sync. The moment the corpse is out of sight, the boat is moving toward the vacant shore.

No one speaks until the bow hits the sand. Everyone gets out of the boat except me. My arms are wrapped around myself, and I'm staring at the spot where they just sunk the guy who supposedly was trying to kidnap me—although, I think I'm with the five men who actually are.

They gave me no evidence that the dead man was going to harm me. All they did was show me that *they* are no strangers to murder.

My gaze shifts in their direction. The group is huddled up and speaking in low, stressed voices. No one is watching me.

I carefully get out of the boat and step into the sand on the opposite side from them. They're still having a heated conversation—about me, I'm presuming. I don't even think about where I have to run to. I just know that anywhere is better than here. There has to be a cabin or fire trail somewhere nearby.

The forest's underbrush isn't too thick, so I'm able to slip into the forest without much noise. *I know that path is around here somewhere.*

I make it a decent ways away before I hear the guys start shouting. That's my cue. I pump my legs as fast as I can and tear across the forest floor. It's still hot out, and I'm sweating from traversing the steep incline.

Their voices are all over the place, so it's safe to assume that they have no clue where I am. I slow down a little so I can be more strategic. I can't outrun them all. I'll have to hide.

After walking for what feels like a mile, I find a large grouping of boulders. There could be some adders in there, but it's the best hiding spot I've found and I don't know how much longer I can walk. I'm dehydrated and my legs are trembling. I must be far into the woods…or I've been going in fucking circles. Once I lost view of the lake, I lost all sense of direction.

Their shouting eventually grows distant. By sunset, it's entirely silent.

No one will be able to find me after nightfall. I'll be able to get my bearings and then I'll hike the trail all the way to the parking lot, follow the road to the highway, and hitchhike until I'm as far from here as I can get.

I'm in survival mode. These guys are going to get me killed one way or another.

I should've listened to Roman that first night and left. I press my palm against my temple before letting my head rest back against the boulder. Did he *have* to throw my phone into the lake? I brew on that for a while as I watch the sky slowly fade into richer colors and the hours drag on.

A cold breeze brushes over me, waking me up from my unintended nap, and I shiver.

It's already pitch-black outside. Crap, how much time did I lose? I need to get moving.

My legs are stiff as I maneuver my way off the boulders. I fall a few feet and my knees buckle, sending me straight into the dirt.

A soft groan escapes my lips. The earthy scent fills the air around me, making me freeze with fear. The memories of Callum and how he pursued me after I escaped stir in my head. I hope Roman isn't as committed to his cause as Callum was.

I've been through worse.

This is nothing, I tell myself over and over.

I furrow my brows and grit my teeth, standing and forcing myself to move.

But it doesn't take long for me to realize that no matter how long I try to find my way back to the lake, I'm utterly lost. After aimlessly wandering for what feels like hours, I finally collapse and pull my knees to my chest. I'm covered in cuts and shiver like I've been dumped in ice water.

"Are you done?"

My body jerks in response to hearing Roman's voice.

I slowly lift my head and meet his icy gaze. "Are you done?" he repeats calmly. Weird, I thought he'd be pissed at me. I narrow my eyes suspiciously—or is this how calm he is when he's ready to end someone?

How long has he been stalking me in the dark?

"Why did you w-wait this long?" I stutter, shivering and rubbing my bare arms.

Roman crouches before me, studying my features as usual but perhaps with a bit more curiosity this time. "Because you needed to wear yourself out. You're more sensible when you're exhausted, or maybe I just like to watch you exert yourself, Squirt." *Really? Sarcasm?*

I can't even muster the energy to glare at him.

"I don't want you guys in my house. I'm fucking l-leaving, even if I have to walk to the next t-town."

He blows out an annoyed breath. "I'm getting tired of this. I'm not letting you go anywhere. You had your chance and you blew it. Besides, the guys are already making the place cozy for us. You know, since you suck at cleaning."

"What?" I say with a little more emotion before a wave of exhaustion has me trembling once more.

"Tonight it'll be just me. But tomorrow we'll all be outposted there." He stands and offers me his hand.

I swat him away and struggle to my feet. The direction I start walking in feels right.

Roman grabs my hand. "Wrong way."

I tear my hand out of his hold. "I don't care," I snap.

He doesn't bother trying to stop me again; instead, he just follows behind me a few beats. My shivering worsens, and it pisses me off that he's just casually taking in the night while I suffer.

I look back at him. His eyes are half-lidded, stuck in that place of so tired that his eyes are rimmed with red, yet burdened with many thoughts that keep him awake. I can't help but take him in. His hands are shoved in his pockets, patiently waiting for me to just give up rather than taking me back by force.

I stop and face him.

His eyes flick up to my face, and he stops a foot away, expressionless yet as beautiful as midnight rain.

"Done?" he asks again.

My body is aching from head to toe. This has gone on for so long now that I feel like a complete idiot. It's clear that he won't stop no matter what I do. All I'm doing is dragging out the inevitable.

I give him a defeated nod.

He bends to my level and looks at my face. "Feeling okay?"

Damn my pride. I nod again, even though I'm ready to crawl into a hole and die.

Roman studies my trembling hands and glances back up at me. "It's good to know that you're a shit liar." He muses before turning so his back is facing me. He takes a knee and looks over his shoulder. "Get on."

My cheeks warm at the offer, but before I forget what a dick this guy is, I double down. "No thanks." My chattering teeth and crossed arms don't help my cause.

He rolls his eyes and takes his vest off, tossing it at me. I snatch it and give him a stubborn firm of my lips. "It won't help much, but it's better than nothing."

His bare torso is covered in scars, much like the rest of him. It hits a chord in my chest. This man is so fucked up that he's barely even holding himself together. What is he caught up in?

I let my eyes trace the grooves of his abs until they catch on the handgun on his left hip and that military-grade knife on his other.

Roman smirks. "Want to know how I killed that guy?"

My grip on his vest tightens. He steps up to me, takes the

113

vest from my hands, and sets it over my shoulders, intentionally pulling it tightly against my throat.

"I stuck him once. That's all it takes if you're quick and know where." He brushes the pad of his finger down my throat and grins, locking eyes with me.

My pulse leaps wildly where he touches my skin, but the longer he stares down at me, the more the alarm shifts into heat. Roman glides his hand over my jaw and gently runs his thumb over my lower lip.

"John could never live up to your expectations," he murmurs with a slight undertone of what sounds like jealousy.

I lick my lip unconsciously. "What makes you think I have expectations?"

His gaze narrows. "I have eyes, Briar. I know a longing girl when I see one. You're a squirter, remember? I can tell. You just need someone to show you."

There are at least ten things I want to say in reply to that, but they all get swallowed up when Roman bends down and kisses me.

My eyes widen, and my heart all but stops. It lasts for only a moment, but it ignites a fire within me. His scent invades every inch of my lungs, and to my utter horror, I find myself leaning into it.

Roman pulls back and stares down at me while I'm blinking up at him with awe. Did he just kiss me? I want to slap him, but I also want to kiss him again.

"Now, get on. I want to try to get a few hours of sleep tonight. You don't want to see me when I don't get at least two hours, Briar." He acts as if he didn't just make me second-guess every decision I've ever made. My cheeks are hot and I'm thankful for it being so dark.

He already looks like he only sleeps a handful of hours, so I really don't want to find out what only two get him.

When he turns, I hook my arms around his shoulders and he wraps his arms under my knees.

The warmth from his skin instantly hits me. I let out a small whimper of relief and let my cheek rest against his shoulder. Did he kiss me only because John did? What game is he playing? I firm my lips, probably thinking way too deeply about it. But it doesn't help that I'm so attracted to him. His villainous vibe is what my darkest dreams are made of.

Roman walks steadily, as if he's not fazed at all by having to carry me or by the dark. I find myself squeezing my thighs around him tighter and trying to ignore the heat that's igniting in my core.

After ten minutes, I can see the reflection of the moon in the lake. It's still a ways away, but at least I know he was aware of where we were the whole time, unlike me. I'm so embarrassed that I got lost that quickly.

"What was your plan anyway? Run away into the woods and live like an animal?" Roman breaks the silence. He doesn't sound nearly as annoyed as he could—more amused that I thought I could escape him and the others.

Arrogant prick.

"Do you really want to know?" I mumble against his shoulder.

He's quiet for a second. "Yeah. I do."

"I was going to hitchhike until I could find some other place to live, at least until I could save enough to move to another country. I know it sounds stupid, but all dreams sound a little silly at first, don't they?"

"Why are you trying to leave?" His voice is threaded with confusion.

115

I consider telling him, but a branch snaps somewhere behind us and makes Roman's muscles seize. His grip on my legs tightens, and he takes off running down the mountainside toward the lake like a banshee out of hell.

"If you let go, you're dead," Roman growls, teeth gritting and his feet crashing through the underbrush.

There's someone else out here.

CHAPTER 10

BRIAR

My heart races as we're relentlessly smacked with branches. Roman slips a few times but catches himself, not letting us fall. I've never held on to somebody so tightly in my entire life. A few times, I think I'll lose my grip, but he's holding me just as fiercely.

"What's happening?" I whisper shout.

Roman doesn't reply. His breaths are labored and he's entirely focused on running as far as possible from whatever is behind us. I dare a glance over my shoulder and see something moving, then another figure shifting off to our left.

"Um, Roman, there's another one!" My voice quivers, and he nearly drops me as he takes a hard right.

Oh my God. Are we being hunted by people? Grahm isn't one of them, is he? The roar of my heartbeat nearly washes out all other sounds, and I have to bite into my lip to stay alert.

My arms are losing their strength to hold on. We're so close to the lake now that I can smell the fresh water and sand. We're going to make it. We're going to—

Bang.

A gunshot rings through the forest, and the bullet whizzes right by our heads. I muffle my scream, burying my lips against Roman's shoulder.

"Almost there. Get ready to swim as hard as you can," he says with a raspy voice. His breathing is labored, but he doesn't let up.

My stomach coils. "Swim? The lake is too big to cross!" The words come out shaky. The adrenaline is already coursing through my body.

It's the same feeling as the night Callum tried to kill me.

Another shot and something hits the back of the vest. Pain instantly flares up in my shoulder, and I choke on a breath. My muscles seize up. I can't hold on, and I'm slipping from Roman's arms. I hit the sand and roll a few times before I'm being dragged up to my feet and thrown into the lake. The cold water hits my body like a lightning strike.

"Go!" Roman shouts as I practically inhale a mouthful of water. My body isn't responding—I think I was just shot. I start hyperventilating and stare with horror as three figures erupt from the tree line around the beach.

"Goddamn it." Roman gets in the water too and grabs my arm, hooking it around his neck. "Don't let go," he growls as he starts pumping his legs.

The water is so icy that each breath feels heavier than the last. Not to mention there's a fucking dead guy in here somewhere. I shudder at the thought.

That could very likely be us soon.

"W-who are they?" I barely get the words out past my clattering teeth.

118

Roman's growing tired. I can feel his muscles trembling. "Men who want me dead and you likely dead or alive." He leaves it vague, but at least he answered me.

Either Roman's cult is a lot crazier than I initially thought, or he's in something much worse. But why me? I have nothing to do with any of this.

They start shooting at us from the beach. Bullets pelt the water inches away from us, and I barely have time to inhale a deep breath before Roman dives under.

We get separated, and I can't see a fucking thing. I swim desperately in what I think is the same direction we were going. My clothes are pinching around my joints suffocatingly. It feels like they'll drag me under if I don't keep swimming like my life depends on it.

I can't hold my breath any longer. The last time I had to hold my breath with my heart racing like it is right now, I was in a grave. The second the water breaks, I inhale sharply and muffle my coughs in case we're still close enough for them to hear.

It's a sobering predicament to be in: swimming alone in a vast expanse of black water. Night swimming is an ultimate fear of mine, alongside being hunted by people. Two for two.

I blink furiously to unblur my vision and scope the beach. It's empty; the men either left because they're worried their gunshots will attract others, or they're waiting for us to swim back to shore.

Oh my God, I might actually die out here. A knot balls in the back of my throat, and I have to take a few steadying breaths before I get my bearings.

Wait, where's Roman?

I look all around me but don't see any sign of him.

Was he hit? There's a strong chance of it, the bullets were

pelting the water all around us. My eyes widen and terror sends another wave of adrenaline through my veins.

"R-Roman." I wince at the scratchiness of my voice. "Roman." I'm not speaking over a whisper, yet with the stillness of the night, I may as well be shouting. Any sound has a chance to give away our location. The dark water is smooth like glass and gives me a foreboding, worried itch in the back of my throat. For a forest so big, it doesn't sound like there's a single creature stirring. Maybe they're all watching, waiting for the lake to take its next victims.

I run my hand on the back of the vest over my shoulder and knock something metal loose. A bullet hit me, and Roman's vest stopped it. *It's bulletproof.* Why the fuck would he be wearing a bulletproof vest as casual wear? My thoughts are muddled with exhaustion and fear.

I continue to search for him, spotting something floating a handful of feet away finally. I swim over to it and let a breath of relief out when I see that it's Roman.

He's on his back floating, taking shallow breaths that wrench at my heart. I mean sure, he's not likable, not even a little, but it hurts to see him like this.

"Are you okay?" I hastily ask, pushing away every thought about my own safety. I try to help him float, but it only pushes me down more.

Roman winces and takes a few more short breaths. "I'm…" He groans. "Fine."

He's acting like he's been hit. It's too dark to see if there's blood in the water, but Roman wouldn't just be floating here if he wasn't wounded. He's conscious, but it's like his muscles have seized up.

"Tell me what to do. Where do we go?" My tone is nothing

short of determined. Although my limbs are already so exhausted, I feel like I could sink to the bottom of this lake any second. *Spending energy on him might mean I don't make it either.* I push the fears away and focus. As tempting as it is to save myself and flee, it's not who I am.

I can't leave him.

Roman looks at me with narrowed, distrustful eyes. He must see the scared, unsure flicker in mine because he relents and sighs painfully. "We need…*ugh*…to get to a different shoreline."

I hate how much agony he sounds like he's in. It makes everything I'm feeling seem so pathetic—the cold that reaches into my bones, the weight of my arms and suffocating grip of the jeans.

"I've got you," I say steadily, grabbing beneath his arms and starting to slowly kick. We're moving at a sluggish pace, but it's better than not doing anything. I have to stop frequently and roll onto my back and float to catch my breath.

Roman groans every few minutes. After the fifth time I stop, I have to start talking to keep myself from going to a really dark place in my mind. I can't stop thinking about both of us drowning.

"Have you e-ever come close to dying before?" My jaw trembles despite my best efforts. Our heads are close together, and Roman's hand softly bumps against my neck as we float side by side.

He's quiet for so long that it becomes obvious he won't respond. I give myself a moment's reprieve and shut my eyes.

"Is this your way of flirting, Briar?"

I ignore that slight and tug on a strand of his hair. He grunts with a short laugh.

"Yes, I have. Many times in fact." His voice is as gentle as the ripples of water around us. I shut my eyes and listen deeply. "This isn't one of those times. So don't panic."

My brows pull together. "How can you be sure?"

He makes a sound that people make when they smile and exhale. "Because you just know when it's close. Death is a cold, vile grip against your ribs. A knocking at the cusp of your hopes and dreams. You'll know." He tilts his head a bit and looks at me. I do the same, feeling my chest lurch at the closeness of his weary eyes. Darkness consumes every fracture of the world, everything but his lonesome stare. It's captured me. He spares me the smallest of grins. "Perhaps you already know."

A secret so dark I dare not share it.

"What are you, Roman?" I bring my hand to his cold forehead and trace the scar there with my forefinger. He observes me, motionless and digesting every move I make.

He blinks as if he'd been lost to his thoughts and then lets his eyes shift back to the sky, the stars our audience.

"Something that should be locked away and forgotten."

It feels like it's been hours by the time we reach another bank. Neither of us said another word after his comment about him being locked away. Is that truly how he sees himself? The thought weighed heavily on my mind and kept me moving.

I didn't stop or get close to the beach until I was sure I didn't see anyone moving. The shoreline we end up on has a lip of rocks that surround the top, edging the forest and making it impossible for someone to reach us from behind without considerable effort and noise.

A small break that we really needed.

I'm not sure if Roman's conscious anymore. I checked his

pulse a few times along the way just to make sure he was still alive. It seemed silly to think someone like him could...I don't know, just die, but I worried enough to check frequently.

I manage to drag him onto the sand after struggling for a few minutes and collapse beside him. My limbs are trembling from overuse, and it's impossible to tell if I'm actually freezing or not.

Everything I learned in survival classes from university seminars indicates that I'm likely cold and should seek warmth. Roman needs to warm up too.

My hands won't stop trembling as I check his chest for a wound. *Nothing.* That's a relief. He's definitely out cold, so I roll him onto his side and let a gasp escape my lips.

There's a bullet lodged between his ribs, almost beneath his shoulder blade. It's odd though, because it pierced his flesh, but didn't go in all the way. It's as if something stopped it. This must be why his breathing was so labored and he couldn't move.

Lucky son of a bitch.

I brush the bullet softly with my thumb, and it falls into my palm. Roman's blood streams down his back and wets the sand.

Cursing, I take off the vest and my tank top. The vest won't help in stopping the bleeding, and I'm not sure how much a wet shirt will help either, but I press it against his back regardless until the bleeding slows.

Once I'm satisfied, I pull the shirt away and stare at something metallic from beneath the entry wound. It looks like a metal meshing of some sort, like chain mail but much smaller. He must've had a surgery at some point that required it to be placed there, but I can't shake the odd feeling that accompanies that idea.

Why would anyone need metal meshing like this under their skin?

The wind stirs, and it's almost as if the forest itself beckons to me. I glance over my shoulder at the tree line. This would be the perfect time to escape and leave Bane Falls and all its devils and secrets behind. But… I stare at Roman's peaceful expression. It's the first time I've seen him without his poker face. He's almost unrecognizable without his signature scowl and heavily furrowed brow.

To leave him alone and cold would burden my mind for the rest of my life. Not knowing whether he got back home safely or not would haunt me. I can't leave—not when something so cruel and vicious is in a vulnerable state.

I shake myself from the trance he seems to always put me in and recover his wound with my tank top. The idea of trying to get help crosses my mind, but I'm so tired that I know I'll drown if I go back out there. It's a miracle I was able to get us to this beach.

With reservations, many, *many* reservations, I press my chest against Roman's back so we can share body heat and I can keep pressure on his wound.

It doesn't take more than a minute of our warmth blooming between us before I pass out.

t's cold. So cold that the chambers of my heart ache viscerally. I know it's because I'm there again. Standing in the foot-deep snow as my friends are slain in the Under Trials.

There was once a time that I rebelled against returning here, in the darkest confines of my mind. I'd often try to change the horrors and stains of the past. But it never did any good. No one was spared. Not in my memories, not even in my foolish dreams.

Now I only watch as my comrades impale one another, *betray* one another. Stab me. Hurt me. Try to kill me.

I never understood why the lessons I learned had to be so heinous. Why it was me who came out alive.

Why?

My eyes open, and I'm met with sand and the sound of water lapping at the shore. I'm not cold like I was in my dream. Or was it a memory? I can't tell anymore.

Warmth surrounds me… Someone is holding me tightly.

I haven't allowed someone to touch me like this for half a decade. The sensation is foreign and sends chills across my arms. I glance down, ready to throw the hand clasping me, but when I see her small, bruised, and cut-up hand, I pause.

My eyes widen, and my chest grows heavy.

Briar.

That's right… We were in the water, and the last thing I recall is her not letting me go—her pulling me through the cold water even though she was so exhausted already.

After my cruelty toward her, why did she risk her life saving mine?

She brought us to a secluded beach. I take in our surroundings. Being stationed out in a small town with damn near nowhere to go and nothing to do means I know every square foot of this lake. The cliff shore. She must've swam most of the night to get to this one.

Slowly, I manage to move out from under her arm. She's so tired that she doesn't notice my absence, but I notice hers. The bleak chill that reaches into my back is arresting, and the pain from the gunshot wound flares.

I wince as I rub my shoulder gently. The pain is welcome, as is the scar it will become. This was a major fuckup on my part. I never should've allowed her to stay in the first place. I should've known that we'd be followed out here since Grahm was there when the guys grabbed her from the café. But things are too messy now. They want her dead or as a hostage, that much is clear.

Fuck, I didn't think they'd actually shoot at us if I was carrying her. I brush my hand through my hair and let out a tight breath.

Whatever she knows is more important than I thought. They

don't want me to have it, which means Grahm and Sub-Rosa must be getting suspicious of us. *We're running out of time.*

I check my belt and find my pistol and knife still attached. Thank fuck. At least I didn't lose anything.

Before I get up to go fetch John, I catch myself watching her slow breaths. She's only in her bra, and it's been soaked through. Even if it wasn't, the pads are so thin they barely offer any coverage for her perfect breasts. Her nipples are pebbled from the brisk air, and suddenly I have the urge to suck on them.

I bury my teeth into my lower lip and force my eyes to her relaxed expression. Against my best judgment, I run my thumb over her lower lip and think about our kiss last night. It was a stupid thing to do, not like me in the slightest. But with her, I couldn't stop myself. Seeing John kiss her pissed me off so much. I wanted to see what she tasted like.

A slight chuckle warms my tenured, bitter smile. She may have caught my eye and stirred something ancient inside me, but it will end there.

I won't let her warm my frozen heart too.

Something crawls over my back and spooks me. My body jerks, and I sit straight up. Pain instantly shoots through my entire body, making every muscle and joint scream out in agony.

"Ow," I murmur to myself as I look around, remembering where I am and what the events of last night led to.

Holy shit, that's right, we almost fucking died.

I look down beside me, where I was cuddled up next to Roman, only to find no one there.

You've got to be kidding me. He wouldn't just leave me out here like this, would he? Did he take my fucking shirt too? After I saved his ass? My face heats, and all of a sudden I'm not cold anymore.

That piece of shit.

I force myself to my feet and look toward the rocks and the forest. The sun is up but not yet peeking over the treetops. My hair is still wet, and there's no sign of Roman.

"You dick." I bury my teeth into my lower lip. That's what I get for helping him instead of helping myself.

Does he want me to leave and is giving me my chance to escape? Is that why he left me here? No, because he took the vest and my tank top. No one would traverse the mountains in just a bra. So he ditched me?

For some reason that hurts a bit, even if it's what I wanted. I guess it just feels a little like being abandoned. That's so dumb though, because I knew he was a jerk. There shouldn't have been any expectation, and yet I thought he might've actually appreciated me.

Stupid asshole.

There's no sense in doing anything until the sun comes back out, so I decide to wait. I pull my knees up close to my chest and glare at the mist collecting above the lake. Once it warms up more, I'll try to find the fire trail again.

I feel a bit more sensible today. Even though I'm exhausted, it dawns on me that I might be doing more harm than good if I try to hitchhike without a phone and no shirt… Yeah that sounds like a recipe for disaster.

Fuck.

Every time I shut my eyes all I hear are the gunshots. But instead of the fear I experienced last night, all I feel is the horror from the night Callum attacked me. The cold in my bones isn't far off from the way it felt to be buried in the earth, left for dead.

I set my forehead against my arm and let a few tears fall.

I'll never forget how Callum looked at me like I was less than a person, how he pushed me into the hole he'd dug while I had lain lifeless a handful of feet away. We never come back the same, do we? Not after surviving something as heinous as that.

The lull of the waves hitting the shore stirs me back from my memories. I glance up, and my breath catches in my lungs.

Roman's expressionless, gorgeous face has never been such a welcome sight. He's with John, who's driving the same motorboat from yesterday.

I remain where I am, huddled with my arms around my legs and shivering. *He didn't abandon me.*

John beaches the boat and runs to my side. He comes down hard and kicks sand up. "Jesus, are you okay, Briar?" His hands are warm on my bare arms as he checks my body. I shut my eyes with the peaceful knowledge that I won't have to swim again or trek through the forest half naked. "Fuck. I knew I shouldn't have left last night," he says, flexing his jaw and giving me worried eyes.

I lean into him as he lifts me up and cradles me in his arms. He carries me to the boat. "I'm glad you weren't here. You could've died—it's a miracle that we didn't. We were ambushed out of nowhere." I cough a few times before shivering again.

John looks away with guilt before wrapping a blanket around my shoulders. "I would've been able to help." He seems so sure. My eyes dip down to his waist, and I recall the handgun he was carrying yesterday and how paranoid they all were.

"Did you guys know they were out there looking for us?" My anger gets lost in my raspy voice. I just sound so tired—or on my death bed, more accurately.

John furrows his brow and helps move me to the rear of the boat without saying another word. That doesn't exactly make me feel any better. Which means they must've known. *Of course,* why am I not surprised?

I almost forget that Roman is sitting here on the boat as well. His hair is wet and he has a thick grayish-green blanket wrapped around his shoulders. His face is covered in scratches from the chase last night, like mine probably is.

I'm so relieved that he's okay.

"I'm almost sorry that you pulled through. I told John I thought we'd be picking up a corpse," Roman says smugly.

Any confused feelings I had about him get thrown into the wind, and my cheeks flare with heat. "You left me," I snap at him. "After I saved your worthless fucking life."

Roman gets a cruel grin—it's wider than his usual ones—and glares at me. "You saving anyone's life is laughable. Don't go giving yourself little awards, Briar."

My cheeks must be as red as cherries because they are on fire. I move to stand and shove him off his seat, but my legs give out on me and I fall onto the floor of the boat.

John shouts as he backs us off the beach, "Would you two knock it the fuck off! You're both being idiots."

I set myself back onto the seat and stare daggers at Roman. "I won't be helping you *ever* again, don't worry."

He gets a smug expression as he lets his eyes dip down to my chest and then back to my face. Goddamn it. *I forgot I'm only in my bra.*

"Are you sure? I could always use a little help, *whore.*" He spreads his thighs, and I see the massive boner he has currently tenting his wet pants.

Furious tears prickle in my eyes. I feel so insanely stupid for everything I did last night. I should've just left him in the lake and let nature take its course. Rationally, I know no matter how much I hate him, I could never actually do that though.

I remember how weak and vulnerable he looked. The way his shallow breaths made my chest wrench like a broken clock.

"Shut the fuck up, Lieutenant."

Roman jolts at that name, and shock moves across his features. John curses and shakes his head like he's pissed at himself.

"Lieutenant?" I repeat with a set frown. "Like a military officer?"

Roman sets his loathing eyes on me, lips twisted like he's not sure he wants to talk about it. "Sort of."

If this psychopath is in the military, then I'm a butterfly named Pancakes.

John interrupts. "Briar, look, we're going to explain everything once we get back to the farm, okay? We need to get out of here while we can, and that will be easier if you two just *stop* talking."

"What makes the farm safe? These guys had weapons, and there were at least three that I could see last night. We should leave Bane Falls while we still can."

John shakes his head. "No can do. We can't leave and neither can you. The farm is safe because your uncle wasn't a simple farmer. Just trust us, okay? We'll explain everything once we're there." His eyes are pleading.

"Trust the guy who calls me a whore, *right*. Because that's so easy." I don't bother trying to ease the sarcasm from my tone.

"You're the one who took off your shirt." Roman has the audacity to keep it going.

"To stop you from bleeding, asshole!"

"Could've fooled me," he fires back, rolling his eyes. Our jaws are flexed and we're glaring daggers into each other. We look utterly stupid being this agitated with shivering frames, each huddled under our blankets like two grannies arguing over tea.

John lets out a long breath. "No one say another word until we get back to the farm, or I'll stop this boat and you two can swim until you're too tired to argue. How does that sound, hmm?"

We stop with the comments, but the tension and loathing that dances between us still couldn't be severed with a butcher's knife. Although, once the sun rises and we're on the road back to Bane Falls, I notice Roman's reflection in the window glancing over at me more than once.

It could just be that the image of him in the window isn't as clear, but there's a soft, almost tortured set to his expression.

ven after taking a scalding shower, I can't stop shivering. Taylor sits down beside me on the sofa and hands me a cup of tea.

"Thanks." My throat is sore from the labored breathing in the cold last night. The air is much dryer in Montana than it was in Seattle.

Bensen and Gale are standing by the small foyer with their arms crossed, while John is sitting forward with his elbows pressed to his knees. Roman walks in last with a towel over his head and plops down across from me on the other sofa.

They all watch him expectantly. I refuse to meet his gaze, so I stare at his legs instead.

"No one knows what darkness truly looks like until it already has a hold of you," Roman says cryptically. It sounds like a rehearsed statement. "No one knows how vicious the shadows are until the Dark Forces are upon you."

My eyes flick up to his, confusion pulling at my brow. The dark *what*?

He's the only man on earth who could pull off being serious with a goddamn towel on his head. But he looks fucking sexy as hell with strands of his hair falling over his forehead. The tight black shirt doesn't leave much to the imagination either—not that I'd need one after seeing his bare chest last night.

"We are the ones they send when the job is too dirty for the officials to handle. We are the violent leftovers of society, recycled into weapons for the secret underground forces no one dares utter a word about. We're crafted for one thing and one thing only: to kill whoever the fuck we're ordered to and clean up messes the uniform-wearing forces can't be tied to." Roman's face is a display of unconcerned truth.

My breaths become shallow, and I hold on to the mug a little tighter. Taylor sets his hand on my knee and gives me a sympathetic smile like he feels bad that they have to tell me this.

I look each of them in their eyes and mutter, "You're serious."

A collective nod.

"Why are you telling me this? I shouldn't know this if you're in some secret branch. Isn't that, like, a security breach?" I move to stand, but Taylor firms his hold on my leg, silently telling me to stay put.

Roman's eyes darken, and he tilts his head to the side as he unwraps a piece of candy and slowly places it on his tongue. "Because the enemy of our enemy is a loose end."

I glower at him. "It's supposed to be *friend*."

"We don't do friends, Squirt. Not when it comes to work," Roman says with a crooked grin.

Work? This is beyond work.

"Uh-huh, I'll believe that when I don't see you guys fawning over every woman that looks your way," I shoot back.

John huffs. "Stop. We are tasked to blend in. It's okay that we—"

"Get your dick wet?" I deadpan. Taylor bursts out laughing beside me. I spot Bensen quickly smothering his grin with his hand.

"Why here of all places? And why me? I'm useless. I don't have anything to do with…whoever you guys are fighting with." I set down the tea before I spill it all over myself.

"We've been digging up the black market's gatekeepers. This particular group is known as Sub-Rosa, but you wouldn't believe how much shady shit goes down in small, insignificant towns like these, where no one bats an eye at anything happening," Gale adds.

Bensen leans against the wall and grunts. "Think hard, Briar. What do you have or have knowledge of that would be useful to an underworld operation? Because honestly, it's been pretty damn quiet around here until your uncle was terminated and you showed up out of nowhere."

My uncle was terminated? My eyes widen and my stomach drops.

Was he working with the black market? Like dark web shit or illegal weapons trade? My heart beats faster, and the few sips of tea I took are already bubbling like they might come back up.

They all stare at me expectantly. Like they genuinely think I'll have the answer they want to hear.

"I don't know anything. Especially about my uncle. Maybe important documents or the item I'm supposed to be looking for that's worth money…but other than that, I don't know." My fingers curl into my palms, and I hesitantly look up at Roman. His gaze could cut stone. I consider clarifying that it's a flash

as it pierced my flesh. I'm glad it was a deep cut—it's the only reason he believed me to be dead.

"Fragile? You couldn't fathom the shit I've survived," I whisper with venom stinging my tongue.

He smiles—like an actual boyish smile—and by the grace of God, it's so lovely that I'm too stunned to do anything as he turns me and grabs my jaw, tilting it so I have to look up into his cruel eyes. "Couldn't I?"

My heart hammers in my chest so wildly that I worry he can hear it. The artery in my neck flutters as I watch his eyes move down to my parted lips.

Roman sucks in his lower lip and bites it before dipping down and stroking his tongue up my chin languidly. Then he kisses me, and my brain detaches from the world. His hand still has a firm grasp on my jaw, and his other is latched to my waist. Our connection is as magnetic as it was last night.

I whimper at the rush of adrenaline that moves through my body. An emptiness grows where I want him to fill me up. My eyes crack open, and I'm met with Roman's starved gaze. His crackling scent of teakwood warming my senses.

He licks his lips and groans. "Just as sweet as the first time."

"Why was there a second?" I whisper over his lips, scared of what the answer will be. The attraction between us is undeniable, but everything else has me questioning more than just my morals.

He chuckles and kisses me again. "Because some sick part of me wants to hear you scream and writhe beneath me." He lowers and dots a kiss on my neck before looking up at me with querying eyes.

I suck in my lower lip. There are a billion reasons why I should tell him to go eat a pile of ants, but I'm transfixed by him.

Roman slowly presses kisses down my chest, eyes still locked with mine. When he reaches my breast and strokes his tongue over my supple skin, my knees threaten to buckle.

He smiles with his lips against my bra, biting the edge and pulling the fabric down until my boobs are free. I inhale as the cold air hits my nipples and whimper as he sucks one between his lips and swirls his tongue around it. Roman's hands dig into my hips as he guides me back onto the bed and makes me sit down with my legs spread to him. "Hold perfectly still, Briar. That's an order, and you don't want to know how I would punish you."

A small cry escapes my parted lips as he pushes my chest so I'm lying down. He hooks his hands around my thighs, dragging me to the edge of the bed.

Oh my God, this is actually fucking happening.

Roman makes quick work of pulling down my sweatpants and underwear. "Your smart mouth was going to get you in trouble, and you know it. It's about time I teach you some manners, don't you think, Squirt? No one talks to the lieutenant of the Icarus Squad like that and gets off scot-free."

He positions himself between my legs and lets out a low rumble from his chest. "Such a pretty pussy."

I want to close my thighs and lock him in place, but I'm so scared of what his punishment would be. It makes my pulse race and turns me on. I just stare down with my heart in my throat as the most terrifying man I've ever met strokes his tongue through my slit.

My head instantly drops back, and I fist the sheets desperately as pleasure jolts through my body. A whimper just on the cusp of being too loud escapes my parted lips. I have to keep my jaw clenched to keep myself from moaning.

Roman flicks his tongue over my clit so aggressively that it almost feels like a warm, wet vibrator that begs me to buck my hips into his face. I'm on the edge of crying out. I need to be filled, I've never felt so empty in my entire life.

He answers my needy pleas with two fingers buried in my pussy. This time I can't stop the moan that wrenches free. The thickness of his knuckles spreads me so fucking good. Roman finger fucks me and looks up, licking my juices from his lips like a depraved, starved man.

I cover my face with my hands and moan as he rocks me on the bed until I'm bucking into each thrust of his hand. I've never felt this way before—something huge is building up. Roman works me closer and closer until he bites my clit, and it's my complete undoing. I come unlike I ever have before, thighs shaking and crying out into my palms.

When the convulsions finally taper off, I'm a trembling mess, legs sprawled out to the sides and breathing heavily like I've just run a marathon.

Roman chuckles. "Told you you're a squirter." I smack his arm, but he only finds it amusing. *I've never fucking done that before.* He totally was right. My cheeks burn.

The other guys definitely heard me moaning. *Crap. What am I doing?* Hot tears prickle my eyes, and I cover my face with my forearm. I'm pissed off with myself for letting him do this.

"Oh, don't be shy. They're about to hear a lot worse." Roman chuckles as he stands and pulls his shirt off.

I should tell him to fuck off. But the second I see those sharp abs and the damage that his body has seen in his short life, I can't help but let the defiance in my gaze shift into longing.

He leaves his pants on and climbs over me, wrapping one strong arm beneath me and tugging me up to the pillows.

Roman's scent cascades around me like silk. I could exist in his presence forever.

We're lying on our sides, facing one another as he pulls me closer against his chest. His warmth holds me in a vise grip. I tilt my jaw up, and our lips are crashing together before we can waste our breath on words.

I know he'll be mean to me after this. He'll probably call me a whore again.

But there's a piece of me that wants this part of him. We are so different but much the same. We share an emptiness that cries to be filled.

He's going to hurt me. And the fucked-up parts of me rejoice in that. Because it's better than feeling nothing.

Roman kisses me so fervently that I'm certain he's going through the same emotional turmoil I am.

Why do I sabotage myself with the softest of kisses from the cruelest men?

I moan as our arms twine around each other. His hair is still a little damp from his shower and feels so smooth as I thread my fingers through it. Our stomachs are pressed together, and his hand is secured tightly around my waist.

He dry humps my pussy, and I swear to God I've never been weaker for a man than for one who knows how to dry hump a girl into desperation. His bulge is begging to be released from his pants, and yet he continues to move his hips into me.

Patience is this man's secret weapon. Or maybe it's that he really enjoys the ache that comes before you actually give in and fuck. That utter feral-ness that grows until the dam is about to break.

"You like being scared, Briar?" He asks as he rolls us so he's on top of me, straddling my hips. I swallow drily as he unlatches his belt and gazes down at me like he's in a daze. "Because I want to fill your cunt and hear you whimper with fear. I want you hopeless."

My eyes widen, and I can feel the blood drain from my face. At the same time, the ache in my core becomes unbearable. The darkness in him is insatiable, and I want to take a peek inside.

I slowly nod, deep down knowing that it's the dumbest decision I'll ever make, because where do you go from here?

CHAPTER 14

ROMAN

Briar looks up at me with fear-filled eyes, and it makes my balls swell. Her lips are puffy from our kisses and her cheeks are red with fever.

I smile and move off her so she can turn around. "Put your arms behind your lower back," I borderline command her. She's a good girl and obeys me. That needy little cunt is already weeping again, even though she just came all over my face.

Her breathing quickens as I secure her wrists with my belt. I wrap my hand around her pretty throat and squeeze enough to get her pulse racing and to hear those sweet little whimpers that make my cock throb eagerly.

"You'll never be the same after tonight, Briar," I confess against her temple, breathing her in and savoring her delicious scent. She shudders and moans at my depraved words.

Fuck. I might never be the same. I swallow as I stare down at her curves. Her pussy is just waiting for me to pound into it and fill her to the brim with my come.

I let her neck go, and she collapses onto the sheets. My pants and briefs are off in a matter of seconds, then I'm fisting my veiny cock in my hand and dipping the precum beading at my tip into her pussy.

Oh, she likes that. I grin as she lightly pushes her ass out for me to give her more than just a taste.

"I'm into raw, and I don't pull out, baby." My voice is raspy as I push the tip in. "Are you on the pill, Briar?" I have to brace my hand on her back so I don't just start rutting into her as hard as I can. She's so fucking tight that it feels like my dick is getting sucked.

She whimpers and mewls, "No."

Fuuuck. Breeding is my biggest goddamn kink. I suck in my lower lip and squeeze her ass with one hand while securing her in position by holding the belt at a tight angle.

I'm about to resign and pull out when she glances back at me from over her shoulder and says in the sexiest voice, "But it's a safe week."

That's all I needed to hear to fall just a little bit deeper into the idea of her.

CHAPTER 15

BRIAR

Roman's fat cock is seated completely inside me after one hard thrust. He doesn't continue to move his hips; instead he bends and bites my shoulder while I adjust to his thickness. My cry is instant, and his dick throbs deep inside me.

He groans and rewards me with a soothing stroke of his tongue over the bite. "You'd let a monster like me scar you, Briar?" His dick feels like it's getting harder inside me as he reaches down and presses on my stomach, adding pressure there.

I moan into the sheets and wiggle my hips in an attempt to get him to start fucking me and stop teasing so much.

Roman chuckles before his demeanor shifts quickly from slow and patient to aggressive and rough.

A scream tears out of my throat as he pounds into me so hard and deep that my core instantly cramps up and squeezes him just as ruthlessly.

His moan is pure ecstasy as he pumps his cock in and out,

balls slapping my clit and making my eyes roll to the back of my head. I'm already close to coming again when he abruptly stops and pulls out.

I'm so dazed that I don't protest when he flips me over and positions himself over me with my legs hooked over his shoulders. For a lucid second I notice movement at the end of the room.

Oh my God. The entire squad is gawking at us. All of their eyes are wide and shocked except John. I've never seen his face so contorted and red.

"Eyes on me, baby. The boys can watch, can't they?" Roman murmurs over my lips, and I don't know if it's because he's so fucking hot or because it turns me on that they're watching, but I don't decline. I moan into his deep kiss, and our tongues chase one another as he slowly seats his dick back inside me.

This position allows him to fill me to the absolute brim. It feels so fucking good, even though it also feels like he's rearranging my insides. The pace is brutal, and knowing that the other guys are watching makes everything feel ten times more extreme. The high that runs through my bloodstream is unlike anything I've experienced.

Roman's thrusts get rougher, and the veins in his neck protrude more as he kisses me again, moaning into each one as I do until I'm trembling with another orgasm and squirting for the second time of my life.

"Oh fuck, she just came on his dick," Bensen says, sounding like he's fully immersed in watching us. I don't care. The only thing I care about right now is that Roman pumps his cock deeper into me a few more times before he stills completely, throwing his head back and moaning his pleasure.

His dick throbs inside me, filling me up with so much come it feels like I'm going to burst. He presses kisses to my forehead as he remains where he is, his cock pulsing a few more times before going still.

Roman's sigh is filled with relief. He stares down at me with hooded eyes and grins like an absolute menace. "That was fucking crazy."

I'm still trying to catch my breath. "Yeah, it was."

"Jesus Christ, that was…inspiring." Taylor laughs, but his tone is dead serious.

My cheeks warm at their awe-filled eyes and flushed faces, but I'm so tired that I don't care what they saw. They literally kill people all the time, and I'm still trying to process that. Their opinion of me means nothing.

"Can we start calling her Squirt too?" Gale cracks a wry grin and winks at me.

My lips part, and I can't help but laugh.

"All right, guys, get the fuck out. You had your show," Roman barks, and they grumble a little before heading out. John stares a second longer before furrowing his brows and leaving.

Roman spares another look at me before he withdraws and stands at the bedside.

I'm an aching mess and struggle to even sit up with my arms still tied. He offers a small smile and helps me up. "Shower?" he proposes as he unbinds my wrists.

"Together?" I ask with a shocked tone.

He shrugs. "Saves water."

I'm not buying the nice-guy act, but I nod.

The hot water feels amazing, and with the lights on, it's impossible not to let my eyes scour over his body. He puts a dab of shampoo on his palm and lifts a brow at me like he might—

My brows shoot up as Roman starts washing my hair for me. I stare at his face. He's so close and so focused on the task at hand. He senses my eyes and glances down at me. I flinch but don't look away.

I've never met anyone so dangerous with such tender hands.

"What are you thinking about?" he asks, letting his gaze move back to my hair.

"Can you tell me about them?"

"About who?"

I lift my hand and delicately brush my finger over the jagged scar that runs across his forehead. "How can someone as gentle as you have such gruesome scars? How did you end up becoming an underground soldier?"

His hands stop moving at the nape of my neck and his grip tightens there, making me uncomfortable, but I know he won't hurt me. No matter how much he wants me to believe that he will.

"I've never once been described as gentle, Briar." He has such a broken, empty expression as he peers down into my soul that it shatters my heart.

I purse my lips and brush the *VI* scar under left his eye. "You were just now. So? Will you tell me about them?"

His eyes narrow, but I can't read what he's feeling. He blinks slowly and then leans his cheek against my palm, shutting his weary eyes. "It's not your type of story, Squirt."

"I love horror stories," I joke. Well, sort of.

He chuckles and tips my chin up with his forefinger and thumb. "Don't say I didn't warn you."

CHAPTER 16

ROMAN

There never really was much left for me in the real world.

Not after my tour overseas. Four years in the military changed me into a man-made monster. I never did figure out how anyone got through it without losing themselves. Although to be fair, I never really was all that sane.

I liked breaking things. I liked watching the chaos unfold and the aftermath more so.

I liked breaking myself too.

It wasn't long after that I found myself in the Dark Forces for my sins.

"Why six?" Dalton asked me as he poked my face. The scar was still a little tender, and I didn't particularly enjoy him jabbing at it.

I swatted his hand away. Of all the people in the Under that I could befriend, he's got to be the most annoying. "Because there were six of us," I grumbled.

The Under Trials were the Dark Forces' version of boot camp Essentially it was created to weed out the weak and find out how far criminals were willing to go in order to make it onto a squad. Only the best survived, and there were limited open spots.

Dalton frowned and looked at Nyla. She lifted a shoulder and let it fall. "Six of who?" she pried.

Six of my comrades that I led to their doom on my last mission when I was on a normal military unit, effectively landing me here. Booked in as a fucking criminal.

I smile. "I had five siblings." It was easier to lie—better that they didn't know the kind of guy I really was. The kind that liked to toy with things until I was ready to decide what to do with them.

"So is Syxx your real last name or one you made up?" Nyla grins. Sometimes I think she sees right through me.

"I'll let you decide." I would always tell them when they asked.

My lies didn't help though. Not when I was stupid enough to trust the people I thought were my friends. Why did I expect them to tell me the truth when I was lying to them?

There are no truths in the underground military. Not between cadets.

The Under Trials were ruthless, yet I flourished so much that Nyla saw me as a threat. Someone to be taken care of before the final trial. In many ways she was right. But I would never betray my friends the way she did.

After the second trial started, we were supposed to team up and make sure the three of us made it to the boat. It didn't take long after I cleared the path for them to turn on me.

Dalton at least looked like he struggled with his decision, but Nyla was another beast. The moment she thought I was down, she didn't waste any time spearing Dalton right through his throat.

I won't forget how much of myself I lost that day. Somewhere between bashing her head into the shoreline rocks and being one of twelve remaining cadets on the boat, I lost my humanity.

General Nolan saw that in me more than I'd like: a machine of madness for his wicked plans.

Nolan had a terrible dream of creating the ultimate soldiers. I heard that over a decade ago. He even went as far as to test capsules that made soldiers feel no pain. Wouldn't that have been something?

I was his current muse. He wanted more than resistance to pain. He wanted someone impenetrable.

Someone bulletproof.

He had mesh specifically made that stops bullets from going farther than a few centimeters into your body. Apparently, I was the ideal candidate for such an experiment. It started slow; the first one was installed over my heart. Then he had them placed everywhere: over my shoulder blades, knees, abdomen, my forehead, neck, *everywhere*.

The scars are brutal, but they're worth it. I was skeptical at first. Everyone was, I think. But after I was shot square in the chest and the bullet didn't go more than half an inch inside me, it changed the game.

After the surgeries were done, I became addicted to the pain of healing scars. So I'd brand my skin. The Dark Forces' psychiatrist said that it was a mental illness, this self-punishment. I never let him get too far into my head, so I never figured out what I was punishing myself for.

The deaths of my friends in the Under Trials perhaps. The

lack of trust and faith I have in anything anymore. The way we are constantly sent to snuff out people like candlelight.

I think I scar myself just because I like it.

Although, the sense of loneliness that burrows in my chest only seems to get deeper. I can't fill it with pain forever.

Sometimes I wonder if the only part of me that's actually bulletproof is my wicked soul.

Roman tells me fragments of his past for hours after we dry ourselves from the shower and lie in bed. Obviously I think he leaves out a lot of the finer details, but it makes me see him differently. With more sympathy. Not that it excuses the terrible things he's done, but I can understand why he acts the way he does.

From what I gather, he's done horrible things to stay in the Dark Forces. It sounds like he didn't have much of a choice. He didn't explain much about what the boot camp entailed, but it's clear that it's a series of trials that only few survive.

No one should have to endure what he's been through.

"Your turn," he murmurs as he glides his finger down the scar on my forearm. "Who did this to you?" Roman's brows knit with sorrow, and his eyes shift back to my face.

I swallow the knot in my throat. "My ex."

His eyes darken, and he flexes his jaw. "What?"

I look away and nod. "He… He tried to kill me." A pathetic, anxious laugh slips from my lips. "He got so close that he actually thought he did, and unknowingly buried me alive."

Roman's face twists painfully. He opens his mouth a few times to say something but shuts it each time before he shakes his head and pulls me close to his chest, embracing me in a hug that I've needed for months.

We stay like this for a few moments before I pull back and gaze at him. We're laying facing one another with sleepy expressions.

I touch his forehead and murmur, "There's truly metal mesh here? You can't see anything except the scar. It just feels like flesh." It's hard to believe, and if I hadn't seen the metal in his shoulder wound firsthand, I probably wouldn't believe him.

His eyes are half open, as weary as mine are.

"Yeah, it's as thin as a few sheets of paper and is malleable like chain mail. When struck, it interlocks and seizes up, which allows it to stop the weapon. Cool, huh?" Roman's smirk is sadder than I think he realizes.

My lips press together, and I try to keep the emotion out of my voice. "Is that why you couldn't move after being shot at the lake? Your shoulder seized?" I whisper.

He shakes his head. "No, it's not supposed to immobilize me like that. But like all experiments, there are flaws and weak points. Mine happens to be my shoulder."

"It's awful," I say, my heart aching.

His body stiffens at my words, and he stares at me as if I've just stabbed him. He recovers quickly, blinking away the split second that his mask was down.

"I didn't mean—" I try to explain, but he cuts me off.

"And so was sex." He glares at me and sits up, letting the blankets pool around his waist.

He knows what to say to be an asshole. I shouldn't care what he says, because deep down I want to believe that he's only doing it to protect himself, but that was pretty cruel.

I slide out of bed in nothing but my bra and panties and reach for my sweatpants. "Fuck you, Roman."

His hand is around mine before I can pull my pants up.

I shoot him a death glare, but his eyes are apologetic.

"I didn't mean that."

My chest constricts at his admission. "Then why the fuck would you say it?"

He pauses and shakes his head. "I don't know. Just…" His face twists and he forces his gaze to his hand, still gripping mine. "Just please don't go." His voice is still raspy from our escape on the lake last night. And I'm too tired to deal with any of this.

"Fine, but I'm going to bed." I crawl back into the sheets. He pulls me against his chest, and damn it if that doesn't make my heart flutter. I can't help the smile that spreads over my lips as warmth dances between us. It's been so long since I've been held this way.

I close my eyes and pretend it's anyone but Roman holding me, but the funny thing is, no one I imagine in his place makes my chest feel heavy like he does.

———

Gale and Taylor set up a few glass bottles about fifty feet away from where me and John are standing.

They seem to think it's imperative that I learn how to protect myself in case we get separated. The squad must've had a serious conversation last night once Roman snuck out of my bed. They haven't questioned me too much, which makes me think that they know a lot more than they're letting on. Could they already know about the flash drive? My stomach drops. Maybe I should just come clean and tell them.

I slept like the dead, so I actually feel great today. Minus the house being infested by men. They ate all the food and drank all the coffee I had. Bensen promised they'd get more tonight.

The thought makes me grin. It's only been a day, but I haven't been plagued by the urgency to leave and keep running from my past. In a weird way, it's like having them tell me that they're in this fucked-up underground operation makes my misfortunes not seem as bad. Not that I should be comparing our circumstances, but I can't help it.

I know the likelihood of Callum finding out I'm not actually dead is slim to none, but worry is a seed that doesn't tend to stop growing. So I'm glad they are teaching me some self-defense, it makes me feel a little surer in my ability to protect myself.

"What are you smiling about?" Roman asks stiffly. His arms have been crossed tightly since we got out of the car. Bensen drove us to one of the huge fields outside of town, and no matter what direction you look, all you can see are tall stalks of corn shifting in the wind.

Apparently their auto shop is around here somewhere. John promised that we'll stop by after this because they need to check in with their general or something. I'd be lying if I said I wasn't interested in seeing their headquarters.

"Nothing," I say, with an implying tone. Roman being a grump only makes my smile wider. I can't help but find his broody persistence amusing.

John unlatches his gun from his hip and sets it in my hand. "It's fully loaded, Briar." *He's been so awkward with me after he saw our little show yesterday.* I give him an uneasy look, but he ignores it. "We don't keep our safety on because we need to be able to act fast out here." He angles my arm so I point the weapon at the ground. "So that means don't point it at us."

I roll my eyes. "I wasn't going to point it at anyone." I'm so used to talking with my hands, I accidentally point it at Roman.

His expression goes completely focused, and he kicks the gun out of my hand in half a second. "Ow! What the fuck?" I cry and clasp my hand.

John lets out a long breath and checks my hand while I glare at Roman.

"What did he *just* fucking tell you, Briar?" he shouts a few inches from my face, and it scares me. My body reacts, and I flinch, tears prickling my eyes. "Jesus Christ, of course you're going to cry about it."

"Hey, fuck off. Respectfully, you don't need to be a complete dick to her, Lieutenant." John shoves Roman's chest, so he has to take a few steps away. I bite down on my cheek as hard as I can to get the tears in my eyes to go away.

Why is he being an asshole again?

Roman glowers at both of us and ruffles his hair aggressively. "I bet you thought I'd be nice to you after I fucked the shit out of you, huh? Whoreton." He sneers at me before stomping away, and I lunge to chase after him so I can slap him across the face.

John hooks his arm around my stomach before I get more than a foot away. "Trust me, he's not worth the energy." I hate that John sees my lower lip trembling with rage and shock. He tilts his lovely head to the side, and a few blond strands of hair fall over his brow. "You all right?"

I fist both hands at my sides and give him one short nod. I can't bear to talk right now; if I try, the knot in my throat will only become more tears.

"For the record, you're not a whore," he adds, setting his

hand at the small of my back and guiding me to our mock shooting range.

"*Whoreton*," I mimic Roman's stupid voice, and it makes John snort with a laugh.

"Sorry, you're not a *Whoreton*." He cackles and shakes his head at how stupid that word is. *Very clever, Roman. Standing ovation.*

"I know I'm not. So why does he keep calling me one?" I glance over my shoulder and hope Roman's long gone by now. But of course he's leaned up against the car, a cigarette between his lips and staring at me.

I give him a smug look before flipping him off and turning back around.

John pats my head gently. "You know, Briar, I'd say it's because he probably has fucking mommy issues." He can't even get through the sentence without laughing, and it pulls a few laughs out of me too.

"That's not funny," I try to say without the giggles, but it's impossible.

"It's not. But just look at how angry he is." We both make a *pfft* laugh as we simultaneously glance at him, indicating we're talking shit. Roman's jaw ticks, and he snaps his cigarette between his fingers before he can even light it.

It takes us a few minutes to stop laughing over it, but I feel much better after.

"I fucked up yesterday, I guess," I mumble, accepting the gun again from John and making sure to not point it at anyone this time. "Moment of weakness, I suppose."

John chuckles. "We're all adults here, and we all have needs. Roman's fucking hot, I get it." He elbows me playfully. He makes it sound so casual, and perhaps it really is that simple.

161

Taylor and Gale come trotting back over to us with curious expressions.

"Where's the lieutenant?" Gale inquires.

"Taking a time-out, I'm afraid," John says sarcastically. The two of them laugh.

"That didn't take long, did it?" Taylor smiles at me and plops a headset over my ears. He points at the mic that's attached before he puts a headset on himself too. "Thornton, you read me? Over."

At least it's hard to stay in a down mood around their group. A small mercy.

"Copy that. Over." A big smile curls my lips because I feel so ridiculous.

"All right, Private Squirt, we need you to take out two hostiles. Eastern ridge. Ten o'clock. Over." Benson's voice comes through, and I blink, looking for him but not finding him. He must be pretending to scout. I roll my eyes at their dramatics, but a giddy sense of fun rushes through me.

John moves behind me and raises my arms to where they should be. He pulls back one of the ear covers and murmurs, "Make sure to line up the scope with the center of the object, account for the fall direction due to the wind, and—"

Bang.

He sets his finger over mine and squeezes the trigger. The gun kicks back really hard. I'm glad he was holding on because I didn't expect it at all. The glass bottle in the center of the table shatters.

A huge smile and inaudible laugh escapes from me.

"Nice work, Private Squirt. There's one more, though. Take them out." Bensen sounds like he's actually talking to a comrade, well, or I guess he would if he wasn't calling me *Private Squirt.*

I'll never live *that* down.

John lets go and moves to stand beside me. I take a deep breath and focus on lining up the scope and the bottle.

Bang.

Nothing happens.

"Crap, I missed." I let out a frustrated huff.

Taylor pats my shoulder. "Trust me, you're going to miss a whole bunch more."

And he's right. I miss nineteen times before I finally hit one. When I do, I about jump into John's arms.

"Finally. Let's get going. This took much longer than expected," Roman retorts, apparently feeling like he had to add an insult. I don't even bother looking at him—I'm not even sure when he rejoined us at the firing line.

John's right. I won't extend him any of my energy.

The guys start packing up the SUV when I notice a car pulling up through the field. It's noisy out here with the rustling grass, so I'm not surprised we didn't hear it coming sooner.

"Um, guys, someone's here," I call and they all snap into movement.

"Get in the car, Briar." John moves in front of me and gives me a little nudge. I'm not going to ask any questions—not after last night at the lake.

I climb inside, and Gale joins me. "Stay low, just in case this is a decoy and there's an ambush in the grass." His voice is cold and focused.

A chill moves down my spine as I try to stay as low as I can while watching the approaching truck.

It could just be a civilian or neighboring farmer, couldn't it? My stomach churns when my eyes flick to Roman and I notice he has his gun clutched tightly behind his back.

Jesus, I bet he has the most blank expression right now too. No one would even know their death was coming. *Would I even know?* I work my jaw, not putting it off the table that Roman would take me out if he was ordered to. His history is chilling, and it sounds like he always does as he's told.

The truck rolls to a stop twenty feet from the guys. John and Bensen approach casually, waving and not giving away that they have weapons strapped to their hips.

The driver's side door slowly opens and a tall male steps out. I shift up in the seat a little more to get a better look.

Gale is facing the other way and watching the fields with his pistol in his hand. "I don't like this. Something doesn't feel right," he whispers.

I swallow thickly. "Why?"

The man leaving the truck is Grahm. My eyes light up, and I'm about to tell them that everything is fine, that he's probably just out here looking for me, when Roman lifts his pistol in the blink of an eye and shoots toward the SUV me and Gale are sitting in.

My heart stops, and I instinctively close my eyes.

For a moment, I think I scream, but all I can hear are sharp shouts and gunshots as everything around us gets turned upside down.

My hands are clasped around my ears, and I force my eyes open when I feel the car trembling and roaring to life. Gale is already in the driver seat, shifting into gear and flooring the gas.

The SUV tears up the ground as it speeds through the field. The corn is still standing tall in the areas where we didn't flatten it to practice shooting, and it's so loud in the car that I can barely hear myself yelling at Gale.

"We can't leave them! Gale! *Gale!*" I try to lean forward to touch his shoulder, but he takes a hard turn and my body is thrown against the door. It must not have been closed all the way because it busts open and I'm sent rolling out into the field.

I hear the brakes after a few seconds and a door slam.

"Briar? Shit, are you okay? Briar?" Gale says in a low voice, just above a whisper. The sound of men shouting and shots being fired ring through the air, though they are much more distant now.

"Here," I rasp, clutching my ribs.

Gale's on his knees inspecting me swiftly before picking me up in a fireman's hold and carrying me back to the car. His gaze is steady and not full-blown panic like mine.

"W-we have to go back," I stutter as he sets me in the back seat and clicks a seat belt over me this time.

Gale's brows are firm. "We are, but promise me you'll close your eyes when I tell you to, Squirt." I don't even blink at the nickname as I nod.

He gets in the driver's seat and extends his hand back, offering me a black pistol.

"Uh, Gale, I'm not ready to use that." I stare down at it, and although it was so easy to use earlier, now it holds an entirely new weight. I can't shoot at a person with that.

"Just in case I need you," he says genuinely. "If they need you too."

They need me? I swallow my fear and steady my trembling hand as I take the gun.

"Ready?" Gale asks, eyes shifting to mine in the rearview mirror.

"Not even a little."

CHAPTER 18

BRIAR

'll never underestimate Gale's ability to drive after this. The fact that he has complete control over the SUV in this terrain is next level.

I brace myself and make sure I'm holding the gun the way that John taught me. *What if I can't pull the trigger when the time comes?* It's impossible to not let the intrusive thoughts crowd my mind.

The second we break free from the field we're met with a gruesome scene. We're not close enough to see the gory details, but there's a lot of red from what I can make out.

Gale white-knuckles the steering wheel. "Eyes closed!" he shouts.

I mean to listen to him, but my eyes stay open as we enter the shootout scene. The truck is gone, but there are at least four bodies on the ground that aren't moving. My heart races, and all I can hear is my blood pumping through my ears.

My mind instantly goes to the worst: Taylor, Benson, John, and Roman are dead.

Gale swerves close enough that someone's motionless body is only a few feet away from us. He throws the car into Park and jumps out. He pulls another handgun from a strapped vest under his jacket. *Good God, they really are prepared for anything.*

I watch as Gale moves from body to body before he whips out his cell phone and calls someone.

My attention shifts back to the body closest to me. The deep red of the blood that's soaked into the ground around the man makes me nauseous.

That's when I notice movement to my left. I look up and spot someone moving out of the cornstalks. My lips part to shout and warn Gale, but I think twice about it since it might cause panic, so I lift the gun, aiming it at the man approaching us.

I take a deep breath and aim at the man's legs. There's no fucking way I can aim anywhere else on him without feeling sick to my stomach.

My eyes flick to his face for a split second, and instantly I wish I hadn't looked. I can never forget his face—dark locks of chocolate-colored hair that make his skin look so pale. The sharp angles of his brows; the soullessness in his brown eyes. A beautiful killer.

Callum?

The blood drains from my face, and I drop the gun. What the fuck is he doing here? Why is he in Bane Falls?

I duck so he can't see me. Even though the windows are blacked out, I won't risk the chance of him spotting me. I crawl over the center console and slam on the horn.

Gale's head is up in a heartbeat, and he aims his gun at

Callum. I shut my eyes and brace for the gunshots, but there's only one, and it comes from Callum's direction.

I'm looking out the window in the next moment and let out a strangled sound as I watch Gale fall to his knees. He's clutching his side, and red spills from his sweatshirt.

No. My hands are shaking so badly that I can hardly hold the gun, but I can't let Gale die like this. Callum is stalking closer to Gale as I exit the car and shout, "Drop your gun!"

Callum freezes.

I wonder if it's from the shock of hearing my voice because he thought I was dead or because he didn't expect someone to sneak up on him.

I refuse to believe that he never had feelings for me. I could see it in his eyes that night that he didn't want to bury me—I only wish that it had been enough to stop him.

He stops walking toward Gale but doesn't turn to look at me.

"You…really are alive," Callum says slowly, voice devoid of emotion. He makes it sound like someone has told him but he didn't believe it.

I have the gun pointed right at his back this time, finger caressing the trigger, but I can't find the strength to pull it.

His head starts to turn my way, but I'm suddenly scooped up into someone's arms. Gunshots tear through the air once more, and I catch the faint sight of Callum taking off back into the field as a few guys chase after him.

I look up at whoever is holding me and meet Roman's gaze. He's covered in dust; dried blood is all over his face and neck. His hazel eyes are bright and only spare me a moment of attention before shifting back up to the SUV. He carries me there and plops me in the back row.

"Stay." His voice is low and demanding.

I nod absently and shrink into the seat, covering my ears with my hands in an attempt to calm my breathing. It must be at least a few minutes before Roman returns to the car.

He gets in the driver's seat just as the back doors open. Relief floods me as Gale gets in and sits beside me. His hand is pressed to his side, but it looks like the bleeding has stopped for the most part.

Taylor, Bensen, and John are nowhere to be seen. Are they in pursuit of Callum? Or are they… My eyes lower to the bodies on the ground. My mouth dries, and I feel a little nauseous thinking about it.

"Are you okay?" I sound so small compared to the loud rumble of the car.

Roman drives us in the direction John told me the auto shop was in this morning. I notice that he's driving with only one hand on the steering wheel while the other is still clutching his gun.

My mind can't even begin to process what just happened. I can only focus on breathing and the very imminent threat of Callum being in Bane Falls.

Gale groans and offers me a light nod as he pulls a bottle of pills from his pocket. "Yeah. I'm okay. Thanks for helping me back there," he rasps as he throws back three capsules. "What did you say to that guy to get him to stop?"

The last thing I need is for them to know that he's someone I know. As luck would have it, it seems that Callum is tied to the underworld gatekeepers they told me about. But how deep does this go? Why are we all meeting here in Bane Falls when it would seem so unlikely?

"Briar?" Roman's voice shakes me from my thoughts.

"Huh?" I look up to find him and Gale watching me.

Roman's eyes narrow in the rearview mirror. "Did you know that man?"

My hands go clammy, and I have to force a straight face as I shake my head. "No."

Gale groans again and seems to steal Roman's attention. I let out a short breath and grab Gale's hand in an attempt to comfort him since there's nothing I can do.

The car ride isn't long. It's maybe fifteen minutes before we're approaching a small building. It's easy to miss because it's buried out here in the tall cornfields. It has a long driveway that extends off a back road. When we get closer I realize that it's their auto shop.

Roman helps Gale get inside while I stand shivering by the SUV with my hands in my pockets, staring up at the old structure. It looks like it was built when the town was, in the early 1900s. The bricks have white stains from years of rain. It's one story tall, but I wonder if it has a cellar. I can't imagine why else they would choose a place like this other than it's in the middle of a freaking cornfield.

Footsteps come from behind me. I quickly turn around and point the gun. Three men who are bruised and covered in dirt and blood step out of the corn.

"We made it." Taylor tries to sound bright, but his weary smile gives him away.

My shoulders relax, and I'm about to lower the gun, but the smell of teakwood and oil spills over me as a broad chest meets my spine. Roman's hand wraps over mine and he pulls my arm up so I'm not aiming it at his comrades.

For some reason my head follows the movement, and I'm looking straight up at him as he stares down at me from behind. That stony expression falters, and he slides his hand down my wrist. It's so soft even though there's nothing gentle about the way he looks right now.

"What did I tell you about pointing guns at my guys?"

I stare longer than I should and blink a few times to clear my head before slipping out of his gravity. He takes the gun from my hand as I do.

"How did you guys get here so fast?" I mumble.

Bensen lets his shoulders slack with a few deep breaths. "We cut through the field. The road goes around the long way." He shakes his head gravely. "We lost him."

"Lieutenant…" John says slowly. Their grave expressions make my chest sink.

Roman just looks at them for a beat. "I know."

Their collective frowns set the tone, and quietly we all move into the building. I quickly find a spot on the only sofa in the shop garage, which is essentially just a big cement room. It's spacious and clearly used for their auto shop facade—it really does look like they work on cars in here. The smell of oil permeates the air.

The guys are all in the smaller room off to the right. I hear Gale groaning in pain and don't have to guess that they're working on him.

My eyes shift down to my hands; they're covered in dried blood.

When did I get blood on my hands? My breaths start to come in uneven waves. I don't know if it's mine or Gale's or someone else's. The last thing I want to do is draw attention away from Gale getting first aid, so I pull my knees up and wrap my arms over my head to keep my cries muffled.

Seeing Callum means I can't stay here any longer, no matter what. Now that he knows I'm alive, I don't know to what ends he'll go to finish the job.

Roman has no idea what monster just walked into Bane Falls.

CHAPTER 19

BRIAR

EIGHT MONTHS AGO

love you." Callum pushes my hands over my head and kisses me deeply. "I can't get you out of my head, Chloe. You know that? You take every thought from me."

I giggle against his lips. He pulls back and looks down at the mess he's made of me. It's rare that we go less than at least twice. I swear to God he's insatiable. It was fate that we met at the bar the night I was ditched by Uncle Arnold. My uncle was supposed to meet me for a drink since we hadn't seen each other in a few years, but something came up and he couldn't make it.

I didn't mind though, because Callum found me. That was a year ago and we've been inseparable since.

"Even when you're working?" I ask sweetly against his lips.

His soft blue eyes warm, and he pushes back brown strands of his hair that fall over his brow. "Especially when I'm working."

I've always wondered why he fell for someone like me,

someone who has a tragic past. He's also clearly way out of my league.

He says he's only successful because of his family wealth, but he's just being modest. I know he works harder than anyone else in his IT firm. I don't know the specifics of what he does there, but I've seen him a few times surveil footage and travel a lot for his boss. He's gone for days at a time, coming home with bruises and cuts. Every time I ask how he gets so hurt, he just shrugs and says that he has to get into tight workspaces with machines. When he's at the apartment, he's working on his laptop into the late hours of the night.

My lips curve, and I lean up to kiss him again. Callum moans and chuckles over my lips. It's my favorite thing that he does. His gravelly voice is impossible not to yearn for.

We cuddle up on the couch after a shower and turn on a movie. I nuzzle into his chest and try not to fall asleep as he gently runs his fingers through my hair.

"Don't fall asleep, baby," he whispers.

I don't reply since I'll likely be asleep in a few minutes. I think it's fun to let him think I'm already dreaming, though. He continues to run his fingers through my hair, leaning over and pressing a kiss to the top of my head.

My chest warms, and I start to doze off when his phone vibrates a few minutes later. I'm barely conscious but I hear him answer.

"Yeah?" he whispers, sounding annoyed that his night is being interrupted. His hand stills on my head and his entire body tenses. A long silence stretches—so long that I think he just got bad news. "You're sure?" he says in a cold, distant voice I've never heard him use before.

Who called him?

Callum's gentle hand curls into a fist in my hair, not pulling anything, but I can feel him trembling. Is he angry?

"Understood. Consider it terminated," he mutters before ending the call.

I slowly lean up and rub the drowsiness from my eyes. "Is everything okay?" My shoulders stiffen when I see his tortured expression. Tears stream down both of his cheeks. "Callum?" Concern is evident in my tone, and I lean forward, pressing my hand against his cheek.

He shuts his eyes and leans into my palm. "No, baby. Nothing will ever be okay again," he chokes out.

Worry tears through my chest. Did someone die? I pull him closer and wrap my arms around his shoulders. "What happened?" I hold him tightly as he lets his shoulders shake with emotion.

He pulls away slowly and looks at me like it's the last time he ever will. His eyes trace every dip and curve of my face.

Before I can ask him what's wrong again, his hands are wrapping around my throat. At first it's gentle, like he's going to pull me in for a kiss or a hug, but I quickly realize that's not what he's doing. His grip gets tighter.

I cough, and my hands fly up to my throat. "Callum, that hurts."

His jaw trembles, and he's looking at me with more misery than a man should hold in their gaze. He shuts his eyes, and more tears spill out as he tightens the pressure around my throat.

Panic hits my nervous system, and I try to struggle out of his grip.

"Fuck!" he cries, shaking his head, but he doesn't let up. "I'm sorry, Chloe. I'm so fucking sorry. Please forgive me. Please don't fucking hate me." His voice becomes distant, and before I hear anything else he says, I lose consciousness.

When I wake up, I'm in a heavily wooded area. It's damp, cold, and everything is hazy. My mouth feels so dry. Why does everything hurt so bad? I try to remember what happened, but my head hurts so badly that I can't think. My lips part, and I'm about to call out for Callum when I'm struck with a sharp pain in my throat.

It all comes back to me.

Adrenaline hits my veins and horror sets into my bones.

He's trying to kill me.

I carefully lift my head and look around. I hear him digging somewhere nearby. *Holy shit, this is really happening.* I'm not tied up, which surprises me a bit. Did he think I was already dead? The idea of that sinks like a stone in my stomach.

Being betrayed like this by someone I love feels like my heart is literally being torn out of my chest.

Why would he do this to me? He just told me he loved me, didn't he? *Why would he do this…* Tears brim in my eyes, and I try to see past them as I slowly get on my hands and knees. I crawl as quietly as I can, trying to breathe equally as silent.

The scent of moist dirt burns my nose. It used to be a smell I loved, from all my time gardening when I was young. There are few memories I have with my parents, but among them are pancakes at diners and gardening on hot summer nights.

I'm colder than I've ever been, hurting more than I thought was physically possible. I can't tell which is more painful: the rawness of my throat or the aching in my heart.

I've been crawling for a few minutes. Small pebbles and sticks are embedded in my palms and knees, but I keep going. Hot tears drip from my chin and hit the backs of my hands.

That's when I hear Callum step on a branch behind me.

I thought he'd give himself away when he noticed I was

175

gone. I thought he'd start calling out my name, and I'd have time to run. But I suppose I didn't know Callum as well as I thought I did. Or at all.

I don't turn to face him. I clench my jaw and continue to crawl.

I know it's the end. There's no sound for one moment, and it feels drawn out into many more insignificant moments—moments in which I wonder if our memories and shared love turn into ash between us. Something sharp glides over my back, making a long cut down my shoulder blade.

Hot liquid spills from my body, and chills pebble my skin like rain.

It's strange. I don't cry out and I don't feel anything except the warmth of my blood. Even the pain in my hands fades.

All I am is numb—already dead maybe, and this is hell.

My body falls to the side, and I face Callum. He's not remorseful like he was earlier. The light has gone from his eyes, and all that's left is an evil I've never known. It's then that I realize how truly mortifying his beauty is, how it only ever masked what he kept hidden underneath.

I lift my arm right as he swings his knife down. He cuts my arm, and more blood blooms into my clothes. Tears are streaming down my temples and choked, rasping sounds escape my throat.

"W-why?" is the only word that comes out.

He doesn't even blink as he smacks the side of my head with the butt of his knife. It dazes me. I don't pass out this time, but I know pretending to be dead is my only hope.

I let my limbs go limp and stay as still as I can.

The fucked-up thing is that the second you're in survival mode, you dissociate. It's like my brain just flipped a switch and everything that is based in emotion evaporates. Like smoke, my heart has all but vanished. I'm just a creature surviving its predator.

Callum stares at me for only a few seconds before he gets up and starts dragging me by my legs back to the hole he dug.

My arms are trailing up over my head, and I'm staring dully into the breaking points of the trees above. The stars are barely visible, but I hold on to them. I wonder if he will hear my question in the back of his mind for the rest of time.

Why?

Callum shoves my body into the hole with one hard boot to my stomach. I hold my breath to keep from gasping as I hit the bottom. It's damn near six feet. I don't have anything to measure the distance other than the despair in my soul.

I watch as he shovels the dirt on top of me until my face is buried. I hold my breath, and the second that I hear him go for another scoop, I cup my hands around my mouth to keep a pocket of air. As he adds dirt, I try to make the pocket as big as I can, like they tell you to do in case of an avalanche.

It only takes him a matter of minutes to bury me. The dirt is loose, so it's not too hard to move my way back up, but I wait for a few minutes without hearing dirt hit the pile before I start moving. It's like climbing mud, fighting for every scrap of life I have left in me.

And after I take that first breath of crisp air, I run.

I run as fast as my wounded body will allow, and I don't look back.

Chloe is dead.

CHAPTER 20

ROMAN

What happened back there?" My voice is low. I don't want Briar to hear us, but fuck, we were just attacked for the first time since settling in Bane Falls. Why now? Everything is escalating so quickly, and I've never seen the man who shot Gale before... Is that the connection to the underworld we're looking for?

"Jesus Christ, Hopper, you are so lucky this hit your side. It's just a flesh wound. Nothing vital was struck," Bensen mutters as he retrieves the bullet and drops it into a bowl we normally use for bolts.

Gale winces and sighs once the tweezers are out of his body. "Stopped by abs and not the full metal." He coughs and chuckles as he shoots me a wry look.

I give him a disinterested frown.

John folds his arms and glances out the small office window into the shop to make sure Briar is still okay before answering me. "We can't ignore that she arrived right around the same time that this all started escalating. They knew where we were. They were likely watching us for a while and we had no fucking idea."

I drag my hand down my jaw. How could we allow ourselves to let our guard down? I know yesterday was a surprise too, but this close to our auto shop, especially during the day, is unlike them. Grahm must've reported in yesterday when the guys grabbed Briar. That's the only reason this new fellow would show up and shake their routine of only making moves at night.

Taylor nods slowly. He's leaned up against the far wall, smoking a cigarette and tapping his forehead with his thumb, brainstorming. "That guy wasn't from Bane Falls. He has to be the connection, but did you see the way he reacted to her voice?"

I nod gravely. He knows her.

She knows him.

"I'm going to report in to the general." My words hang in the room for a few awful beats. The men sit with it because they know as well as I do what it means.

General Nolan doesn't leave loose ends. Tired of his work or not, he's not the kind of man to let innocent people live.

I guess neither am I.

"Syxx?" John looks at me, not as his superior but as a friend. "What do we do?"

My jaw feathers, and I tap my finger over my arm. "I don't know." I pause and look each of them in the face. Gale shifts up to his elbows now that Bensen has him all patched up. I take a deep breath. "You trust your lieutenant, don't you?"

They all nod in unison, without hesitation.

I hold their gazes—a heavy burden I've learned to shoulder.

"Good," I mutter as I walk out of the room and head downstairs. There's a distinct mildew scent that lives in these old bricks. I sort of like it, if nothing else because it reminds me how cruel nature is.

The lights flicker on as I step into the room I've been staying in. It's always cold in here; the cement walls have been crumbling for at least the last decade.

I lean up against the sink in my room and glance at the mirror. My face is covered in dust and dried blood. None of it is mine, and that thought used to bother me—being drenched in others' blood was a living nightmare until I realized that it was either them or me. Then it became simply my reality.

I'm no stranger to the man in the mirror. I'm indifferent to him. He's cruel and callous, pushes people away because he knows they die easily. And humanity, of all things, is what almost killed him once.

Before calling Nolan, I take a shower. I let it run until the water is no longer red and my thoughts don't seem as dreadful.

The phone rings once.

"Lieutenant Syxx." The general's voice is clipped as usual.

"General… We had a situation come up. I'm reporting in for clearance and orders moving forward." I sit at the edge of my bed, my head hanging down.

He's quiet for a second. "Proceed."

I tell him about the attack and, reluctantly, about Briar.

"Our intel shows that the man you mentioned arrived in Bane Falls yesterday. If you suspect that he has ties to this girl for any reason, I want you to use her to lure him out. He's likely our ticket in, and I want him *alive*. Find that fucking flash drive too." I hear Nolan slam his fist against a table across the line.

My leg bounces. "Use her, sir?"

He's never asked me to use a civilian for a mission before.

She could get hurt, and she's already been put in danger twice now because of me.

"Yes, I want their hideout exposed by the end of the month. She doesn't need to be recovered, so discard her when you're done."

My mouth parts, but no words come out.

How did it come to this? How have I lost so much of my humanity that Nolan knows I wouldn't have a problem doing something so heinous? My eyes widen. I guess it's because if I didn't have this weird attachment to her I would follow his order with no hesitation. Because *I* am heinous. I picture her sweet smile that she still extends to me even though I don't deserve it.

Nolan notes my silence with a dramatic breath. "You've done much worse, to more innocent people, Syxx."

I swallow thickly, letting that notion sink in. Is it because she sees me in ways I didn't think anyone else could? Why do I care what happens to her when I didn't the others? My jaw feathers as I clench my fist. "I'm aware."

"But?" His tone is unreadable.

But you don't know how she caresses my scars and yearns for every horror story I have wrapped up in my bones.

I clear my throat. "Nothing. I will carry out the mission and we'll find their hideout." The words taste like poison on my tongue. A loathing I've never felt for myself fills my chest.

"Good, and Lieutenant?"

"Yes, general?"

"If she does end up surviving your use, I want her disposed of, got it? This isn't something we can let a civilian live with."

My throat is tight, and a knot forms.

"Yes, sir."

The phone clicks, and I let it slide out of my hand. It falls to the floor and I stare at it for a few minutes. This shouldn't be a big deal to me, so why is it? I want to covet her. Not hurt her.

What is it about Briar that drives me insane? Why do I see myself in her?

I let out a long groan and run my hand down my face.

If I don't follow orders, my squad could be terminated, so there's not much of a choice. Once an order is given, it must be seen through.

I've never not delivered, and I don't plan on letting the general down.

CHAPTER 21

BRIAR

When the guys come back out from the room, Roman isn't with them. I force my eyes to meet their gazes. They've all washed up and are clean. Gale's in an unstained T-shirt and doesn't look like he's dying as he did earlier, so I allow a breath of relief out.

Thank God everyone looks okay minus some scratches and cuts here and there.

John lowers to his knee to get to my eye level and offers a small grin. "Hey. You all right?" He presses his wrist to my forehead to check my temperature.

I nod. "I just look like shit because I've been crying," I say with a slight laugh. No one else finds it amusing.

"Here, I'll help you get cleaned up while the guys get a movie going. We're making tacos tonight too," he says in a chipper tone.

I blink twice. "A movie? Dinner? Do you have any idea what just fucking happened? This isn't okay, none of this is okay." I motion my hands to them. How can they just act like this is normal. Gale was fucking shot and people *died*.

John squeezes my hand reassuringly. "I know it seems like that for you, Briar, but this is what our squad has been trained to deal with. You can hold on to the trauma and the shit and let it ruin your day, or you can move the fuck on and enjoy your night. Tomorrow isn't promised, not for me, you, not even Roman."

My chest constricts at the thought of any of them dying. "I get that. But I haven't been trained to deal with this… It's a lot, John. It's too much. I just want to…"

He looks at me as we reach the bathroom, and he has me sit on the tub wall. "Just want to what?"

"I want to go home." *But I don't have one.*

I hate how defeated and sad I sound, but I'm too tired to care.

John wets a towel and wipes my face gently. His weak smile is soft and reassuring. "Don't we all?" He's quiet for a few minutes as he finishes wiping me down and scrubs the blood from my hands. "Do you want a word of advice?"

I meet his ocean eyes. "Home is where the heart is?" I scoff and glance down at my hands.

He grips my chin and tilts it up until I'm looking at him. "Home is where the squad is, Private Squirt." John winks, and it brings a smile to my lips.

I hold on to those words more than he could ever know.

We head downstairs and as promised, Taylor and Bensen have tacos ready for us to eat. We each grab a soda and some tacos and eat them on the sofas where some movie I've never seen before plays. Gale's snoring before the opening credits are over.

Taylor's on his phone, texting someone constantly. I'm so zoned out I can hardly pay attention to the movie. My mind is lost in the past and on what happened today with Callum. Not only him but the people who died too. Was Grahm one of them? I hope not.

I shut my eyes and try not to think about it like John said, but it's impossible.

Bensen hands me a blanket. I blink at him and lift a brow before I realize I'm shivering. "Thanks," I whisper and happily take it.

John scoots in closer to my side and pulls me against his chest. "You're still pretty cold from the other night," he mutters and brushes my hair from his face.

I instantly melt into his arms. His warmth bleeds into me so quickly that I can't help but latch on to it. John sets his hand on my side and rests his head on the top of mine. A thread of guilt moves its way through me, because I wish it were Roman and not John comforting me right now.

Why do I yearn for comfort from someone who is utterly incapable of giving it?

Just as my eyes are starting to get heavy, the lights flick on. It makes me flinch. I almost forgot that Roman was still in the building. Everyone ignores his presence except John.

Roman's eyes burn into me. He works his jaw as he lets his gaze drag over us and where we're cuddling on the couch. He tilts his head and gives me a cruel grin. "Go figure, Squirt makes her way around, doesn't she? Seconds don't look good on you, Bishop." Roman doesn't spare us another look as he stomps upstairs.

My cheeks flare. "That's it, I've had enough of his fucking shit," I grind out and crawl off the couch to chase him upstairs.

John grabs my wrist and shakes his head. "He's just being an asshole."

"That's fucking bullshit and you know it." I shake him loose and follow Roman up the steps. By the time I get to the top, he's

185

already in the garage, revving up his crotch rocket and about to put a helmet on.

He gives me the coldest eyes.

"What's your fucking problem?" I fist my hands at my sides to stave off the fury that has me trembling like a leaf. I'm so sick of being afraid of him.

He just scoffs at me with a nasty smirk and sets his helmet over his head. I storm up to him and try turning his motorcycle off. Roman snatches my wrist and shoves me back.

I fall on my ass and have to swallow the pain that shoots up my tailbone. Roman physically jolts when I hit the ground, and I can hear him let out a furious sound in his helmet before he takes it off and tosses it.

My lungs fill with oxygen, and my eyes widen as he bends down and lifts me up effortlessly. I set my hands on his shoulders for support as he sets me down on his bike.

"My problem is *you*, Squirt," he says with a deeply furrowed brow.

"Why am I always your problem? I'm not doing anything! And—" My words are shut off with a brutal kiss. Does he seriously think I'm going to just let him kiss me after what he's said today? I set my hands on his chest and push him away.

He backs off for only a second before he's licking his lips and gives me another crushing kiss. This time he threads his fingers through my hair and pulls my head back. A cry escapes my lips, and I'm left whimpering as he kisses my throat.

"You are my problem because you're fucking distracting. Trouble follows you wherever you go, doesn't it?" Roman murmurs over my neck and curls his fingers into my waistband. "I hate how much I want to touch you." He leans up and kisses me as he slips his hand into my panties.

Chills erupt over my skin, and all I can do is hang my head back and breathe sharply as he inserts two fingers deep inside me. I bury my nails into his back and he groans, deepening our kiss and devouring me.

The brief moment of pleasure is interrupted by my sensible side. Am I really going to let someone who calls me terrible things and nicknamed me *Squirt* finger me right now?

I'm not letting go of *Whoreton*.

I break our kiss, and he stares at me with half-lidded eyes filled with lust and desire. "If I'm such trouble, then why don't you let me leave. I don't want to be here anymore. I'm a survivor and after today, it's clear that this isn't the place I should be." In an odd way, I want to stay. I've gotten rather close with them, and as much as I hate to admit, Roman did save me earlier.

But a nagging guilt rears up: *Why didn't I shoot Callum when I had the chance?*

Callum would've taken the shot if given the same opportunity. I know he would. So why couldn't I do it? Gale's life was on the line.

Roman's fingers are still knuckle-deep inside me, but his expression is made of stone. "We've already gone over this—you are tied into this as much as we are now."

I look away, even though we're stuck in a very intimate position right now. "Yeah, well maybe it wouldn't be so hard if you weren't such a coldhearted asshole. It's clear you despise me, so instead of messing with me and getting in my head, just leave me alone."

He curls his fingers, and it makes me squirm. A soft moan escapes, and his eyes flicker at my response. "Why? So you can go back to John and let him comfort you again?" Roman says ruthlessly.

He withdraws his hand and grabs my wrist, pulling me over to the Benz. My brows knit, but I'm more worried about why he's dragging me all the way over here to it.

"At least John is nice to me! You called me Whoreton."

"Because he pities you, Briar! For God's sake, look at you." I flinch at his verbal attack.

"What? Why don't you just tell me?" I shove him and he whirls on me, pulling me against his chest and grinning wickedly. Roman Syxx, he's so fucking deranged. He loves when I push his buttons, and damn it if I don't get a high out of it too.

My heart is racing and my thighs warm; need grows there quickly.

"He pities you because you can't keep your eyes off demons like me. It's already gotten you in trouble before. What do you expect will happen this time, Squirt?" Our chests are pressed together, and no matter how much I struggle, he doesn't let me go.

"You're disgusting," I bite out.

He chuckles. "And you're a liar. If I'm so vile, tell me to let you go and I will," he whispers over my lips. His hand moves down my back until he reaches my ass and squeezes it roughly.

I literally can't utter a word because I don't want him to stop.

He smiles at my silence and shamed expression. "That's what I thought," he tuts as he turns me around and bends me over the hood of the car. My pulse leaps as the cold metal hits my stomach.

"You're sick," I say with a breathy voice.

He shoves my pants down, and I hear his hit the floor a second later. His hands are hot as they wrap around my ass and he lines himself up with my pussy. It's already so wet from feuding with him. I don't know why my body reacts like this to him, but I can't help it.

"Oh, you have no idea just how sick I am." Roman lets his hand glide down my back and splays it over my ass before slapping it hard.

I moan loudly at the painful burn.

"If given enough chances, I'll end up stealing everything from you." He thrusts once savagely with his hips and fills me up. I let out a muffled cry.

Holy shit, why does he feel so much bigger than he did before? Is it because he's fucking me on the hood of an expensive, stolen car? Fuck, he wasn't kidding. They really are corrupt as shit.

I try to clamp my mouth closed so we don't attract an audience again, but Roman wastes no time shoving two fingers in my mouth and pumping his hips into me relentlessly.

"Tell me you hate me," Roman grunts as his hand smooths down my side and then snakes around to find my clit. My hips buck of their own volition as he starts rubbing me and building my orgasm.

He withdraws his hand from my mouth and moves his grip to my throat. My pulse leaps with fear and pleasure.

"I hate you," I choke out. Furious tears spill down my cheeks at my inability to tell him to go fuck himself. Because even if I don't like him, I love the way he fucks me.

Almost as if he needs it as much as I do.

Someone to be crazy with and let our dark sides out to play.

He moans at my words and sets his forehead on the center of my back, rutting into me like a fucking animal. "Do you mean it?" he grinds out, grip tightening around my waist as he nears his climax. My hips are practically vibrating on his dick as I'm on the edge of coming.

I hesitate. He makes me mad and says terrible things to me. I *should* hate him. I should hate him as much as I do Callum.

And yet there's something so genuine in the way he lets his soul bleed through his scars. I can't look away no matter how hard I try. They are the constellations of a broken man.

Maybe he can bring beauty out in mine too.

"No," I murmur, and the word brings him to a halt.

He's fully seated inside me, spreading me open and pushing against my cervix. Roman flips me over so my back is against the hood and secures his hands on my thighs in a vise grip as he starts plowing into me again.

He fucks me so hard that tears prickle in my eyes.

"Say you do." He glares at me as he rocks his hips so roughly into me that I'm about to come all over him.

"I'm not going to lie to you, Roman." I hold on to his forearms as he ruts into me. His breaths are getting clipped, and I'm not sure how much longer I can last either.

"Haven't I given you a million reasons to?" His jaw flexes and he thrusts in ruthlessly one more time before he's spilling his come into my deepest parts and rearranging my insides. I writhe beneath him, and he leans against the car, arms braced on either side of my head and staring down into my eyes. "Haven't I been cruel?" he whispers against my lips.

All I can focus on right now is the erratic beating of my heart and the throbbing hot dick that's pulsing come into my deepest parts.

I lick my lips and stifle a moan as I try to form a response. "You've given me one to not hate you."

He lifts a brow inquisitively, almost as if I've offended him terribly. "When?"

A playful smile splays across my lips. "I guess you'll never know." He traces my features with his softened gaze and firms his lips as he pulls out.

I know he isn't mine to fix. But sometimes I wonder if it was fate that brought us together to mend one another's tattered souls.

Roman is like an old worn coat, with holes and tears you could fit your hands through. Something abandoned and left to rot. Yet against all odds, he treks on. He doesn't hide his monsters, yet Callum hid all of his. At least I know what Callum is capable of.

"You aren't as cute as you think you are, Squirt," he murmurs as he collects me in his arms and gently sets me on the ground. He keeps me pressed close to his chest, and when I look up at him, he presses a soft kiss to my lips. Almost as if it's an apology for the rough sex.

Once we have our pants pulled back up, Roman walks over to the wall-to-wall cabinets and pulls out an extra helmet. I quirk a brow and nearly have the breath knocked out of me when he tosses it at my chest.

"Grab the jacket on the hook." He nods to the coat rack by the door leading back to the hallway. "We're going for a ride."

CHAPTER 22

BRIAR

This feels incredibly dumb to leave," I mutter through the helmet.

His voice cuts in with a dash of static. "I told you, we're safe. Sub-Rosa won't make any attempts to attack us. They just lost at least four men."

The nice thing about wearing helmets is that you don't have to try to hide your smile.

"Did Taylor really do all the modifications to the gear himself?" I can't help but be impressed. There are five of them that need gear too, that's quite the job. Taylor spoke about it on the way to the cornfield earlier today and wouldn't shut up about it. He made their jackets and helmets all bulletproof, and even added weapons compartments to their bikes.

Roman nods. "Yeah he did. Hold on tight, Squirt. I'm not letting up until we get to the peak."

Peak? Of a mountain? I swallow nervously but do as he says

and wrap my arms around him. I know the jackets have bullet-proof vests built into them, but my heart is racing so viciously right now that there's no way he can't feel it.

I glance down at his hands and watch him send off a text to a group thread labeled Icarus.

VI: Going out for a drive. Taking Squirt.

Zeus: We'll watch on the surveillance in town and up-date you if there's movement at the laundromat.

"Which one is Zeus?" I ask, not particularly expecting him to answer.

"Taylor."

A beat of silence.

"Is Roman your real name?" I rest my head against his back as he presses a button on the handle, and the garage slowly lifts. It must be exhilarating being in a secret military force.

Music lightly plays in the helmet's speakers. I wonder if he's hearing the same song, "Chandelier." It draws a chuckle from me.

"What? I can't like pop music?" he tuts.

I laugh harder and squeeze his chest a little more. I swear he stifles a laugh of his own. "It's not that you can't so much as I just didn't pin you as a Sia fan." He doesn't answer my question about his name, not that I necessarily thought he would, but I tuck the thought away to ask another time.

Roman pulls out of the shop and onto the highway at high speed. I scream and hold on as tight as I can. Roman laughs again, and my heart weakens a bit at the thought of what a weightless smile would look like on his lips.

I loosen my grip after the first ten minutes and take in the moonlit scenery as he drives us up a different mountain than the party was at. Coming from the city, I never would've thought I'd be able to know what it's like to have so many mountains around one town. But that's just how it is out here. This one is farther away, right next to the lake, I think, but it's hard to be sure in the dark.

As isolating as it is out here in the country, I've never felt more like I could belong in a place. It gives me hope.

We reach the parking lot at the peak's scenic outlook after twenty more minutes of blissful driving. There wasn't a single car on the road, but it wasn't like the first night I arrived in town that gave me uncomfortable pits in my stomach. This is a deep peace.

Roman sets the kickstand and easily steps off the motorcycle. My dismount is much more unceremonious. We take our helmets off and set them on the seat.

The piney air hits me with my first breath. It's fresh and could be wrapped up and shoved into a candle. This mountainside isn't like the night of the bonfire, or even the lakeside. It's quiet—no splashing of water on the shore or music to scare off the bears and wolves. It's bone-chillingly silent. A promise that death is stalking these woods in search of its next victim.

A shudder moves through my spine, and I have to swallow my nerves. "What are we doing up here?" I ask when Roman starts walking toward a wooden fence post.

"You'll see." He glances back at me with a half-grumpy expression but offers me his hand. My heart flips.

Did Roman just… I decide not to question it. I take his hand and ignore the butterflies fluttering in my stomach. I'm too wary of the dark woods to argue with him.

We walk along a narrow trail that has each footstep sounding louder than the last. The path abruptly ends, and we have to trek a handful of steps farther until we reach a random picnic table. It's clearly been here for years, the old wood and chipped paint indicate as much. Splintered areas and initials were carved into the boards long ago.

Roman sits on the top portion of the table and pats the spot beside him without looking my way. I glower at his back and cross my arms. He doesn't talk much, and sometimes it feels so passive.

"Sit, Briar," he grumbles.

I relent, pulling my knees up and resting my chin on them as I watch him. He fidgets with a pocketknife before casting a glance my way. Our eyes are locked for a few moments, our warm breaths fogging the air between us. "Would you change your scars if you could?"

What kind of a question is that? I quirk my brows at him. "Change them?" I whisper as I rub the scar on my arm from Callum. "Wouldn't that hurt?"

I hate pain. So much so that I can't imagine doing it on purpose.

Roman's face is unreadable, but his eyes are curious as they take me in. "Of course it would, but changing them alters our story." He looks down at his forearm and pulls his sleeve up.

It's like a mural of carefully crafted wounds mixed with unintended ones. Smiley faces, stars, barbwire, even some words, although I can't tell what they say in the dark.

"So would you, Briar? Alter the story your scars tell the world?"

Chills move up my arms and I shrink into myself, shoulders lifting and my stomach sinking. *Would I?* I've never thought about it before. I glance over at him and murmur, "What do they currently say?"

Roman hums thoughtfully before offering me his hand. The moonlight finally peeks over the mountaintop as he does, tracing his outline at the highlight of eventide. His raven hair almost has a blue tint, and his hand comes through the cold night as a lifeline. His eyes are brimming with light, taking me in like he never wants to look away.

I take his hand and he guides me into his lap. My breath hitches in my lungs as he slowly lifts my shirt and sets it to the side. I've never felt as vulnerable as I do in this moment with my bare skin exposed to the dark woods—and to the scariest creature within them.

Roman gently runs his hand down my arm over the scar that tells the story of Callum trying to stab me, where my flesh severed in place of my life. Was he thinking about bringing me out here after he saw the scar on my shoulder yesterday?

"This one is loud," he whispers and leans forward, pressing a kiss against my skin. Tears form in my eyes, and I have to bite my lip to keep them there. His eyes lift to mine and the universe stops for a lovely moment. "It tells a story so sad and twisted that I can't give it a voice…but it doesn't have to be. It can say something else entirely, Briar. It can be a story that isn't filled with screams and horror." His eyes don't falter, even as tears stream down my face.

"What would you make it say?" I whisper.

Roman's face softens, and a beautiful smile curves his lips. "That you cannot be overcome. You're bulletproof."

My lips part, and I have to swallow a few times to get the knot in my throat down. He lifts his hand and presses his palm against my cheek, wiping away hot tears with his thumb.

I manage to choke out a few words. "It was a knife actually."

Roman grins and shakes his head. "You don't call bulletproof glass *knife proof*, even though it is, do you?" I let a few half-hearted laughs out. "You're so tragically lovely that I can't stand it. A creature as gentle as you shouldn't be running from the beasts in the dark." He cracks a sarcastic smile.

"What do you run from?" I ask, and he holds me a little tighter.

"Nothing, until you. You scare the shit out of me," he admits.

I laugh and shake my head. "No, I don't."

Roman leans up and guides my mouth to his, not yet a kiss. "You scare me more than anything."

My eyes widen as I stare into his. He's serious. "Why?" I murmur against his lips. "You're the one who's *literally* bulletproof."

A sad smile. "Am I, though? It doesn't feel like it. At least, not anymore."

His eyes narrow as if he's bringing himself back into his thoughts. He firms his lips and clears his throat before I can say anything else. "Do you want to watch how I change my story, then decide if you want me to change yours?" He puts a breath of space between us, pulling away like he always does when he catches himself allowing too much bonding.

Roman pulls my shirt back over my head and hands me back the jacket. I shiver but am grateful to be wrapped back up in the warmth of it.

"Okay," I say skeptically.

I'm not exactly into watching people cause themselves pain, but I'd be lying if I said I wasn't curious about his process.

Roman pulls a small circular container with red powder from his pocket and unscrews the cap. He takes a lighter to the edge of his pocketknife, cleaning the blade and immediately dipping it into the powder.

He pulls up his sleeve and points to what looks like a scar from a medical incision. The bulletproof mesh, I bet. I frown at the painful wrench that twists my heart.

With a steady hand, Roman cuts into his arm. His eyes narrow with pain, but an almost euphoric expression spreads across his face as his blood spills down his arm.

I open my mouth to ask if he's okay, but he shoots a look at me.

"I'm fine, Squirt."

I have to hold myself back from trying to help him and sit patiently as he works. When he's done, he dumps a little of the powder over his wound and lets it sit there for a few minutes before wiping it off.

The bleeding stops instantly. The powder must be a coagulant of some sort. The design that remains is an ivy vine, wrapping around the original scar. It looks like a tattoo almost.

"There." He grins almost to himself, but his eyes flash up to mine. "Much better, don't you think?"

I nod absently as I let my fingers softly touch his raised skin. "Do you come out here often to do this?" The image in my head of him out here alone, carving himself up at night hits deeper than I thought possible.

Roman shrugs. "Not always here. I have a few other places," he says casually.

I can't tear my gaze from the scar below his eye, VI. He was just a young man when he gave himself that. His story about it was haunting. A history of self-loathing that's led to this. I wonder if he'll ever stop. *He's not mine to fix*, I remind myself.

"Did you really lead your squad to their deaths when you served?" He gives me a short nod. "Did you do it on purpose?"

Roman's expression flattens, but he presses his lips together

198

and gives another short nod. "It's what got me thrown into the underground, remember?"

Even though he's admitting to me he's done something heinous, I have a hard time believing it. He kept it brief the other night, yet he has no trouble talking about other things. Is it because he fucked up? I want to know everything there is to know about him.

"Do you regret it?"

He turns his head toward me and we share a silent moment. "No. They were bad people. I know it doesn't excuse my actions, but they were killing innocent civilians, and I couldn't let them do it anymore. I don't regret it." There's guilt in his gaze, though. Roman's guilt looks like storms building behind his eyes and lightning swelling in his veins.

"But?"

"You don't miss a thing...but now that I'm in the Dark Forces, I find that I've become the very man I hate." His eyes linger on my arm, where my scar lies underneath. There's no way I can live the rest of my life without knowing what he'd make of my scar. So, against my better judgment, I shrug off my jacket and pull my shirt over my head, offering him my arm.

"An asshole?" I muse.

He chuckles as he cleans off the edge of his blade on his jeans before using his lighter again to sterilize it. He dips it in the powder and smooths his hand over my skin.

I look away and tense my muscles for the pain to come.

"Someone who hurts innocent people." His voice rolls down my arm and makes me shiver. The cut of his blade comes next. I whimper and fist my hands against my thighs. "I lost the part of myself that cared a long time ago. People became things in my way or objects that I needed to discard. Emotionless beings that are only out to fulfill their own needs over empathy for others. I lost my humanity. I would follow an order over anything." His voice tenses at the last part, and his hands pause briefly before resuming.

Focus on the sound of his voice. I take a deep breath and try to ignore the pain that flares over my skin in slow, agonizing lines.

"That's a terribly miserable way to view the world," I murmur.

"It's a place built on lies, Briar. That's why I find you so interesting. You have every reason to be angry with everything, and yet you let the world move through you like water through a screen." He taps the powder over my arm and rubs it in. I hiss at the sharp sting and then let out a breath of relief once it's done.

"It's because I'm tired," I say weakly. "So fucking tired. Anger requires so much, I'd rather enjoy what little I have…and survive another day."

Roman blinks at me like he wasn't expecting that reply. His eyes dip to my lips before he inhales and refocuses on my arm. He uses his undershirt to wipe the blood from my elbow and stares at my arm with a bit of pride flashing over his gaze.

"There. Your story has been rewritten." Roman sits back and watches my reaction. It's just him, and yet it feels like I'm standing in front of a crowd of people.

Tell him your name isn't Briar. Now would be the time to come clean, but my lips won't part, my voice won't come.

I swallow and look down at my arm. A small gasp escapes me.

He made it look like the ivy vines on his arm. The old scar looks like a branch, and the vines wrap around it as if to swallow it whole. I blink down at it in awe.

"Now I will only ever think of you and this moment," I say sheepishly, granting him a small grin.

"Exactly. You're a part of the squad now, Squirt," he teases. He sets his hand on my knee, and my pulse quickens at the warmth that spreads from his hand.

I roll my eyes at him. "Uh-huh… If my code name is Squirt, I'll resign now." He laughs. But I wonder what we're supposed to do now with Sub-Rosa attacking…and with Callum being back in town. "Where do we go from here? What if they attack again?" My stomach curls at the very thought of that. There's not really much sense in running anymore. It didn't go so great last time, and I have no doubt Roman would just track me down easily again.

I need to get back to the farm and find that flash drive at the very least. If it will help the guys, then it's important to me too.

Roman puts his knife and powder container back into his pocket and stares up at the view as the moon crests over the treetops. "We have to get to them first, don't you think?" His jaw feathers with whatever thoughts are floating through his head right now. "Who was that guy earlier anyway?" His voice lowers, and he lets his heavy gaze shift to me.

I know Roman's not stupid. He likely saw the whole scene with me and Callum unfold and instantly knew something was off. I rub my hands together and try to think of where to even start. I sigh and lift my arm to my new scar. "His story has already been rewritten."

Roman's brow furrows, and he lets out a long breath and nods with understanding, even though he looks like he wants to ask more questions about him. "Fair enough."

"Any chance we can go to my farm and look around for a flash drive? I meant to tell you guys at the house yesterday, but I was just so overwhelmed that I couldn't bring myself to say anything. I think it's valuable for the information it holds."

Roman gives me an understanding look. I was expecting him to look a little surprised that I know of a flash drive, but he doesn't. Did he already know? "I'm glad you told me. I actually sort of knew about it and was going to root through your farm today after the shooting practice, but one thing led to the next." That's an understatement. "We can go there, but it might be dangerous. They know you've been staying there, so it's not as safe as the auto shop."

"Do you know what's on it?"

He shrugs. "I think I have an idea. Remember Sub-Rosa and their gate we discussed? Well, our main goal is to infiltrate so that we can put a stop to it."

"And the sooner you guys have what you need, the better, right? Then you can take out whoever you need to deal with to eradicate this underworld outpost in Bane Falls?" I want his word that this isn't going to be for nothing.

Roman stands and shakes his jacket before zipping it up, his back facing me.

"Yeah. And then you can have a nice, quiet life somewhere, Squirt." He sounds distant. And I have to admit that the idea of living somewhere quiet without troublesome boys like them sounds a bit boring. I refuse to invest too much thought into that feeling in this moment.

"Well then, let's go." I brush by him and head toward his motorcycle, glancing over my shoulder and shooting him a playful smile. "Can we stop by the grocery store first?"

thought she wanted to look at wine. I didn't expect her to be on a mission of her own to find some lady she's worried about after the race over a week ago. I snag an orange and toss it in the air as I trail her in the store.

It's probably a good idea to watch from afar just in case some of Sub-Rosa's guys are out here waiting for us to leave the store. I've already checked my cell a few times and haven't heard anything from the squad, so we're more than likely fine. I'd rather err on the side of caution than leave anything to chance, though.

Briar's brow is furrowed and she looks down every aisle before she stops and talks to one of the other store clerks. It's pushing ten p.m. already so I wouldn't be surprised if the lady she's looking for is off for the night.

My attention gets pulled to the front of the store, where a group of four men enter. They are familiar enough; I think I recognize them from the races, but they don't look like any of the Sub-Rosa men, so it's not enough for any concern.

I glance back at Briar and watch as she gently rubs her arm where I rewrote her past. A subtle warmth blooms in my chest. I wish I could reach in and tear that feeling out with my bear hands. There's nothing good that can come from having emotions again. Especially not for someone like her.

Someone I could never be with.

Unconsciously, I rub my thumb over my fresh scar that matches the ivy leaves to hers. I can't believe I let myself share that with her. I've never shown anyone my process before, nor have I met someone who would let me mark them in my fucked-up methods. But I felt…vulnerable tonight.

What the hell does she see in a man like me? Especially after her ex hurt her like that… I'm cruel to her, at best. Why doesn't she hate me?

She will once I use her as a lure to get that guy to show himself again.

Guilt is a heavy burden to carry, one that I haven't endured in years. But the thought of using sweet, unsuspecting Briar puts a weight in my chest.

Briar calls me over, her eyes bright with answers she got, I'm assuming. The corner of my lip curls up, and I have to shake my head at her relentless care for others. Does this Hailey person even know her very well? I doubt it. I've been watching Briar since the party. No one except that damn Sutherland boy has been around her.

"They said she just clocked out and we might be able to catch her in the parking lot if we hurry. They're worried because she hasn't been looking so great this week." Her eyes narrow, and she bites her lower lip—an unfortunate habit that makes me want to be balls deep in her.

"Let's go then." I toss the orange onto a shelf, and it earns me a glare from her. She should know that I don't give a shit. About the orange or her judgy looks.

The parking lot is fairly empty, so it's not hard to spot the only other person in it who happens to be walking with a limp toward her car.

"Hailey! Hey, are you okay?" Briar shouts as she trots across the asphalt toward her. I shove my hands into my jacket pockets and survey the parking lot as I follow.

Hailey visibly stiffens and quickly looks over her shoulder at Briar. Her eyes widen, and she hurries to her car.

Briar freezes for a second before resuming her pursuit. "Hailey?" Her tone falters.

That's a strange reaction to have to someone coming to see if you're all right. I look around the parking lot one more time before jogging to catch up to Briar.

We get to the car before Hailey can start it. Her expression is filled with terror, and she's trembling.

"Um, Briar." I reach out to set my hand on her shoulder and stop her from pursuing this, but she's already talking.

"Hailey. Oh my God, what happened to you? Did Grahm do this?" She opens Hailey's door and inspects her. Briar's breaths are heavy now, and I can see why.

Hailey's face is a bit swollen, and she's clearly using makeup to hide some bruises on her face and throat. Her eyes are blood-shot, and I'd bet beneath her jeans and jacket are many more bruises and potentially worse.

I frown. "Sutherland did this?"

I knew he was likely in on the black market, and that he's likely the one who killed Briar's uncle, but I didn't pin him for someone who beats on women.

"P-please just leave me alone." Hailey's voice is shaky, and she finally successfully starts her car.

Briar takes a few steps back, tears brimming in her eyes. "I'm sorry. I just wanted to make sure you were all right. I didn't see you at the party after Grahm followed you into the trees."

I give Hailey a dull glare and set my hand on the hood of her car and lean in. "Did Sutherland do this? I'm not going to ask nicely again."

The blood drains from her face, and she forces her eyes to her steering wheel where her hands are gripping it tightly. "If I say yes, I'm only putting myself in danger." Her tone is clipped but with fear, not anger.

I lean in closer so Briar can't hear what I say next. "Are you in the underworld? A gatekeeper for Sub-Rosa?" I mutter coldly.

Her eyes flash wide, and she finally looks at me. I don't know what she sees, but her teeth start clattering. "Yes," she whispers. "I used to be."

Unfortunate.

"I see. Well, you'd better get home before trouble finds you again," I say in a normal volume. Briar looks worried, even though Hailey wasn't very friendly to her. "I'd be quick about it too," I tack on at the end, and she seems to get the message loud and clear.

She shuts her door and tears out of the parking lot.

Briar's holding her arms as if she could make herself smaller than she already is. "Will she be okay?" she asks quietly.

I glance down at her and firm my frown. "My bet is that she's going to go home and pack all her shit. She'll likely leave town before morning." Briar covers her mouth. "At least she will if she's smart. Things in Bane Falls are escalating."

The farm is as lifeless as it was the first night we met. I cut my headlight a mile out from the house in case we have company out here. This is probably a really stupid boundary to push with everything that happened today. But Nolan was clear. He wants the flash drive and the gate location to the underworld.

And selfishly, I want more time with Briar.

The flash drive might have enough secrets on it to satisfy Nolan. If I check off all his boxes, he might allow me to spare Briar. I know he wants me to discard her after, or let her die in the raid, but I don't think I can do that.

It's much too late for me to walk down that path. Whether I like it or not, my humanity stirs around her. Like a beast being coaxed from a long hibernation.

Briar, why did you wake me?

Some might say I'm more dangerous when I'm willing to save someone out of emotions. I think about Dalton and Nyla and how horrendous I became after. Yes, one is willing to be much more vicious when it's for someone they care about.

I park in the barn and clear the area with my silencer pistol up and ready before I give Briar the nod to let her know it's safe.

She quickly unlocks the back door of the house, and we slip inside.

"Best to keep the lights off," I mutter, grabbing her hand softly as she reaches for the switch.

Her eyes fill with horror. "Oh shit, yeah, good call. But how will we look through all this crap?" She motions to the hoard that Arnold built. I have no doubt that he intentionally filled it with clutter to hide the flash drive and possibly weapons.

I don't release her hand as I guide her down the hall. "Let's start upstairs, there's a full moon tonight so we'll have a little light. I'll work on getting the windows blacked out so we can light some candles. That should be safe enough, but not the overheads."

Briar nods, and we spend the next two hours sorting through a bunch of trash.

I found black garbage bags and was able to completely cover the windows in the entire house. We work in silence. I appreciate that about her—she needs time to her thoughts just like I do.

Her hand brushes over mine when we reach for the same pile of books. Our eyes meet, and neither of us move our hands away from the other.

"Are we wasting our time here?" she asks with an exasperated sigh.

I brush my thumb over her hand and smile as her cheeks flush. "No. We need to find it, even if it takes all night."

"Did you let the guys know we'll be out late?"

A devious grin pulls at the corners of my lips, because I already told them we won't be coming back to the shop tonight at all. "Yeah, I did. They're monitoring for us, so don't worry, Squirt."

She nods and sets her other hand on top of mine. I startle, which is fucking weird for me, but the warmth and softness of her hand makes my chest flutter.

"I never thanked you for saving me today." Her voice is like a song I can never forget.

I find myself staring at her and have to blink and clear my throat to reset my expression. What the fuck is this girl doing to me?

"We're even. You know, since you helped me out at the

lake." I rub the back of my head and force my eyes away. I hate intimate things. It makes me uncomfortable, but with Briar it's in the best way. I want her to follow me into the dark. More than anything, it's what I want.

She looks at me like she's waiting for more, but I shift and start looking through the books. I know what she wants me to say. She wants to know why I keep pushing her away and saying terrible things to her. But how could she understand? *I'm calling you a whore and being a dick because it's in your best interest* sounds like an asshole excuse—even if it's true.

I set aside a book and lift another, flipping through the pages and freezing as I find it's been hollowed out. I tilt it, and a USB drive falls into my hand.

Relief sets into my bones, and it feels like for the first time in months, my shoulders relax. I clutch the flash drive like it's a lifeline. This might be what saves Briar. I won't let anything bad happen to her if I can help it. Not a fucking chance.

I slip the USB into my pocket and continue searching as if I haven't found it yet. It might be selfish, but I don't want to go back. She's all mine tonight, and I still have to convince her to help us on our mission to draw out the guy who shot Gale.

An awful, guilty feeling seeps into my marrow. I shake it off and ignore the morality of it.

This is for her. I'm using her to save her life, I reason, and it makes me feel a little better.

Briar stretches her arms over her head and yawns. "I guess we should head back. I'm so tired. We can keep looking tomorrow morning, I guess." She seems bummed out about it.

I give her a sly grin. "Let's just stay here. We'll risk exposing the hideout if we keep going back and forth, especially at night when they're most active."

She doesn't say anything for a few seconds, then nods in agreement. "Yeah, you're right. Okay, fine." She levels me with a suspicious glare. "But you're sleeping on the couch."

I chuckle and grab her arm, pulling her into my lap and thoroughly enjoying the surprised gasp that breaks from her lips as she falls against my chest. "Baby, you know I'm not doing that. I need to stay with you, for safety reasons." I wink and suck my lower lip in.

Her cheeks burn red and she mimics me, sucking in her lip. We both know I'll be buried seven inches inside her for the remainder of the night.

"You make me crazy, you know that?" she whispers over my lips, eyes searching mine like she'll find a man and not a beast behind them.

"Funny, you do the same to me, Squirt."

I clutch the nape of her neck and bring her soft lips to mine. She smells like vanilla and honey—a warm and consuming scent that has irritatingly reached into my heart.

Our kiss ripples through the empty halls of my haunted soul. She lets out a small whimper and melts into my arms. I slide my tongue into her mouth, and she eagerly lets me in.

I forget time.

I forget that we are wrong for each other.

I don't fucking care.

Slowly, I lower to my back and lie in the scattered pages we sorted through. Our kisses don't break, they become more sensual, and she starts grinding that perfect pussy over my cock.

I groan into her mouth and bury my teeth into her lower lip. She moans and smooths her hands down my chest. I watch as she slowly lifts my shirt, pressing kisses down my scarred abs and tracing her finger over them thoughtfully.

She glances up at me with those lovely eyes and continues down to my pants, unbuttoning them and freeing my cock.

The candlelight halos her figure. She's so lovely it hurts. Flowers couldn't bloom bright enough to rival her.

Briar wraps her hand around my thickness and starts pumping. I let my head fall back and moan as she watches what she does to me.

"Fuck," I say in a breathy voice that I didn't know I had until meeting her.

Her lips are coming down around the head of my dick in the next moment, and I inhale sharply, arching my back as she sucks me in hard. The urge to start fucking her mouth is so strong that I have to will myself to keep my hips planted to the ground.

Briar works my cock with her hands, pumping me, while taking me in her mouth deeply. I'm shocked that she hasn't gagged once.

Another moan falls from my lips as she deep throats me. I'm so fucking close to spilling into her. *Fuck, I want to rut into her so bad.* I fist my hands in her hair and stop myself from jerking my hips up.

It's goddamn painful to restrain myself.

She pops my cock out of her mouth and licks her lips as she smiles seductively. "You can fuck my throat. I don't have a gag reflex."

My jaw drops, and my dick throbs with another wave of precum from her unexpected, filthy mouth.

Jesus Christ, I think I just fell in love. My eyes widen at the intrusive thought.

Oh, I'm so fucked with her.

CHAPTER 24

BRIAR

Roman's eyes fill with lust as he bites his lip. "You sure, Squirt?"

I nod with a cheeky smile and put my lips back over the head of his dick. He lets out that deep moan that makes my pussy so wet. I hollow my cheeks and start taking him in deeply. His hips buck lightly at first, with restraint, and it's cute that he doesn't want to hurt me. But that doesn't last more than a second before he's forcing my head down over his dick and fucking my mouth ruthlessly.

I moan on his thickness, and it draws a groan from him as he pumps his dick so far down my throat that I can't breathe. He pulls out enough to give me a small breath before he's fucking my throat again, his thrusts getting more erratic until he's blowing his load and holding my head down until he's done. A few stray bucks of his hips make my core ache.

When he finally pulls out of my mouth, I'm gasping for breath and savoring the salty taste of his come.

He holds my jaw in his hand and tilts it so I have to look up at him. "That was the craziest shit I've ever experienced. Now it's my turn." He gets a wicked smile on his lips as he scoops me up and carries me into the room I've been staying in.

There's only one candle in here, so it's significantly darker. Roman's movements are hasty, like he can't wait to taste me, and that does something to me.

I wriggle out of my pants as he helps pull them off.

"Someone's already soaking wet for me," he teases as he pushes my legs up. "Hold them like this, Squirt. Don't let go until you're fucking vibrating for me." Roman dots kisses down my leg until he gets to my pussy.

I inhale sharply as he drags his hot tongue through my slit and ends with his lips over my swollen clit. God, it's so sensitive with my legs up like this.

My moans are loud and echo through the entire house as Roman flicks his tongue rapidly over my clit. I'm writhing and trying not to let go of my legs because it feels like I'm already going to climax.

"Oh my God," I cry out as he pushes two fingers inside me and starts pumping them and hooking up toward my G-spot. My hips are bouncing of their own accord, and I let out a scream as my orgasm finally hits. I'm squirting all over his face, and he's dipping down and lapping up my juices greedily. I realize that he's dry humping the edge of the bed, dick fully out and precum already getting on the sheets.

"Fuck, baby, that was so hot. You better come on my dick just as hard," he says darkly with heat burning in his gaze. I can't even muster up a response because I'm still reeling from my orgasm.

Roman chuckles as he kisses his way up my chest, lifting the shirt from over my head and kissing me deeply as he prods my entrance with his cock.

I smooth my hands down his broad chest, feeling all of the grooves in his muscles and the softness of his skin. He palms my breast and breaks our kiss, moving his lips across my neck and whispering filthy things between our moans.

This is starkly different from the last few times. This isn't rushed, angry sex to get out our sexual tension. It's sensual, beastly in the way that we taste one another and take our time discovering the scars on our bodies.

"Briar," Roman moans as he bites the skin beneath my ear and pushes the head of his dick inside me. He spreads my core so perfectly, even though we're wrong for each other, it's as if we were crafted by the stars themselves to meet.

"You feel so good, Roman," I murmur as I dot kisses on his shoulder. He growls and works his jaw against my neck as he thrusts himself all the way inside. I cry out and dig my nails into his back as he pumps his hips relentlessly.

He wraps me in his arms, holding me so close that our chests are pressed together as he fucks me.

"*Briar*," he whispers again, and it makes my walls clench around him. He moans and starts thrusting harder.

"If you keep saying my name like that, I'm going to lose my mind," I whimper beneath him.

Roman chuckles as he pulls out of me. I pout in protest, but he flips me on my side so that we are facing the horizontal mirror set above the dresser. My naked body is on full display in the candlelight. Bite marks and hickeys are all over my neck and chest. The lust-filled lull of my eyes and Roman's starving gaze make my core ache to be filled again. It's not just an ache, I'm *desperate* for it.

"You're telling me you haven't lost it yet?" Roman breathes against the nape of my neck as he moves up against my back so he's lined up to my entrance. He wraps an arm under my head and kneads my breast while he lifts my left leg up with the other. "You will when you watch me break every last piece of you and become your utter undoing."

I watch in the mirror as Roman's huge cock enters me. He does it agonizingly slow so that it's obvious how much he spreads me open. It's entirely different watching it go in. I can hardly believe it fits.

Holy shit. This is the sexiest thing anyone's ever done with me. I melt in his arms as he starts to work his dick into me and presses hot kisses to my neck. I let my head fall to the side and moan with each thrust that hits my cervix.

"You like when I fill you, don't you, Squirt?" he murmurs against my jaw. I nod, drunk with lust.

"Yes."

He buries his face into my hair as his thrusts get stronger. I watch as I come undone on him, hips vibrating as I come on his dick and soak the sheets.

Roman pumps into me as I'm squirting and goes deathly still, holding me as tightly as he can as his dick throbs deep in my pussy, his hot seed filling me to the brim. "*Oh fuck,*" he groans as his hips buck lightly. Then his entire body relaxes, and he lets out a long sigh. "You're so fucking amazing." He chuckles and slowly withdraws from me.

I'm left lying in our mess and breathing hard.

"Come on." Roman offers me his hand, and I let out a whine

in protest. He rolls his eyes with a big smile as he dips down and picks me up in a cradled position. "Look at you, Squirt, living up to your name," he teases, and I can't help but laugh into his shoulder.

"It's not like I try to do it."

He carries me to the bathroom right down the hall and starts the shower. "You make it sound like it's a bad thing." His tone is light, but I can see the weariness in his eyes. I'm bone tired too.

The hot water hits my back, and I let out a relieved sigh. We shower quickly and with great reluctance, I'm able to resist Roman's playful kisses. There's no way in hell my pussy can take another ruthless pounding tonight.

We crawl into bed after changing the sheets. One look at the clock has me groaning. "We stayed up way too late," I complain as I pull the comforter up to my chin.

I figure Roman is going to go right back to his cruel antics, but to my surprise he snuggles up and spoons me.

"Four a.m. isn't so bad," he murmurs sarcastically. He seems so at ease, if I wasn't there myself, I wouldn't believe what went down today in the cornfield. It puts a weight in my chest, how desensitized they are to the horror of their lives. In a way, I guess I am a little bit too.

My eyes are heavy and start to shut when Roman presses his forehead to my shoulder. "Hey, Squirt?" His soft whisper warms my skin.

"Yeah?"

"Do you care about us? About me?" His touch is gentle as he glides his hand soothingly over my hand.

My brows pinch. "Of course I do."

"We need your help. *I* need your help." His voice sounds pained, like he wouldn't ask me unless he had no other choice. I worry my lip.

"My help?"

He nods against my neck. "That guy today that reacted to you? I think he's our main target. We need to get him alone, and I think the best chance we have of getting him to come out again is if you reach out."

Chills erupt over my skin at the thought of seeing Callum again. I swallow nervously. "I don't know, Roman—"

"Please, Briar. We need you," he pleads, rolling me to my back so he can stare down at me. He's so beautiful in the dim light, every angle of his face is etched in shadow. "Please. I won't force you to do it if you don't want to, but you should know that Lieutenant Syxx doesn't beg. Not for anything, but I will if it's you."

His eyes trace over my features, and damn it if my heart doesn't flutter every time he's this close. "You promise you won't let him hurt me?" I whisper, and it sounds so pathetic.

Roman's eyes soften, and he presses his forehead to mine. "I promise. I won't let him touch you, Briar."

I wish I believed him completely. But it's enough. "Okay."

His eyes light up and he sits up a bit. "You're sure?"

I swallow. "Yeah."

He kisses my cheek and nuzzles back beside me, holding me in his strong arms. It makes me feel like the most precious thing to him. Even if it's a delusion, I entertain it for this moment, in the dark, early hours.

"He hurt you before," Roman says in a low voice, yet it feels like a shout. It's because he isn't asking, he's affirming. "He's the ex that tried to kill you. What's his name?"

That old wound twists in my heart and festers. I manage one small nod. "Callum."

Roman brings his lips to my shoulder. "Can you tell me

what happened? Why did he try to kill you?" His finger coasts over my new scar, where he's already rewritten my past.

I smile sadly at the thought. "It's the oldest story in the book, Roman. He betrayed me, and I was dumb enough to fall for it. I ended up buried because of it. I never really got an answer as to why."

His mouth firms into a frown. "I'm sorry, Briar."

"Me too." My voice is so weak, I'm surprised he hears it.

"After this mission, I swear you'll never see that mother-fucker ever again." I hope he's right, and I never cross paths with Callum again.

"Will you kill him?"

Roman is quiet for a moment, as if he actually needs to contemplate it. "Yes."

A small smile curves my lips.

CHAPTER 25

BRIAR

The squad returned to the farm the next morning. Apparently they didn't pick up on any suspicious activity for the rest of the night and morning.

It felt much safer having everyone back together. I understood why John said that the home is where the squad is. I'd never felt like I truly belonged anywhere more than I do with them. It solidifies that it's not the places we find our home in, it's the people.

The next few days are spent formulating a plan for drawing out Sub-Rosa and trying to figure out a plan for delivering the message to Callum and what will happen thereafter. I've been nervously listening and trying not to let my fear of Callum change my mind about helping them.

He's a terrible man who needs to be stopped no matter what. The guys filled me in that his group stationed out here have been responsible for many deaths and even one of their prior squadmates. The fact that he's involved in the black market and moving illegal weapons just means he's going to continue hurting people, and we can't allow him the chance to do that.

We remain holed up at the farm, continuing surveillance and staying quiet until Bensen gives us the all-clear that we can resume target practice and return to town without bringing danger to the civilians. As boring as it sounds, it's actually not so bad. Movie nights with the squad and tucked in Roman's arms hasn't been anything I'll complain about.

"We're going out tonight, Squirt." Roman draws me against his chest. We're tangled in the sheets and a stream of daylight is filtering in through the tear in the trash bag we have taped over the window.

I long to stay wrapped up in his embrace like this every morning…or afternoon. I have no idea what time it is anymore since we do most things at night now. It's been a shock to my system, but it's also been sort of fun to live like a secret agent.

"We are?" I whisper drowsily. Roman brushes his hand over my face, coaxing my eyes open to see his ridiculously handsome face. His morning hair is my favorite, all tousled and soft like he's a normal guy in a sleepy town.

He nods, eyes barely open like mine are. "Bensen hasn't seen any activity from Sub-Rosa, and we're clear to stir things up again in town." He winks at me, and I chuckle.

"Let's not cause trouble, but I wouldn't mind going out. Where to?" I nuzzle into his chest, and he gently holds me. I wish he was this soft around the others. He still puts on that cold front, like he's indifferent to me when everyone is watching. But at least he isn't calling me Whoreton anymore.

"The Rose Diner," he says, and it makes me flinch.

It's just now occurring to me that it's called Rose's Diner. That can't be a coincidence. I pull away from him and quirk a brow.

Roman smirks. "Smart girl. Exactly what we've been thinking, but we haven't been able to prove shit. We think it's their gate, but after all this time we've had nothing to show for it." He slowly sits up and glances down at me. "We're going tonight, and since they've been escalating their tactics, it's time we did too."

Oh, I don't like the sound of that. I frown and sit up. "Escalate how?"

It's incredibly uncomfortable sitting in the diner after Roman ran me out of it when we first met. We're all even sitting in the same booth. Although I seem to be the only one who feels weird about it because the guys are as rowdy as ever.

Roman grins at me from across the table, interlocking his foot with mine and making my cheeks flush. God, this man does things to me. My mother would roll over in her grave if she knew this is where I'm at in life right now.

Lana is working again tonight. She looks like a completely different person from the first time I met her. Her eyes are sunken and her hair is frazzled like she's been skipping brushing it. Has she been crying?

My stomach drops as she sets down six coffee mugs for us. I catch eyes with her, and she's just as venomous, giving me a glare that sinks below my flesh and into my bones.

Did she know one of the men killed in the field? I haven't built the courage to ask Roman if he killed any of them. I know he likely did, and it wouldn't change my opinion of him given that he already showed me the guy he killed in the lake. But now that I'm seeing her state, I wonder who they were as people. What could've led them down this dark path?

"I'll be back to take your orders," she says with a raspy voice. Her eyes connect with John's before she walks back to the kitchen behind swinging doors.

Taylor and Gale stop chatting and Bensen looks at John, nodding. I feel like I'm playing catch-up, trying to follow their nonverbals. But obviously they caught on to the same thing I did.

Roman glances at the kitchen window cutout that overlooks the counter before returning his attention to the table. "It seems safe to say that she's definitely rooted with them. Just like Hailey."

I lift my head in surprise. Hailey? "Wait. Is that why she warned me about Grahm? That's why he…" I let my words trail as I remember how beat up she was. She could hardly even walk to her car. His hoodie I found that had blood on it comes to mind.

My chest constricts.

"Did Grahm do that to her on the night of the party?" I ask, swallowing thickly as I look at Roman. Gale and John are sitting on either side of him with grim expressions.

"I bet it was Hogan. He was known for being rather violent. Grahm just doesn't seem like he'd get his hands dirty, but he may have helped." Roman stares at the mug of coffee in front of him. None of us have taken a sip. I guess that shows how comfortable we feel eating or drinking here now that it's pretty much confirmed they are a part of Sub-Rosa.

Lana wouldn't actually poison us though, would she?

Taylor shifts next to me and stands, lifting his hand to his hip. "We should check it out in the back, Lieutenant."

Roman nods, and the rest of the squad moves to follow Taylor. I slip out from my seat so Bensen can get up, and then I stand awkwardly by the table.

"I thought we were going to have dinner and escalate, not fully blow the top off this thing," I whisper shout since the squad is already in stealth mode and pushing through the double doors.

Roman shrugs as he pulls out a little packet. It's black and has the letters *DF* on it. He tears the top off it. He pours it into a mug of coffee and I watch as the liquid turns blue. "See that? She started it. We'd all be dead if we took a single sip."

The blood drains from my face. She really tried to kill the whole squad. I hesitantly lift my eyes to the many windows. It's getting dark, and the diner is surrounded by fields.

"They aren't going to do anything with weapons while we're here, Squirt," Roman chides.

I shoot him a worried look. "And why the fuck not? This seems like a choice location." I shudder as a chill runs down my neck. Callum could be out there right now, watching.

"Because Sub-Rosa doesn't want to draw any attention to their existence. There's a reason why they've been so tolerant of us in their town. And that attack in the field the other day? That was the first time they've acted out like that. There were no establishments besides our auto shop in the area, and Callum must've called the order. They're not going to damage their own building and draw the eyes of the town to them." Roman sounds so sure, and I have to hand it to him, it makes sense—the last thing secret organizations want is any sort of attention. They want to move in the dark and stay hidden.

"Empty," Bensen calls out from the kitchen.

Roman nods toward the swinging doors, and I follow him over. We step through and find a pot of boiling water and the back door open.

There's nothing here that would make me suspect Lana

and the chef. It looks like the normal commercial kitchen you'd expect to see in a diner.

Taylor folds his hands behind his head and leans on the metal counter. "Great, that was a wash. *But* I think it's safe to say that Lana and the chef are definitely in on it. Whether or not they are actually a part of Sub-Rosa or just crooked civilians remains unclear."

"I won't be eating here anymore." Gale folds his arms and gives the kitchen a disgruntled frown.

Roman shrugs. "Well, let's go get some food from the gas station before heading back to the farm then. I promised Squirt dinner." He shoots me a heated look that the others might interpret as a glare. But they don't know the side of Roman that I do.

After Bensen and John finish ensuring there aren't any secret doors or a basement in the diner, we all head back to the motorcycles.

I'm embarrassed to admit how much I enjoy clinging to Roman when he drives. It's an excuse to hold him and rest my head against his back. The helmet keeps me from hearing his heartbeat, but listening to the same song as we ride is a good substitute.

For the drive to the gas station he plays "Titanium" by David Guetta. My lips curl up, and I can't help but laugh. "Seriously?"

His voice cuts in over the headset. "My hype song." The amusement in his voice makes me giggle more.

I squeeze him tighter and try to forget that our lives won't stay this simple and normal for long.

We pull up to the gas station and park on the side of the building that's not lit up by the streetlights. It's the only place to get gas in town, so it's relatively busy. A few pickup trucks are parked out front with a handful of people in the backs of them.

Heading to a party I'd presume. I grin because you don't see this in the city. Only out in the small country towns.

Five of us head in while Taylor hangs back to watch the motorcycles and check his surveillance apps.

We divide and conquer. Roman splits off and heads down the beer aisle while John follows me through the snacks. We grab an assortment of chips and prepackaged cookies.

Gale and Bensen meet us back up front with sandwiches and yogurt parfaits. Gale gives us a sour look when he sees what we grabbed. "What are you guys, ten? What kinds of snacks are those?"

John shoves him playfully. "Live a little, Hopper. These cookies are fucking divine."

Bensen laughs as we head to check out. Roman sets down two boxes of beer, and I glance up at him in surprise. "I don't think I've ever actually seen you drink." I chuckle.

He lifts a shoulder and lets it drop. "Unlike you, I'm actively working, Squirt."

"Whatever." I crack a smile. "I'm still looking for the flash drive and cleaning up the farm. Those count." I'm reaching, honestly.

He chuckles and crosses his arms before giving me a smooth smile. I forget that the squad is here with us, watching. Roman seems to have forgotten too, because he flinches and looks over at them the same time I do.

Bensen's eyes are wide, and Gale's too distracted to take his change from the cashier. John elbows Gale to get him out of his thoughts, and everyone snaps out of it.

My cheeks warm, and I hesitantly glance at Roman. He's looking down at his phone as a distraction, but I don't miss how red the tips of his ears are and the blush that's racing over his nose.

Not so tough. I bite down on my lower lip to keep my smile from spreading.

The ride back to the farm is bliss. The cold air moves through us as I listen with my eyes closed to "Orpheus" by mgk. Roman has this one on repeat. By the time we're back at the house I have it stuck in my head, and the grin on my face couldn't be scrubbed off with a wire brush.

The rest of the night we hang out with the guys and finalize the plan to get the message to Callum. It's decided that we're going to try to find Grahm at the next race party this coming weekend. I'm going to break away from the squad and tell Grahm I want to talk to Callum in private.

It takes me a few minutes to agree to seek out Grahm on my own. I have to assume he's just as dangerous as Callum. Hailey's bruises flash through my mind and make me angry again. *Fucking asshole.* Even if he didn't do all of it, I know he hurt her at some point because there was blood on his hoodie that night.

"We'll be close and watching, so don't worry." John smiles reassuringly.

Roman stares at him and narrows his eyes at the glimmer we all see in John's gaze. "Sub-Rosa isn't going to do anything with that many people around. They won't risk their parties. It's the main way they distribute their drugs and products."

I flinch. "They what? I didn't know they were the ones that threw the parties."

Bensen shakes his head. "Originally, they might have started them, but that was years ago. It's become such a town ritual that they no longer host them."

It's disturbing to think about, but how many "traditions" have been started with ill will? Using civilian gatherings like nightclubs and church events or even parties like this to make trades without authorities picking up on it—something that should be fun and harmless is used to cover for an underworld so dark and gruesome.

"Okay, I'll make sure he gets the message." I wish I sounded more courageous, but this isn't a game. Not after what I've already seen the Icarus Squad do and knowing Callum.

We finish eating with small talk and end the night with a movie. Roman has a few beers, and I enjoy the laughter and ease with which he speaks to his men.

I fall asleep in Roman's lap halfway through the movie and only wake when the credits are rolling and Taylor's obnoxious snores are the only sound that moves through the room.

Roman's hand moves through my hair gently, and I decide to leave my eyes closed. Why ruin a moment like this?

"Are you sure, Syxx? I like her…but I don't know if I trust her with this." It's John's voice. My heart skips a beat. *He doesn't trust me?* I didn't think that would hurt coming from him, but it does.

Roman's hand stills over my head. "I trust her, Bishop. That should be enough of a reason for you."

My chest blooms with warmth, and I fight the smile that dares to spread at him sticking up for me.

John sighs, and I hear him shift to stand up. "All right, I hear you loud and clear, Lieutenant," he says with the lift of his hands. "Come on, boys, we have training tomorrow. Get up." He smacks Taylor's head, and he grumbles awake.

They all sluggishly leave the living room.

My head is still in Roman's lap when I look up at him. He's staring down at me with an intensity that looks through me. I offer a small smile, lift my hand to his face, and brush the dark strands of hair that cover his forehead.

"What?" I ask with a soft chuckle.

He continues to look at me like he can't tear his eyes away. "Nothing." He dips his head down and slowly presses his lips to mine in an upside-down kiss.

My heart flutters, and I nearly lose my breath.

Roman pulls back up and smiles down at me. "Care to join me in bed?"

I lift a suggestive brow. "To sleep or…?"

Roman laughs as he cradles me in his arms and lifts me up with ease. "Guess we'll find out when we get there, Squirt."

I smile into the crux of his arm. He looks tired and like he has a lot on his mind, so I don't expect him to pursue me in bed. To my delight, the moment our heads hit the pillows, he's slipping his hand beneath my shirt and burying his face in my neck and shoulder, making me giggle.

"I can't get enough of you," Roman murmurs as his lips coast over my ear. "Why do you let me in, Briar?" He sounds tormented by the thought as he kneads my breast softly.

My back arches into him, pushing my ass into his hard cock. He rolls me over as he shifts to lie on his back with me over him. His hold on me is firm, one arm wrapped around my lower back and the other hand threaded in the hair at the nape of my neck. He kisses me again and again, until I have to push myself up just to breathe.

"Why do you let me in?" I echo his question, our breaths heavy from our kisses.

He sets his hands around my back and stares at me thoughtfully, the lust slipping away from his eyes as he traces my features drunkenly. I study the scars on his face, yearning to kiss away all the pain he's ever felt.

"Because you wouldn't leave when I pushed you away,"

he says with a wry smirk. I laugh and shake my head, trying to roll off him, but he follows the motion and our positions are reversed. His arms are braced on either side of my head. "Because you didn't let a grumpy, broken thing like me keep you from seeing the real me." His words are vulnerable, and his eyes reflect as much.

I stare into his gaze and slowly reach my hands up to his face and cup his cheeks affectionately. Tears brim in my eyes. "I let you in because you crashed in headfirst."

A wide grin spreads over his lips, and he starts laughing so hard that it makes me burst into it too.

We hold hands, side by side, and share our warm laughter until we can't anymore.

"Go to sleep, Squirt. We've got a busy week." Roman wraps me back up in his arms.

It takes forever before I shut my eyes. How am I supposed to sleep when I know I'll have to face Callum and Grahm in a few days?

CHAPTER 26

BRIAR

For the next couple days we go over the plan for the mountain party. Over and over and over, until it's seamless and we all have the details memorized to a T.

Roman has been much less harsh to me when we're around the other guys since they all saw him be affectionate to me at the gas station. Although, he's still most tender when we're alone, drawing over each other's scars and kissing through movies we should be watching.

We moved the practice shooting range to another location. This one is inside an abandoned building that has a second story so Bensen and Gale can keep a better lookout. They've still been on high alert and ensuring they don't allow another ambush.

I've gotten pretty good at shooting too. Not as much as them, obviously, but at least I can hit an unmoving target every other time now.

Annoyingly, we still haven't been able to find the damn flash drive. We go back to the farm every afternoon and turn the place upside down. *Nothing.*

Roman seems to have lost his desire to find it, but Taylor and John help me as much as they can. Bensen and Gale have been strictly on surveillance, which seems unfair, but they told me that they switch every few weeks and it's just their turn for the time being.

Taylor drapes his arm over my shoulder as we sit down in the break room of the auto shop. There's a cheap folding table in here, which technically makes this their war room. It's tacky, but that's how my boys are.

I keep catching myself thinking of them as my own squad. I know I'm not really a part of their group, but our time together has really made it feel that way. We sleep, eat, and train together. And for someone like me who has no one, it means the world to have something that feels like home.

"All right, one more time. Hopper, you start," Roman says as he leans against the old white fridge with his arms crossed. His gaze skates over me briefly before he quickly looks away.

He's been colder today and has hardly spoken to me since he took a phone call this morning. I let a frown set in. I genuinely thought he was past this.

Gale tilts himself back in the metal folding chair. "Squirt is going to go in as innocent and helpless as possible. She'll convince Sutherland that she needs to talk to Callum. We'll spread out and be watching from five different angles at the party in case there's suspicious activity or he tries to take her."

No matter how many times I hear him say that last part, I still flinch. *Grahm won't do that*, I tell myself.

Roman, satisfied, nods and looks at Taylor. "Zeus, what's next?"

Taylor clears his throat. "After she delivers her message, we'll remain at the party to avoid suspicion. Syxx will participate in the race while we keep an eye out for Callum from the bleachers."

"Good. Viper?" Roman prompts.

Bensen's fingers are interlaced behind his head as he casually states, "We wait for a response from Callum and prepare for a private meeting in a secure location. Fan out and make keeping Squirt safe our primary objective."

Roman nods and grins. "Bishop?"

There's more? This is where it's always ended when we've gone over it before.

John frowns and casts a stray look in my direction. "Once we have Callum, we disband from Bane Falls, as are the general's orders—most likely within twenty-four hours of completing the mission."

My heart drops, and I'm sure my face shows it. Why wasn't I ever informed about that? I stare at John, who looks remorseful, before shifting my gaze to Roman.

He's a wall of no emotions. It feels like a slap across the face.

"Roman?" I ask, voice conveying my hurt more than I'd like it to.

"It's Syxx when we are in the war room, Squirt. Lieutenant Syxx, if you want to be formal." His tone is impassive, and it cuts into me worse than it ever has before.

"Syxx... Are you guys really leaving after this mission? What about..." I almost have the audacity to say *What about me?* but it hits me that it was so stupid for me to ever think that I was a part of them.

"Briar, you know we're only here for work," Taylor says gently. He slides his arm over my shoulders and offers a somber look.

Bensen chimes in too. "It might be well after, so don't worry about it too much." But there's an air of guilt in his tone, which means he's lying.

I nod slowly and pretend to buy it. "Yeah, anyways, I'll be heading overseas once I sell the farm, so it's actually pretty good timing." The lie tastes sour, but I keep a forced smile on my face.

"Good. Well, men, Squirt, we will be commencing the mission tonight. We need to be vigilant and make sure we know exactly how many of their crew are left."

After the attack last week, I thought it would be dangerous for us to attend the party. But Gale explained to me that the Sub-Rosa group has integrated themselves into this town so perfectly that they wouldn't give themselves away just to snuff out our squad.

It's the same vice versa. The Icarus Squad has melded themselves into Bane Falls in the same fashion, under a ruse of being civilians. So even though it seems dangerous to go to the party, unless they know all of our faces and catch us alone, we're good.

"Remember the one rule tonight." Roman looks squarely at me, and I suppress the urge to roll my eyes.

"Stay in the crowd and with one of you at all times…except for when I deliver the message to Grahm," I state matter-of-factly.

Roman nods coldly. "Let's cause some trouble tonight, Icarus."

The party is in the same location, and it's every bit as grand as it was the first time. Only now the weather has grown quite a bit colder and the larches have started to turn yellow.

I inhale the crisp air and grip the edge of Roman's jacket. His steps falter, and he stops and turns to look at me. The dullness in his gaze could carve my heart out.

"Did I do something wrong?" I manage to get the words out before clenching my jaw and looking at the ground. "I'm scared to do this tonight, and you're not making me feel better about it by pushing me away."

Roman's eyes widen, and the light seeps back into them. He bends and presses a kiss to my forehead. "Sorry for being a dick in the war room. I'm... Fuck, I don't know. I spoke to our commanding general, and it put me in a shit place in my head," he says with a guilty tone.

My gaze falters, and I let it shift to the bonfire that's just now catching flame.

"You could've told me that you'd be leaving."

"No, I couldn't."

I look up at him, and he stares down at me.

"Can we make the best of it until then?" he asks and curls a few fingers around mine.

I put on a fake smile. "Of course."

We make our way up toward the party to join the others. We have a mission to see through, after all.

"Do you think I'll make it across the ocean? Or do you think I'll drown?" I swallow my emotions and shove them down into my stomach.

Roman slows until he brings us to a stop, not yet to the crowd that's already half drunk and the bumping, loud music that vibrates through my bones.

His eyes are cold and distant as he stares at something far away. "This world is dark. Greedy. It's so starved for bright little things like you. The Dark Forces taught me that." He lets his words trail off as his attention shifts back to me. "You'll make it, but you'll have to swim like you did at the lake."

I nod and consider my words. "Will I have baggage like I did at the lake?" I tease and give him a wry smile.

That pulls his lovely laugh out from his chest and makes my cheeks warm.

"Nothing to hold you back, no." He quickly turns his head, tugs my hand, and leads me into the party. The moment he's not looking, I let the pain ebb into my expression.

Alone. I'm always alone in the end.

There are at least twice as many people here than there were before. I'm a little shocked but at the same time, there must be a dozen other small towns around this one that have nothing to do but join the one giant party Bane Falls throws every weekend.

The smell of smoke, beer, and a variety of perfumes mingles around a group of people dancing. Kegs are on the ground, and beer cans are lined up on tables where people grab what they need before returning to the grind fest. I spot the one cop in Bane Falls here, dressed in casual wear while tossing alcohol beverages to people who put their hands up. I only recognize him because I saw his picture in the auto shop, pinned up in the war room identifying him as Sheriff Murray.

"And they say Murray isn't vital to this town," I say sarcastically, trying to stay rooted in the moment and have as much fun as I can tonight.

Roman chuckles. "Honestly, I wouldn't be surprised if he was in on the underworld's presence in his town." There's not a lick of humor in his tone.

Now that he mentions it, it would make sense. What kind of a police station shuts down at eight p.m.?

"There you guys are. I thought we'd already lost you!" John shoots me a wink and slaps Roman on the shoulder. I have to admit, they put on a great show of being normal. It fooled me when I first met them. I'd never guess that they had bulletproof vests on under their coats.

Roman groans and gives him a death glare, but that only makes John more eager to piss him off. Taylor lingers at his side and has an entertained look on his face.

"Let's go dance, Briar." John takes my hand and pulls me toward the thick crowd of moving bodies. It's warmer in the center, near the fire, and the music is just as electrifying as it was before.

Although I do have to admit, it's much more fun with people to dance with.

John flirts with his eyes more than anything else, but he lets his hands move down my sides a few times. Taylor and Gale are dancing with some girls nearby, and Bensen is in a heated conversation with a group of people. Perhaps some friends he's made while being here?

I can't help but feel bad that Roman is watching us all have a good time from the sidelines, arms crossed tightly and a dangerous scowl planted firmly on his face.

I wade through bodies and grab his hand, pulling him into the horde against his will. "Briar. I'm not dancing," he whispers with a glare.

My smile is as mischievous as it is curious at how far I can push him. I pass the squad and drag Roman into the thickest part of the crowd, where everyone is chest to chest grinding and dancing with half their minds.

"Who said anything about dancing?" I tease, turning around and lifting the back of my skirt up enough for him to see my thong.

Roman swallows, and his pupils dilate. "Fuck, you are wild, Squirt." He chuckles as he pulls me closer, holding my hips against his tightly. "I'm going to show you what's really crazy."

He unzips his pants and moves my underwear out of the way, groaning when he feels how wet I am already. Roman grinds behind me, teasing my ass with his cock. We're so packed in here that no one would be able to see what we're doing unless they were paying attention.

Roman lines himself up with my entrance, stretching my undies to the side as he thrusts into me with one sharp movement. I cry out, but the sound gets swallowed whole by all the other people laughing, singing, yelling. The music leaves nothing left of our moans as we fuck in the crowd. The bass of the song vibrates my chest. This is true ecstasy.

My adrenaline is piqued, and I can't help but want more. It's fucking addicting pushing the limits with him. And he doesn't give a shit, he just keeps going to greater heights and pushing past where I think he'll draw the line.

My skirt is up and long enough that no one would know we're actually fucking unless they were watching closely at how hard Roman's railing into me from behind. He's gripping my hips so aggressively, burying his fingers into my flesh and pounding my ass with a force.

"Oh fuck, it hurts," I moan, knees turning in toward each other.

Roman chuckles, wrapping his hand around my neck so he can murmur in my ear, "But you love it rough. You like when my fat cock fills you so much that it hurts, don't you, Squirt?" My head bobs up and down lewdly as he ruts into me.

"Fuck yes, I'm addicted to you," I mumble as my eyes roll to the back of my head and he pumps into me once more before I'm coming on his dick so violently that my cheeks turn red.

He stops humping and comes deep into my pussy, growling as he rests his head against the back of mine. "You're fucking milking me dry, Squirt," he moans.

My eyes are heavy as I scan the crowd to make sure no one's looking. As suspected, no one is even looking our way or has any idea what he just did. I smile and bite the corner of my lip. That was the most exhilarating thing I've ever done.

Roman slowly pulls his dick from me and slides my thong back into place.

I frown and shift uncomfortably. "It's all wet. I'm just going to take it off," I complain as I move my hands to pull them down.

Roman catches my hands and spins me so we're looking into each other's eyes. A dark flicker moves across his gaze that makes my breath catch in my lungs.

"You'll do no such thing. You're going to keep my seed snug inside you with your soaked panties, Briar, or I'll put something in you to plug it up." His threat only makes my core ache again, and I moan a little into his kiss. Why is that so hot? I don't question it—I just lean into his embrace.

"So volatile," I murmur against his lips.

He smiles and chuckles. "I'm only a man, Squirt."

Yeah, one who can kill people with no remorse.

Roman's pocket vibrates and he pulls out his phone, sparing it a short glance before dropping it back into his pocket. "Sutherland is by the beer table." He moves my hair behind my ear gently before readjusting my skirt. "Ready? I'll be watching the entire time."

I nod nervously and turn to head toward the beer station. My stomach churns as I get closer. Grahm's talking to a few other men, so I stop at the edge of the table and act like I'm looking for a drink.

I glance back to where Roman and I were just "dancing" and find no sign of him. Nor do I see any of the others. They must already be in position.

This better work. I'm putting everything on the line for them. I fist my hands at my sides and take a steadying breath.

"Hey, Thornton."

The hair on the back of my neck bristles as Grahm's voice settles over me like fog. It's been a few weeks since I last heard his voice, and the last time I saw him he was getting out of the truck that started the attack in the field.

Reluctantly, I turn and give him a small smile. "Hey, Grahm."

His soft light-brown hair is styled just like it was last time. There's no evidence of bruises or cuts from last week, which means he must've gotten away unscathed.

I feel guilty for being relieved that he didn't get hurt. Especially when Gale did. But he's not someone I want to die, even if he's a bad person.

He gives me that easy smile and leans casually up against the trunk of a pine tree. "You never texted me like you said you would," he says with a playful lift of his brow as he passes me a beer as a sort of peace offering.

I take it and hold it with both hands like it's a comfort drink. There's no way of knowing if he was at the lake that night, so I decide to leave it vague. "Yeah, I dropped my phone in the lake right after we got there."

Grahm's brows knit together, and he purses his lips. "Really? That sucks." A silent beat rolls between us. Both of our attention turns to the dancing crowd. "I'm glad you're all right." He leaves his comment open to interpretation. Does he really think I didn't see him in the field?

I decide to cut straight to the point and not dance around this. "I have a message for Callum." I don't let my eyes lift from a glint I spot in the dark boughs on the other side of the fire.

Grahm flinches and, after taking a moment to consider my words, mumbles, "What is your message?"

"Tell him I want to talk about what he did that night. Tell him I..." God, it's like swallowing knives. "Tell him that I still love and miss him. I don't care what he's gotten himself into. Tell him that we can work it out together."

Grahm just stares at me, eyes narrowing with suspicion. "I'll pass your message on." He turns to leave.

"Wait, how will I know what his answer is?"

He looks over his shoulder at me and shrugs. "You'll know. He'll make sure of it." That's fucking ominous as hell.

I think back to the grocery store and how messed up Hailey was. I haven't seen her here tonight, and if Roman is right, she's already left town. I can't let Grahm get off free from that. Before he can get too far, I shout, "I know what you did to Hailey. And I wouldn't be surprised if you get a taste of your own medicine."

Grahm turns and casts a look over his shoulder at me, giving me an empty gaze that holds no answers. I take a deep breath and turn around to look for Roman, but he's already waiting for me a few yards away behind a group of people.

"Delivered," I grumble, pissed off from my short conversation with Grahm. I can't believe my uncle didn't see all his shortcomings. Or maybe my uncle was a part of the underworld too. The thought is depressing.

Is there anyone in my life who doesn't have some dark secret? Why should it stop here? It's not like I can come clean and tell Roman my real name now after waiting all this time. Though, I know he'd understand, given what I went through with Callum. He knows my pain more than anyone else ever could.

But it's been a while, and he might be hurt at how long I've waited.. I *just* got him to start opening up. I don't want that to go away. I grit my teeth as I approach him. I'll tell him as soon as this mission is over. We will apparently be going our separate ways anyway.

I'm hoping we can have a little fun tonight. Well, more than we've already had. My cheeks warm. I can't believe we had sex in public. I giggle, and Roman quirks a brow at me.

"What's so funny?" he asks with a stern expression.

I shake my head. "Our *dance*."

He cracks a smile and shakes his head at me. "I'm guessing

the conversation with Grahm went well then?" Roman extends his hand, and I happily take it.

"Like a charm. He said that we'll know when we get the answer." A chill crawls up my spine. The ominous statement still doesn't sit well with me.

Roman grunts. "Well that was all we needed to do tonight. Let's have a drink and then wait for the race to start?" He grins as I hand him the beer I've been holding, and he pops the lid.

I smile and take in the crisp evening for what it is. "Sounds like fun. Too normal of fun for someone like you, don't you think?" I tease.

Roman takes a few gulps before laughing. "Ah, that's where you're wrong, Briar. I know how to have a good time."

I give him a skeptical scowl. "Since when? You're the grumpiest guy I've ever met. Like an old man keeping tabs on everyone at all times and only letting loose when we're alone." I pout when he finishes the can and tosses it in a bin.

"I'll get you a new one." He laughs and starts walking toward the beer table. "And did you seriously just call me a grumpy old man?" he calls back at me.

A laugh breaks loose from my lips, and I nod. "Yeah, I did."

Icarus spots us as I'm taking the first sip of the beer Roman got for me.

Gale is already half drunk, which is impossible to distinguish because his only tell is getting really chatty. Taylor and Bensen are in high spirits too. It's nice to see them happy. It's been a lot of doom and gloom at the auto shop, nonstop training and planning for this mission.

I wonder if they'll be able to enjoy their lives after Bane Falls.

Will I? I've already grown so attached to the idea of them in my future. Thinking about my life after... It seems as pointless as when I got here. Just a girl trying to survive the dark world and monsters within it.

John glances down at me and grins. "Told you it'd be safe here. As long as we stick together, we're unbreakable."

I nod and smile as he brings me in for a hug. His cinnamon scent wraps around me, and for a stupid few hours, I believe that everything will be fine.

Everyone starts heading down to the racetrack. Much like the first one, the vibe is good. People are having a fun night with their friends, and everyone is nicely buzzed.

Gale leans in. "Let's go get the top seats. I like being up high where I can keep an eye on everything."

I nod, and Taylor shoots him a thumbs-up.

Roman's eyes are heavy lidded, and he looks really tired.

"Hey, are you feeling okay? You look like shit." John grimaces at his superior and pats him on the back a few times. "I can drive this one, Syxx."

Roman shrugs John off and straightens his posture, though his eyes convey how utterly zoned out he is.

"I'm fine." He struts across the gravel toward his Benz and gets in.

The five of us look at one another with concern before Bensen sighs. "We all know that the lieutenant is going to do whatever he wants, so we might as well just head up to the stands."

The others seem convinced, but I hesitate. I'm pretty sure he only had one beer. "Are you sure? He seemed off."

John sets his hand at the small of my back as he guides me up to the stands. "Sometimes he just shuts down. You know how he gets. He won't listen to reason, Squirt. He's stubborn."

Something isn't right. It's a feeling deep in my gut that I can't shake.

We sit at the very top back corner of the stands like Gale wanted. Taylor snagged a bag of popcorn from a lady handing them out and is leaned back, chomping away without a worry in the world.

"Thanks for watching from the treetops while I was talking to Grahm. I really appreciate it," I say to Bensen. His eyes get wide, and he stares at me like I've just sprouted two heads.

"I wasn't watching from the trees, Briar. I was in the crowd."

My heart skips a beat. "What?" My voice sounds panicked and draws the rest of the guys' attention. I know I saw a glint. "Then who was in the trees with a scope?"

Gale and John look at each other, and Taylor's face pales.

We all seem to put it together at the same time. Roman only had one beer but he's acting weird.

"Oh shit," Bensen curses as I stand up and fly down the metal stands.

"Briar, wait!" John shouts, hot on my heels.

Someone fucking spiked that drink. But did they know I would grab it? My eyes widen. I didn't grab it—Grahm handed it to me.

Fuck, this is my fault.

Tears prickle my eyes as I run across the track and throw

open the driver's door. Roman is slumped over the wheel and doesn't respond when I try pushing him back against the seat. He's heavy, and I can't move him.

I choke back the sob in my throat and try again. This time hands come down gently over mine. I flinch and slowly look up, finding John's soft gaze flicker with worry.

"Let me help, Briar."

I wipe my eyes with the back of my sleeve as John pulls Roman from the car and shields him with his body so no one in the stands can see us. The last thing we need is the attention of everyone at the party.

"Is he okay?" I can only see Roman's limp arms and legs as John gets him in the back seat.

"Briar, I hate to tell you this, but you're going to have to drive."

I blink at him like the two thoughts won't connect.

That's right, Roman was about to race.

Race?!

"Um, John, I can't. We should get out and get help," I say with a panicked voice. The flag lady is already walking out onto the track. God, my fucking luck is bullshit.

"We're already in the car and can take the road off the back end to leave. If Grahm spiked this beer, then there's no telling who's waiting out there for us. I need to check his vitals, so don't flip the car. You got this, Squirt." He gives me a weak smile before he lets his attention fall back to Roman.

My hands are trembling, but I manage to buckle the seat belt and secure the helmet that's in the passenger seat over my head.

I spare a look back at Roman. Seeing him passed out with whatever drug was in that beer hits me like a train. He's the strongest man I know, yet he's so vulnerable right now it brings the tears right back to my eyes.

"Don't look. Just focus, Squirt." John sounds stressed.

I try to steady my erratic breathing, but the flags are lifted into the air and the countdown begins.

Go.

I floor the gas pedal, just as Roman did when he roped me into the car the first time. The car lunges forward. I can't see who is in any of the other cars since it's night and everyone has tinted glass.

Is Callum in one of those other cars? The thought is terrifying.

We reach the first corner and I slow down significantly, taking it as carefully as I can, but it's still way too fast. Driving on dirt is like driving on ice. I floor the gas again once we're back on the straightaway.

John's phone rings. I barely hear it with how loud all the cars are around us. "Syxx is down. He's been drugged or something."

I don't miss the air of suspicion in his voice. Does he think I did this? My eyes flick to the rearview mirror, and I meet John's darkened gaze.

"Roger that. We'll try to get there at the same time. Make sure no one trails you." John's voice is sharp.

My grip is tight around the steering wheel and my palms get clammy. "Is everything okay?" I ask, trying to keep my voice from trembling.

John is quiet, and I hear the click of a gun being cocked. A small gasp escapes my lips as the cold steel of the pistol's barrel touches my temple.

"I saw you hand him that beer," he snaps.

My foot comes off the gas, and my instincts are to wrap my arms around myself.

John yells so loud that I see stars. "Don't fucking let up.

247

Drive. I'll tell you when to turn. We're getting out of here while we can." He nudges my head with the gun, and tears spill down my cheeks.

"John, I—I didn't do it. G-Grahm handed that drink to me, and I d-didn't even think about it." My breaths are as erratic as my words. Fear and anguish have never moved through me with such fluidity before.

"We're going to let the lieutenant decide what to do with you after he wakes up." He keeps his response short, making me feel even more like a traitor.

"Are you guys going to k-kill me?" I hyperventilate. Not for myself but because I've lost their trust so easily. Did they ever actually trust me? No, why would they? My name isn't even Briar. I haven't been honest with them from the start.

"Turn right on this road."

I do as he says and turn off the racetrack, taking a small fire trail road that seems to lead deeper into the mountains. "I'm so sorry. I was just trying to help." I cry, biting my lower lip and trying to keep my wits about me.

John doesn't make a sound. When I look in the rearview mirror, I see soulless eyes watching me distrustfully.

I drive, half lucid and with puffy eyes, through the silence. John doesn't say another word until we're on the main road, heading back to the auto shop.

A warm glow in the distance catches my attention. "What's that?" My voice is raspy and I hate how emotionally depleted I sound.

John sits forward more and stares in the direction of the orange glow. It's getting bigger.

"Briar, that's the area your uncle's farm is in." He sounds shocked and not as pissed off. I'm not sure he'll ever look at me the same again, though. I don't think he'll ever trust me if this is all it took.

"The farm?" I suck in a breath and stare in horror.

"Change of plans, head that way," John orders and quickly gets on his phone. "The farm is on fire."

The farm is on fire. His words move through me like ice, and thoughts race through my mind like a million embers. What am I going to do if the farm burns down?

We arrive before any fire trucks do. From what John said in the car, I've inferred that the nearest one is at least ten minutes out and we were the first ones to call it in.

I stumble from the car and stand helplessly as the fire rages, consuming the barn and farmhouse as if they were nothing more than a pile of hay.

It doesn't strike me like I thought it would. Probably because I have no emotional ties to this farm. Which is all it is—a building made of wood and stone. No animals or souls were in there. Nothing good ever came of this place.

But there's a distinct hurt that grows in my chest. For the lies. For the stolen future this offered me. And for the moments that I had with Roman and the squad.

As the embers flicker across my weary gaze, I notice an envelope tacked to the electric pole right by where we parked. I take it down and look at it.

Laundromat. Tomorrow at 2 a.m.

I blink emptily at it.

This was Callum's doing?

John snags the note from my hand and nods toward the car. "Let's go before the firefighters show up."

He makes me drive back to the auto shop. The road looks blurry, and I can't seem to focus my thoughts. Am I having a panic attack? I swallow thickly and try to will away the tingling in my fingertips to no avail.

Gale, Bensen, and Taylor are waiting for us in the garage. In the few seconds it takes to pull in, dread fills me, and I keep my eyes on the ground when I step out.

Their attention is solely on Roman.

John pulls him out of the back seat, and the guys carry him to the sofa in the break room. I follow awkwardly, feeling so out of place.

Taylor is on his knee checking Roman's pulse. He lets out a sigh and then looks at me. I shrink into myself and take a few steps back. Taylor gets to his feet and storms over to me. "You gave him that beer? What did you do?" His voice is loud, and it makes me wince and shut my eyes.

Gale makes a stressed-out sound, halfway between a sigh and a grunt before he sets his hand on Taylor's shoulder. "We don't know anything for certain yet. Don't just jump down her throat." I look past them and find John and Bensen giving me lethal glares.

How little it took for them to turn on me. I bury my teeth into my bottom lip. It's not fair.

"Briar, I think it's best you come with me for now." Gale gently grabs my hand and guides me out of the room. I keep my eyes trained on Roman's motionless body for as long as I can before we pass into the hallway.

I don't ask where Gale's taking me. I know he's going to lock me up until they figure out what's going on. Do they think I'm working with Grahm? My heart aches.

Will Roman believe me?

Of them all, he won't think I'm working with Grahm, will he?

I sit against the cement wall in their water heater room, restrained to a thick pipe, and stare into the darkness until I can no longer tell whether my eyes are even open or not. It's dark.

As dark as it was when Callum buried me.

CHAPTER 29

ROMAN

uck. My head hurts. I press my palm against my forehead and blink past the blinding light.

"Hey, he's waking up." Is that Bensen? Ugh, why do I feel hung over and groggy?

"Syxx, sir, how are you feeling?" John is at my side in a second and helping me sit up. I keep my eyes squinted because everything is so fucking bright in here.

"I feel like I just got done partying for ten hours." Gale shuts the blinds, and it's much easier to see. I blink a few times and look around the room. All the guys are here, but— "Where's Briar?"

Their relieved expressions all but disappear at the mention of her name.

My brows knit, and I look each of them in the eye. "What's going on?"

They fill me in on last night's events. My head is throbbing, but it's coming back to me now. Briar handed me the can, and it didn't take long for me to go downhill from there.

But she wouldn't do this on purpose. It's Briar.

Sweet. Innocent. Couldn't harm a fly even if she wanted to. Briar.

But the men aren't so certain, and it gives me enough reason to doubt her.

"How long has she been down there?" I ask as I drink a full cup of water. My throat is dry and raspy. "And what the fuck was in that beer?" I rub my head again and try not to focus on the headache.

"She's been down there for twelve hours, Syxx," Taylor says with a heartless tone that sets a fire loose in my chest.

"It was a sedative, you're lucky their target was likely Briar and they didn't want her dead." Gale passes me the blood test kit we keep on hand for situations like these. I set the results down to my side, distracted by Taylor's comment.

"*Twelve* hours?" I bark at them.

Gale is the only one who looks a little remorseful about it. "We had to wait for you to wake up, Lieutenant. With the fire, you being drugged, and…well we found this in your vest pocket."

What fucking fire? What the hell did I miss? I'm about to ask when he uncurls his hand and reveals the flash drive. My pulse dashes over a few beats, and I grit my teeth. I wasn't going to tell anyone that I'd found it until after we captured Callum.

It's my only chance at saving Briar.

I glare at Gale. "What the fuck does that have to do with anything?"

They look at one another and share an unspoken silence that makes my stomach feel weak. *They looked through it already?*

253

John grabs his laptop from the counter and plugs in the flash drive before setting it down on my lap. I stare at him expectantly, waiting for an answer.

"I'm sorry, sir. It's better if you just watch it," John says solemnly as he works his jaw before looking away and nodding to the others to leave the room.

I wait until I hear the click of the door and then stare down at the Play button on the black screen. I didn't think what was on it would be relevant to Briar. I thought she only had the code to open a folder on it.

Swallowing the knot in my throat, I press Play.

A man steps into frame. It takes a moment for me to recognize him.

Arnold? I narrow my eyes at the screen as Arnold sits down and threads his fingers together in front of him.

He looks tired and beat to shit. Cuts are all over his face, and deep bruises mark his arms.

"Chloe. I know you are wondering why I left this farm to you. It's because I think you're the only person who can break the ties between the underworld and Bane Falls. You're smart and quick on your feet. I know you think you love Callum, but he's going to do away with you sooner or later." He lets out a long sigh and shakes his head, biting his lip with emotion.

"I might've fucked this up for you. I might've tipped them off that I set up the night you met Callum. I swear I didn't think you two would get as far as you did. I was aiming for a one-night stand to get information out of him. I shouldn't have bugged your apartment, and I should never have involved you in this…

"I know you weren't aware of it at the time, but you certainly are now, if you're still alive and have found this drive. I fucked up, and they are onto me. Everything I found on them, I've locked in the unnamed folder on this drive. Use the code I once told you. If you've forgotten, you'll remember. And if you don't, then destroy this drive."

He curses and runs his hands through his hair.

"I won't survive out here much longer. They're coming for me. Chloe, I know you'll find this. Take it to Mr. Holland. You can trust him."

Arnold stares at the camera for a moment, like he wants to say more but thinks better of it. He turns the camera off, and the feed cuts.

Chloe?

He wasn't talking about… But he had to have been.

My body reacts viscerally—heart racing and breathing off rhythm. It takes my mind a second to connect everything because I so desperately don't want to believe it.

She lied to me.

Her name isn't even Briar. *She's going to betray you just like Nyla.* If she's lying about her name, she could be lying about anything.

"Not again," I whisper and press the heels of my palms into my eyes. "Not again. *Not again.*" My voice breaks as I curl into myself. I can't let her put my squad in danger, and she already did last night.

Was she working with Grahm to poison me? My eyes widen. She knows I wouldn't question it if it came from her. Bile rises up my throat, and I feel like I'm going to be sick.

It hurts. It hurts so fucking much. Why did I let her in? Why did I think she was different? I'm so goddamn stupid.

My hands tremble, and I get the overwhelming urge to hurt myself. I take out my pocketknife and forgo the powder, pressing the blade into the back of my hand and dragging a ragged line across my skin. The second the hot liquid escapes and spills over me, I let out a weary breath.

I have to get rid of her.

If only she'd listened to me the first night.

CHAPTER 30

BRIAR

M y hands and wrists ache. Why does the cold hurt so much? My fingers and toes have it the worst, and I've never shivered as much as I am right now.

I think about a million things other than my situation. There's no way Roman won't believe me. He's going to come down here and see me cold and wrap me in his arms. We're going to take a hot shower, and then I can rest.

Rest. Warmth. Roman. I think those three things over and over.

Hours drag on, and the icy chill sets deeper into my bones. But I don't lose hope. I won't lose faith in Roman. *How long has it been?* I wonder. Is the farm completely destroyed? I hope John passed on the note I found. Maybe they're going there and capturing Callum without me. I keep my mind as busy as I can. But I'm so cold.

Roman is going to hold me.

He will.

He will.

"Chloe?"

I jolt at my name, and alarm tears through me. Roman's staring down at me with the most betrayed eyes. Pain flashes there before he sets his jaw, and everything kind and soft I've grown to love about him is extinguished with one harrowing glare.

He's looking at me like I'm a prisoner.

I can't even begin to conjure any words. Why didn't I just tell him my real name? Of all the things to be the final straw in his trust. Of course, it's my name.

"Roman. I didn't do it. I didn't know the beer was drugged." I try to explain, but his face remains impassive. "Please. Roman, you know me. I wouldn't do this... Please." Resorting to begging is a new low for me. It feels like a pile of stones in my gut.

"Chloe," he says it again. Dully. No anger or emotion. His jaw flexes, and he disregards my trembling body. "You will meet with Callum as planned tonight. We'll prep you five minutes before we go."

"Roman? Roman, wait!"

He slams the metal door behind him and it makes an awful, hollow sound.

I stare down at where my hands are. It's too dark to see a fucking thing, but I'm so disappointed in myself. Why is this happening? I grit my teeth and hang my head.

I cry until there are no tears left to shed. There's no telling how much time has passed by the time I fall asleep against the pipe I'm tied to.

It's long enough that I'm woken by pangs of hunger and ebbing cold that makes it difficult to move my limbs.

He didn't believe me.

He didn't even care to hear what I had to say.

It's pitch-black, and yet I can see all the broken parts of my heart as if I'm holding them in my palms. I'm not sure I can be put back together again for a second time. Not after Callum. Not after Roman.

———

It's John who retrieves me from the water heater room.

He's wearing a fabric mask that covers the majority of his face with only his eyes and brows exposed. A small tuft of his blond hair peeks from just the edge of the mask over his forehead.

"Come on. You should freshen up before meeting him." John helps me up, but I shrug him off and glare.

"I don't need your help." Even though my bones and muscles ache, I force myself to walk with my head held high.

He stands post outside the bathroom door while I shower. Steam rolls off my shoulders, and I breathe a little easier with the warmth creeping back into me.

Roman's just angry that I lied about my name. He's going to keep his promise. I know he won't let anything bad happen to me tonight. Even if everything we had is over, he's still going to uphold his end of our bargain.

I fist my hand against the tiles and allow myself to take a settling breath before rinsing out my hair.

John gives me a bulletproof vest and black casual clothing—a knit sweater and jeans. There are still tags on them, so someone must've gone to the store today and bought them for me.

"Will you guys be nearby?" I ask with a shallow breath.

John glances at me. All softness that existed there before has long since dissipated. "Yeah. This operation is going to be smooth." His cold voice makes chills spread over my arms.

I nod. "And what happens to me when it's done?"

He doesn't answer me, just keeps his arms crossed and looks the other way.

They are treating me like a traitor. I feel so stupid for thinking we were ever closer than that.

When we head back upstairs, the squad is suited up and lingering by their crotch rockets. Their heads lift to acknowledge us as we pass. They are dressed in their motorcycle gear—helmets, gloves, jackets—and yet I know exactly which one is Roman. He's taller than the rest. And he has a terrible habit of leaning on things. He's also the only one who won't look at me.

I straighten my shoulders and force my eyes to the vehicle ahead. It's the Benz. I give John a curious look. Is he going to drive me there while the others follow behind?

He extends his hand. I notice he's holding something, so I lift mine and flinch when he drops keys into my hands.

"Your car was destroyed in the fire. So take this one. Consider it our parting gift. If you don't go to the laundromat, we'll put an order in with the Dark Forces to have you exterminated." John's tone is monotone, and it digs that knife a little further into my heart.

I break and cave to my emotions, turning and looking directly at Roman. "That's it? You're sending me on my way to meet with the devil, and then that's it? You won't even talk to me before I go?" My jaw trembles, and I clutch my fists tightly at my sides.

Roman doesn't move. He doesn't look at me. He doesn't even acknowledge that he heard me.

Fire burns deep in my chest. *I refuse to let them see me cry again.*

I brush past John and don't look back at any of them. Not as the garage door opens. Not as I pull out onto the highway. And not as I drive down the long, dark road toward the laundromat.

It crosses my mind to just say *fuck them* and leave town, but I'm tired of running from my past. I don't want to run from them too.

It's time to face my problems.

I pull up to the laundromat, which is eerily surrounded by nothing but farmland, much like the diner. It's an older building with a flat roof. Windows make up most of the walls, and there's a minty-green glow from the tiles. Lines of washing machines and dryers make up the aisles inside with a few of those old-timey metal laundry carts I remember playing in as a kid.

Two a.m., and there's not a car in sight. Not a soul inside that I can see.

My fingernails curl into my palms as I get the courage to step out of the car and head inside. A small bell dings over the door, and elevator music plays in the background.

The intimate sensation that I'm being watched sends chills up my spine. It's terribly bright in here, and I can't see a thing outside with how dark it is. I swallow nervously and walk slowly around the aisles. I'm the only one here.

Ten minutes pass by agonizingly slow. I sit between the washers and dryers, shielded from the windows. I know the Icarus Squad is out there somewhere waiting for Callum to show up. I can't stand the idea of their eyes on me. At least I'm shielded from that much for the time being.

I go over what I'm supposed to do once Callum shows up and try not to think about the fallout with Icarus.

A soft clicking interrupts the elevator music and draws my attention. I shift to my feet and stand slowly. There in front me, like a ghost from my past, is Callum. Or perhaps I'm the ghost, since he thought I was dead.

His dark hair is now shaved on the sides and tapered on top.

He's not the man I once loved. The eyes that take me in are only that of the man who thought he finished me off and left me to rot, not the Callum I let into my life for an entire year.

Neither of us utters a word. We stare at each other with bitter expressions. His hands are tucked into his black trench coat pockets. He takes me in and looks me over like he's still making sure I'm real.

"Chloe." He says my name as if it's something lovely. "You know, I brought flowers to your grave every week, only to find out you were never in it." His voice wraps around me like a viper. Smooth and filled with dark intent.

I steel my heart. "Sorry to disappoint you." I keep my tone even.

His brows soften, and he takes a step closer.

It takes everything in me to stay where I am.

"Disappointed? Chloe, I've died every day since I thought I killed you. I yearned to pull you from the earth, rotted or not, and hold you again." He closes the distance between us and gently swipes my hair back from my face.

He was always a master manipulator. A wordsmith who was all too easy to fall for. He knows how handsome he is. And he knows how dearly I once loved him.

"You did kill me," I whisper, staring into his beautiful blue eyes. "You killed me in every way a person can be killed. Chloe is dead."

He seems stunned for all but a moment before his lips curl into a dark smile. "Yes, you go by Briar now." He lowers to one knee and presses a kiss to the back of my hand. He looks up at me, hope flickering across his eyes. "And what a rebirth you've undergone. I barely recognize you."

My heart twists, and I try to keep my expression free of the pain that moves through me. I loved him thoroughly. As no one ever should, only to be left for dead. I force a tight smile.

"You look well too." I manage to get the words out without spite stinging my tongue. "Mind telling me why you had to burn my farm down to deliver your note?"

Callum stands and grins like it's some silly prank he pulled. "Because any trace of the Dark Forces is going to be scrubbed clean from Bane Falls. That little group you've been entertaining has been pretty crafty keeping their presence known as the town's bad boys. Grahm had no clue that they were secret soldiers until you came along."

"What have you gotten yourself into, Callum?" I whisper.

A wicked smile spreads across his lips. "You mean what have I *built*. I'd love to show you, Chloe." His tone is as endearing as ever. I'd be an utter fool to fall for his antics again.

I just had to get him alone. I anxiously look toward the windows. *Where are they?*

"Come." Callum grabs my hand and pulls me toward a back panel in the wall. A secret door? We move through it, and the door closes behind us so seamlessly that no light seeps through the cracks. We're cast into the dark for only a few seconds as stair lights flicker on and dimly light the space leading down.

"Where are we going?" My palms are clammy, and my instincts tell me to do anything but follow him underground.

"No one conducts business aboveground anymore. It's not practical." He chuckles at my question. "And once you enter the dark, you can never return to a life of mindless pleasures. Not once you see the ugly underbelly of what those pleasures cost. You entered this world the moment I got that phone call all those months ago."

Callum leads me slowly down the stairs until we reach a

cement platform at the bottom. He glances at me, and regret moves over his features. Now that we aren't in the harsh glare of the laundromat's fluorescent lights, I can see how worn out he looks. The shadows always pulled at his eyes more than most.

He's used to running on little sleep, but it's catching up to him. Time and rest are among the things we cannot get by without.

"Who called you that night? And what did they tell you that was so compelling you had to kill me?" I ask as a tear slips from my eye and rolls down my chin. My expression is stone. It's a tear from the dead girl deep, *deep* in the recesses of my mind because she's still bleeding out in the dark.

Callum looks at me for a moment before pressing his hand gently against my cheek to dry the tear with his coat sleeve.

"It was Grahm. He'd just found out about Arnold Thornton. Did you know he was a sleeper agent in the Dark Forces? Or that he intentionally set us up together in hopes that he could use you as a source of information to get further into my gate?"

My eyes widen, and horror races through my veins. That can't be right… Uncle Arnold wouldn't do that to me. But then again, I hardly knew him. Was I just a tool to him?

"After Grahm made the connection, he found videos on Arnold's computer of us talking. He had your place bugged, Chloe. Which I'm assuming you had no clue about, based on your face right now." Callum smiles weakly before his frown returns. "I was informed right after Grahm intercepted the videos, and it was decided that to protect our gate in Bane Falls, I would dispose of you."

I'm speechless.

My uncle used me? After all this time, why would he do

that to me? "What did he want that was worth putting me in danger?" I ask, pressing the heel of my palm into my eye to relieve the tears that are trying to build up.

Callum tilts his head. "You found the USB, didn't you?"

I shake my head.

Callum's eyes narrow. "Isn't that interesting? Grahm got a notification that it was accessed this morning. The file was observed a few times actually. Although they can't crack the locked file that only you apparently know the code for."

It was? A cold thought moves through my mind and makes the back of my throat feel dry. Is that how Roman knew my real name? But when did he find it? I think back to the night we were at the farm and searching together.

Reality hits me like a bag of bricks. He lied to me and hid it from me. It makes them treating me like a traitor hurt so much worse. Roman intentionally led me on, thinking we couldn't find it. He even asked me to do this for him so they could get Callum alone… Frost sets an inch deeper into my heart.

He used me. He lied too.

They are all the same.

"It's all right, Chloe." Callum stares down at me like I'm a useful tool in his grand plan. Or maybe he's happy to see me miserable.

He shows me the underground facility. It looks disturbingly similar to an underground car lot, except it's void of vehicles and filled with pillars and crates upon crates of goods. We pass a few people working; they barely spare us a glance before nodding at Callum with respect.

This cement tomb is enormous.

"We have tunnels and passages that extend throughout the farmlands. This is *the* hub of the Northwest," he states proudly.

Is this why there's so much empty space out here? All this underground shit that nobody has any clue is here?

Grahm walks around a row of crates with another man at his side. They are examining the condition of them before they notice us.

"Hey, Thornton." Grahm winks at me. "Did you like the gift I sent with our note?"

I give him the most unamused expression. "The fire? No. I didn't."

He laughs and looks at Callum like he doesn't have a care in the world. "Backer Team is en route. You're clear to head back upstairs for the fireworks, boss."

"Fireworks?" A rush of adrenaline floods my veins.

Callum presses a heartless kiss to my forehead and flashes me a manic smile. "It's nothing personal. And if you survive this, you can be mine again, sweet Chloe."

The second we step back onto the main floor of the laundromat, Bensen's shouting, "Move, move, move!"

John's voice sharply follows. "Get on the ground, keep
your hands where I can see them."

They're pointing assault rifles at us and quickly secure
Callum. It's all too easy, don't they see?

The rapid beats of my heart drum through my ears as one of
the guys grabs my arm roughly and pushes me to the floor beside
Callum. They're treating me just like him.

I stare hollowly at the floor. Some small, ignorant part of me
still believes that they'll see the truth.

Callum laughs and licks his lips. "Which one is Roman?
You're in charge, right? Oh, our sweet Chloe told us all about
you. She got in your head, didn't she?" I flash Callum a mortified look before snapping my eyes at the masked soldier leaning

against the far wall, watching all of this unfold. His arms are crossed, and he has an assault rifle slung over his shoulder.

"Yes, she did," Roman states, sounding completely devoid of emotion. It hits me like a bullet.

"Too bad you have to take me in alive. But what about our Chloe?" Callum pushes him further. It makes my stomach turn. What's he trying to do by provoking him?

Roman pushes off the wall and walks over to us until he's standing a few feet away. I can't see his face past his helmet, but I can hear the hatred in his voice as he says, "Our orders are to terminate her."

My pupils dilate, and all I can do is stare up at him. I don't know what he sees in my expression, but it feels a lot like being buried alive. I can't fucking breathe, because I know he's not lying. Roman said he always follows orders no matter what—no matter who is in his way, even if that person is me.

Callum is about to goad him more when a huge explosion shakes the ground and shatters all the laundromat's windows. It's so loud that I can't even hear my own scream.

Smoke and dust hit the back of my throat instantly. I try opening my eyes, but it's hard to see anything through the cloud of debris.

If I don't escape right fucking now, this place will be my grave. Roman is going to tie up the loose end: me.

My heart pounds as I crawl over shattered glass and rocks. I know they are piercing my skin, but I can't feel it. I don't feel anything. Shouting ensues, and a few of Callum's men rush by me, unsuspecting that I'm making a break for it.

My throat burns as if it's on fire, and tears sting my eyes, but I hold in my coughs the best I can and head toward the closest broken window.

Someone grabs my ankle and I gasp, kicking and looking over my shoulder. My eyes meet Roman's. His helmet's glass is broken, and there's blood trickling over the arch of his nose.

The same fear I felt the night Callum tried to kill me resurfaces. The adrenaline rushes through my veins and makes every cell in my body scream to get as far away from him as possible—from both of them.

I kick him again and knock his hand off my ankle. My knees are bleeding and my legs are stiff, but if I'm injured I don't feel it yet. I need to use this time to survive. I force myself to my feet and limp as hard as I can to get away.

"Briar!" Roman shouts. He sounds angry—not desperate for me not to leave or to protect me like he promised. He grunts as someone comes down on him. I look for only long enough to see Callum attacking him with a KA-BAR. The two struggle on the ground, and it's the last I see of them before I turn a corner.

Tears cut through the dust and blood on my cheeks, tasting bitter when they reach my lips.

The second I break free from the building, all other sounds start to hit me. Men shouting, gunfire, and the clinking of metal in close combat. My heart races, and I go in the direction that has the least amount of fighting.

I don't realize I'm being followed until I reach the edge of the field where there's less smoke, and weeds rustle behind me.

My hand flies to my waist, where Icarus at least left me a knife to protect myself. I unsheathe it and clench it tightly. I'm wishing I would've listened to Taylor and practiced more with it and not just focused on shooting.

I turn sharply and come face-to-face with a huge man in tactical gear. It's not like Icarus's, where it's more tailored to look like motorcyclist gear; this guy looks like a SWAT officer mixed with military. He's at least six feet tall and muscular beyond all reason.

A terrified scream tears from my throat when I see him. He's made of nightmares, and there's no mercy in his eyes. He must work for the underworld, whoever Callum works for.

I run as fast as I can and try to put distance between me and the Sub-Rosa soldier. But with my limp and the length of his stride, he swallows up the space I manage to achieve in four steps.

He strikes with his knife, cutting the back of my shoulder blade, and the force of his attack sends me straight to the ground. I gasp from the pressure that spreads over my back. *Holy shit, the vest saved my life.*

I roll to my back quickly before he comes down on me. I try stabbing him in the throat, but the knife only nicks the fleshy part of his neck just beneath his Adam's apple. He wraps his gloved hand around the blade and tears it from my hand, tossing it into the weeds.

Panic takes over, and I try thrashing as hard as I can to get out from beneath him. But it's futile. This guy must weigh at least two hundred and fifty pounds.

"Stop fighting. It'll be quick," he says with a laugh as he pins my throat down with his palm and raises his other arm for a fatal thrust of his knife.

My hands are wrapped around his wrist, and as I stare up at the fire that reflects off the sheen of his blade, time seems to slow.

No one is coming to save me.

No one is coming.

I'll be damned if I let myself fucking die like this. I bury my heels in the ground and twist my body with all my force, knocking his hand off my throat. I inhale sharply and take advantage of his moment of confusion, pushing myself up to my hands and knees and knocking him off balance.

Fire wells in my chest as I grab my KA-BAR and sprint back into the thick smoke and gunfire. I don't stand a chance against this guy without some other advantages.

I don't make it ten steps into the smoke before I trip over a body and eat shit. There's no time to think about the morality of any of this. I quickly pat it down for a weapon and find a handgun in the man's hands. He doesn't fight when I pull it away, so it's safe to say he's probably dead. I don't look at his face or pay attention to his uniform.

Whoever it is, it doesn't matter.

Not if I want to live.

This is who I have become. I check to make sure the safety is off and eject the ammo pack swiftly—three bullets. It'll have to do. I smack it back in and cock it.

The soldier comes after me full bore. I fall back on my ass just fast enough to evade his knife. It goes straight into the chest of the dead body. The man looks into my eyes, seeming to realize his mistake as his eyes shift to what's in my hand.

He's a person… But it's him or me.

I don't hesitate. The muzzle of the gun is lined up with his head in less than a second, and I pull the trigger without blinking. The moment the bullet leaves the gun a different face flashes in front of me—the face is gone in a matter of seconds, and it's the Sub-Rosa soldier once more.

His blood splatters everywhere. My eyes are wide, and even though the smoke burns them, I can't look away from what I've done.

My hands tremble, and I drop the gun. I stare into his vacant eyes for a few seconds before I come back into myself and a gasp escapes my throat. I quickly push myself across the pavement a few feet.

The smoke clears, and the bullets and shouts slow.

I can't bring myself to look up as footsteps approach. My mind feels broken.

I killed someone.

"Chloe." Callum's voice is calm, as if nothing at all has happened. His hand wraps around my jaw, and he guides my face to look up at him. His face is half crimson, coated in blood as if someone threw a bucket of paint over him. But those blue eyes are gentle and seem like he's satisfied with me.

The face of evil.

My eyes are dry, yet I don't blink as he leans down to wipe something wet from my lower lip.

"Come now. It's done." He offers his hand.

Tears spill from my eyes as I take it and struggle to stand. I'm only now realizing how injured I am. Shards of glass are stuck in my knees and palms. The bottom of my left foot is soaking wet and warm, which means I must've stepped on glass or a nail.

I swallow the knot in my throat and let Callum lift me in his arms. *Is he going to kill me?* I wonder as I stare at his sharp features, defined by the flickering firelight.

"Where are the others?" I whisper, letting my eyes fall back to my torn-up hands so I don't have to look at the dead bodies Callum steps over as he walks me back into the laundromat.

He chuckles. "Did you think I'd just kill them? That's not how you get a message across very effectively. I've learned *that* much," he says with an amused tone.

I'm not sure how to process the warmth that dances in my chest at his words. Roman is alive… Everyone is still alive then. At least, I hope.

Only once we're in the center of the room where the washers and dryers are covered in debris do I let my gaze move to the ground. All five of them are gagged, their arms tied behind their backs. At least twenty men stand behind them, holding assault rifles and decked out in tactical gear.

They never stood a chance at capturing Callum. Not with this many men at his disposal.

Roman's eyes are filled with loathing unlike I've ever seen before. His face is smeared in blood, and his brows are firmly pinched together.

Why is he looking at me like that? My jaw flexes.

They're all looking at me like that.

Callum sets me down gently and nods to Grahm. "Ungag Roman."

Grahm does as he's told, forcing Roman to his feet before he pulls down his gag.

"Fuck off, Sutherland," Roman snaps at him. Grahm smirks but keeps his hand firmly around Roman's bound wrists.

"I have a message for your general." Callum grasps the cowl of Roman's jacket and gets a few inches from his face. Roman's jaw feathers, and he bares his teeth. "Tell him that if he wants the key to Bane Falls' gate into the underworld, all he has to do is ask." His voice is ominous and cruel.

My leg gives out on me, and I fall to my knees. A pained groan slips from my mouth as the glass pushes farther into my body.

Roman's eyes flick to me, but his expression is impassive.

"Tell your general of the Dark Forces that I know his game. I know what he really wants, so tell him to come here and ask for it himself." Callum shoves Roman back and pats off the lieutenant's jacket as if he's right as rain now. "Off you go. Take this as a mercy. *Oh*, wait."

Callum squats down next to me and wraps his arm around my shoulders and tilts my jaw up so I have to look at Roman.

"Are you going to take Chloe with you? She helped you, didn't she? You fucked her? Chloe doesn't belong down here with devils. Take her with you. If you don't, I'll make sure she's buried right this time around."

I don't like Callum's tone. He makes it sound like he knows Roman won't take me with him.

I hate that hope ignites in my heart.

I hate that I remember Roman's promise to me.

I *hate* that my soul is on the verge of shattering as I wait for Roman to soften his gaze and help me up. To take me in his arms and carry me home with him. I want to curl up in bed next to him and let him hold me.

The silence in the room is thick like oil.

Roman looks at me for only a handful of seconds before he turns the other way, offering his hands to Grahm to untie him by walking over and standing in front of Grahm.

Callum nods at his men, and they untie the Icarus Squad.

I hold my breath as Roman leads them slowly out of the laundromat. Not one of them looks back at me or questions their lieutenant's decision.

Roman sees how hurt I am. I know he does. He knows from what I've shared with him that Callum will likely kill me.

Does my blood mean nothing to him? Tears race down my expressionless face as I watch them leave.

You promised.

274

FOUR WEEKS LATER

Callum's bluff had power behind it. *"You see a person's true colors when you give them the worst-case scenario and they still let you go."*

Those were the words he said to me when I woke up a few days later after surgery. Roman thought Callum would kill me, and he let him take me anyway.

The cards are down; I lose.

My heart is dead.

Grahm sets down a hot cup of coffee as I move the chess piece across the board and take his knight.

"Cheater," he says as he wrinkles his nose at me.

I smile and take a sip of the bitter drink. "You can't keep saying people are cheaters just because you keep losing, Sutherland."

He crosses his arms and frowns as he stares down at the board to figure out his next move.

One month is a long time to be physically underground. It's

long enough to forget about the world above and all the problems that came with it—it's also long enough to patch up the scars on your heart. It's enough time to forget the things that you've done and whether or not you'd have done them differently.

"Briar, we'll be heading out to the lake today to drop off some dead weight. Care to join?" Callum runs his hand down my neck. I startle—he always sneaks up on me somehow. Or maybe it's that I keep getting lost in my thoughts.

I glance up at him and smile. "I'd love to."

He stopped calling me Chloe after my third day down here; after the worst of my distress and depression at being abandoned by Icarus. I refused to answer to my old name, and he finally relented.

Callum smiles down at me, his brown eyes warm like they used to be. I don't know if I find comfort or defeat in them. He never said what he wants from me, but he treats me like he did when we lived together in Seattle. Like the kind man I once thought he was. I know it's a facade. I just don't know what he truly wants. And honestly? I'm too tired to ask.

I'm not being treated like a prisoner. He knows I can't get out of the underworld by myself. Even if I did, I have nowhere to go. The Dark Forces are waiting for me; they'll hunt me down because I'm a loose end.

Roman's pained eyes flash through my memories, and I have to shove them away. *I hate him.* I hate him for what he did to me. For how he broke me.

Callum buried me.

But Roman destroyed everything else.

"Another one? I don't know why you do this to yourself, Briar." Callum smooths his thumb over my stomach where I cut a smiley face with X eyes over a scar I got from fighting with the man I killed. They kept me under anesthesia for a day to do surgery on all my wounds. I guess I had more injuries than I thought.

My knees are riddled in scars from the glass. My palms are too. Somewhere between lucidity and heartbreak, I altered all of them. Anything to forget that day. Callum doesn't like that I keep aggravating the wounds, but I can't help it.

"It makes me feel good," I say as I stand up and throw on a sweater over my loose white-collar button-up. It's technically Callum's, but I took it for myself. It suits me better anyway.

"You should find other ways to self-sabotage, Briar." Callum smooths his hand over my jaw and presses a kiss to my cheek.

Callum entertains my wild side. At least he doesn't look at me like I've lost my ever-loving mind like Grahm does.

I can't complain, though. For someone like me who is just going through the motions and giving up on everything, this is all I need.

Not giving up. Giving in. I correct my thoughts.

Because apparently there's a difference.

We take Grahm's pickup truck out to the lake with a pile of corpses in the back. There's a rug over their frozen bodies. I don't feel anything for them. And I don't care to ask Callum who they are or why he's dumping them out by the lake. The only thing I care about is going for a chilly swim. It's not that cold, and I know they'll take care of me if I get sick.

I just want to feel again.

It's only two in the afternoon, but the sun is already dipping below the mountains. I stare out across the dark water and wonder why I helped Roman that night. I should've let him drown.

Why didn't I?

My fists curl tightly, and I bite my cheek as I step out of my boots and let my pants fall to the damp ground.

Grahm gasps and drops the feet of the body they're carrying. "Thornton, what the hell are you doing?"

I unbutton Callum's shirt and shrug it off carelessly, glancing over my shoulder at them. "Going for a swim." My voice is impassive.

Both of their eyes flash down to my bare breasts. Grahm takes a step toward me like he's going to try to force me back into my clothes, but Callum puts his arm out across his chest and stops him.

"It's cold out there, babe."

I lift a brow at Callum. "I know."

His eyes narrow, but he nods. "Be back in twenty minutes." Callum lifts his end of the dead body and Grahm follows suit, although he looks more hesitant.

"Will do," I say with a small smile. At least he lets me do whatever the fuck I want.

The cold sand pushes up around my toes, and a shudder moves up through my body. I don't know what I'm doing, and one step into the icy water makes me think twice about going farther, but the rush of adrenaline and fear of freezing in this lake makes me feel everything again.

I hold my breath as I force my legs to continue wading into the water. A sharp gasp escapes my lips when my breasts are submerged. It hurts for a matter of seconds before everything goes numb and a sense of euphoria tears through me.

The mist that clings to the shoreline and the clouds that hang low as if to observe my movement hold my attention as I swim out as far as I can to the center of the lake. My mind clears of all my troubled thoughts, and my limbs become harder to move.

I turn to float on my back and stare up at the crows that fly overhead. They must be the ones that decided to stay behind for winter.

No one is coming to save you.

A drowsy grin spreads over my lips as I force all the air from my lungs and allow myself to dip below the water's surface.

The cold feels like a million needles over my skin.

I open my eyes and take in the way the light dances over the water's surface. It's beautiful for all of ten seconds before my eyes start to close and my consciousness falters.

"Briar." It's his voice.

Roman.

I focus my mind and swim to the surface, gasping for breath and looking around to make sure I'm alone. It's not fair that people can haunt you when they are still breathing.

I don't care about him. Just like he doesn't care about me.

But the thoughts are weak. I can't lie to myself, even if I wish it more than anything.

At least the cold water staves off the aching in my chest.

CHAPTER 33

ROMAN

've never been so tortured by sleep as I am now. For years, I've faced my memories of the Under Trials and the ghosts I've left behind. But now all I dream of anymore is the moment I betrayed the one person I care about. Is this what Nyla felt after she killed Dalton? Is this the suffering she endured before I bashed her head in?

Briar. I think her name a million times every night. I stand and watch her look at me with so much misplaced hope. Did I do it because Nolan ordered me to? Or did I do it because I was hurt by her lies?

Her broken body and desperate eyes haunt every waking moment of my days. There is no reprieve when I sleep. There is only horror and despair. As I watch myself make the same mistake over and over again.

I let her go. I handed her over to the monster she feared most, knowing very well that he might kill her.

I'm the true monster.

But she betrayed us… She lied to me and made me vulnerable, I reason. I did what Nolan said and disposed of her…even if it was indirectly. Deep down I'm hoping that Callum didn't kill her.

And yet, I find myself frequenting the fields and trails where we've seen Sub-Rosa bury bodies in the past. I look for her even when I don't realize it. I find myself doing strange things lately, lashing out at the squad and sitting in places that will make me cold to the bone.

I cannot sleep.

I pound my fist against my bedroom wall and tap my forehead repeatedly to it. Why did I do this to myself? I knew she was trouble. I knew it, and yet I still tried to save her. I should've sent her on her way out of town instead of asking for her help.

A sharp knock comes at the door.

I still and straighten my posture. "What?"

Gale's voice comes in urgently from the other side of the door. "General Nolan is here, sir."

My eyes widen. *He actually came in person?*

"Icarus Squad. I didn't anticipate on many of you surviving that mission, but as fate would have it, Sub-Rosa is more merciful than we are. Or at least that's what they would have us believe."

Nolan's hair is streaked with gray and white strands. His fade cut reveals the scars on the side of his head and the wrinkles of time that have burned through his weary soul.

I knew he'd take great interest in Callum's bait, but I didn't think he'd really show. The least he could've done was let us know ahead of time that he was coming to Bane Falls.

We've been sitting like ducks for a fucking month. No

contact, no orders, *nothing*. Maybe it's part of our punishment for failing to get Callum.

My jaw flexes as John leans forward and asks, "General, why have you come to Bane Falls? You're not seriously thinking about meeting with that psycho, are you? We found their gate and supply bunker. Why don't we just demolish it? We don't need to keep waiting."

Because he isn't interested in getting rid of the gate. I sit quietly with my hands folded in my lap, a smoldering cigarette perched between my lips as I analyze the situation. Whenever I think Nolan will zig, he zags.

Nolan's in full tactical gear under his winter trench coat. I don't think I've ever seen him dressed like one of us before. In all my years in the Dark Forces, he's always in his officer attire with badges and polished shoes.

Why now? What is he up to?

"Bishop, you observe the world around you like a Dark Forces soldier, but you never truly see our purpose. Why would we want to destroy the work they've done? The fluidity they've created in this town," Nolan says with a mystified voice, like he's excited for what's to come. "I've never seen anything like what they've built here in Bane Falls. It's why I sent your squad here to watch and observe, to infiltrate and find them naturally. Everything was going flawlessly until Arnold went AWOL. Did you like the package I informed you about, Syxx?"

My squad turns and slowly looks at me. My heart sinks. I meant to tell them about it, but the timing never felt right.

"Did you send her here?" I ask, sounding dangerously close to accusing him.

Nolan laughs. "No," he says with a sly smirk, obviously lying.

It takes everything in me to stay seated and keep my calm

facade. "Sir, please get to the fucking point. Why aren't we eliminating the gate?"

Gale and Taylor shift uneasily in their seats, and Bensen shoots me a worried frown.

Nolan doesn't drop his sinister smile. "I've been chasing the black market in one form or another my entire career in the Dark Forces. And every time I thought I was close, someone tore it from my hands one way or another. Either they got to my forces first and stole them away or they killed them. This is the closest we've ever been, and I'm not letting this chance slip from my hands. We are going to use Callum to get into the deeper veins, the dark cities, they call them."

My eyes widen. No way it goes that deep. Dark towns like Bane Falls that have been infiltrated by the underworld are one thing, but entire cities where the network of corruption controls the baseline of a metro area is insane. There'd be hundreds of men like Grahm and Callum.

They can't keep an operation this big hidden throughout the world… Could they? Is that what's on the flash drive? All the locations of their cities? My throat feels dry, and my hands grow clammy at the thought. I've had it this whole time. I told Nolan we couldn't find it because I wanted to spend more time with Briar. My stomach twists with anxiety.

Bensen tilts his chair back and balances on the back legs. "But what does that get us?"

"It gets us a map—a glimpse at the end of the campaign I started. Once we have all the dark cities, we can finally unleash the full capacity of the Dark Forces." The general's voice sends a shudder up my spine.

Full capacity? "Have you not been already, sir?" I slowly stand from my seat, placing both my palms on the table.

"Lieutenant Syxx, you know you're not the only test squad, let alone the only experiment." Nolan's face hardens, and his features are like glass.

I flinch at his comment.

"But you are one of my favorites. Which is why I sent you here specifically. Now, if we're done with that, we need to go over the plan. We have an audience with Callum tomorrow."

———

Blood drips from my thumb and causes ripples in the dark water.

I shouldn't have shown Briar my spot on the mountain. I haven't been able to go back, not once. The second I get to the fire trail, bile always rises in the back of my throat and I see the way she looked at me again when I left her—the pain of realizing I wouldn't keep my promise to her.

Fuck. I squeeze my hand so more blood drips out.

A promise can look like a lot of things.

My promises look like Briar's bleeding hands and knees—eyes so filled with misery and hurt that it will haunt me to my grave. I will never escape what I did to her.

I press my knife deeper into my thumb. I don't even alter my scars anymore. Now it's just self-punishment…because I deserve to hurt.

She's not a scar I want to alter. She's one I never want to heal.

My hands tremble as I let myself fall to my back in the sand. My legs are in the frigid water while my torso is splayed on land. I stare up at the crows that caw annoyingly above. They must think I'm dead; most days I wish I were.

I watch them linger near the center of the lake. Curiosity gets the best of me, so I sit up and stare out there.

Something is bobbing, causing ripples in the glassy water.

Who the fuck is swimming in this weather? They must have a death wish.

Drowning. How terribly romantic.

CHAPTER 34

ROMAN

The auto shop is quiet when I pull into the garage. The lights are all off, and it's as if no one's here.

But I can sense Nolan's heavy gaze through even the darkest shadows. It has a weight that bears down on your shoulders and makes you uncomfortable.

"General."

"Lieutenant." He strikes his lighter, and a small flame discloses his location against the far wall.

I let out a long sigh and walk over to him. He extends his pack of cigarettes. I take one and light it, standing beside him and staring out into the dark like he is.

"You've done good here, Syxx. I'm sending your squad back to home base after tomorrow," he says flatly.

My body jolts at his words. "Nolan, you made me a promise."

He chuckles and inhales deeply off his cigarette. "You made

that girl a promise. Did you keep it?" My eyes widen. Nolan stares at me, something calculated in his gaze.

How would he know about my promise to Briar? I swallow thickly as my fingertips smooth over the phone in my pocket. *They've been listening to everything.* A breath escapes my lips because I feel stupid. Of course, they've been listening.

"That's what I thought. It seems we aren't so different, Syxx. That's why I like you so much. You get the job done, even if it means you discard the people who care about you the most." His words are an axe to the throat. Nolan flicks his cigarette to the cement and steps on it as he heads toward the office. "Pack your shit, you won't have time to do it tomorrow."

I don't pack. I just sit in my empty room and stare at the flash drive. With everything going on with Callum, I don't think anyone has said anything about it to Nolan. And maybe he's forgotten as well, or assumes that it burned in the fire.

What's in the locked file that's so damn important that they brought Briar into town? I tap my knee anxiously before grabbing my laptop and booting it up.

I click on the locked file and enter words I think Arnold may have used as passwords. Nothing.

I drag my hand down my face and think. If there was information that was locked because of the Dark Forces, then what would I put as the password? I close my eyes and picture Arnold and remember who he was as a person. He was like most of the other high-ranked officers. Cold. Disconnected. Someone who likely didn't crave anything perhaps other than...

My eyes widen.

Freedom.

I punch in the word, and the file opens. I sit for a few

seconds, just staring at the screen and the unlocked file. If the password is indicative of anything, it's that whatever is in it could potentially give not only Arnold the freedom he sought, but perhaps all Dark Forces soldiers.

I click on the folder, and it opens. There are hundreds of documents and videos labeled with dates alone. I open the most recent one. The date is the same day that it was reported Arnold was terminated.

The video plays; it's footage from the war room at the main base in California. My brows knit. How could he have access to this if he was here? Shock ripples through me. Arnold either hacked into the Dark Forces' security cameras or he had a connection on the inside, likely the IT department.

Nolan and Captain Bridger are discussing the Bane Falls operation. They skirt over the Icarus Squad and focus mainly on Arnold and the underground he's been infiltrating to get information on the locations of the dark cities.

"This has to be their entry point there," Captain Bridger says slowly as he smooths his hand over a map. "It's the only one Callum visits often aside from Seattle."

Nolan nods thoughtfully. "And you're sure Callum is the gatekeeper? We still have a few other candidate towns that have the potential of being the entry point too."

I frown. It sounds like Nolan wants more than just the cities. Why does he care so much about the entry point? Who are they looking for? Callum's boss? I didn't consider it before, but of course, he's reporting to someone just like we all are.

Captain Bridger slides a few documents to Nolan. I can't make them out in the grainy footage.

"Right. Well, Arnold won't last the night. He's been discovered by one of Sub-Rosa's men, and satellite footage indicates that they're on the move to his location. So at least that ties up that loose end." Nolan's tone is indifferent. I'm not surprised in the slightest that he'd let his elite soldiers die so easily when he's harvesting more and more each year in the Under.

"And Icarus?" Bridger leans on his hand pressed against the map.

Nolan shifts in his chair, the first sign of discomfort I've seen from him. "I haven't decided yet."

The video cuts to black, and a sick feeling coils in my stomach.

I don't trust Nolan to do good by us in any sense. I thought we were here to shut down the underworld, not tap into it and get our hands even dirtier than they already are. What is he really after in all of this?

A document next to the video has the same date on it. I click on it, and a one-page PDF comes up. My eyes skim through it with little interest before catching Chloe's name. My jaw flexes, and a knot grows in my throat.

I read it.

My heart starts pumping faster, and I start sweating.

I read it a second time.

Then a third.

"What the fuck." I stand abruptly, dropping my laptop to the ground and not blinking when it breaks and sends keys across the floor.

My hands are trembling, and my jaw works with horror.

"No." I shake my head and fist my hands in my hair. *"No!"* I shout and fall to my knees, pounding my fist against the cement. "Not her. *No.* Not her. What have I done?"

I don't stop when my hand starts to bleed, and I don't fight the wall of emotions that crashes over me like a tidal wave.

289

Gale bursts through my door, followed by Taylor, Bensen, and John. The four of them have panicked expressions. They've never seen me like this before. *Fuck*, I've only seen myself like this one other time, and it was when I killed my friends in the Under Trials.

I force my head up and catch my reflection in the mirror on the wall. My hair is tousled, and blood is smeared over my jaw. I look fucking insane. Tears are in my eyes, and that's the most shocking part of all.

I bite my lower lip as my tears fall…before I start laughing.

My men stand in the doorway, staring down at me in horror. They've never seem me like this before. Fuck, *I've* never seen me like this before.

"Lieutenant… What's going on?" Bensen asks hesitantly.

Gale is the first to step closer and kneels beside me, setting his hand on my shoulder and furrowing his brow. "Roman," he says softly. As a friend, not as my subordinate.

I look at him and then behind him at the others. General Nolan is standing with them now too.

I glide my tongue over my teeth and force myself to stand.

Gale follows my death glare and lets his eyes land on Nolan.

"Tell them," I say with a lethal tone. Blood drips down my knuckles and peppers the ground with red dots.

Nolan takes me in, then looks down at the laptop on the ground with the flash drive in the port.

A weary smile moves across his lips. "Which part?"

Fire burns in my chest, and I feel like I'm going to be sick. "All of it."

The general lights a cigarette and slowly takes a seat in the chair by my closet, completely unbothered. I'd dare even say he seems a little relieved. "Briar doesn't have time for me to tell you all of it," he says smoothly.

"What?" I whisper. It feels like a shot to the heart. "She's—"

Nolan grins. "Alive."

I stumble and brace myself against the wall as I take that in. The overwhelming sense of hope and hurt mix together until I can't tell which is which. I rush to my bag and start getting my gear on.

John walks up to me and grabs the collar of my shirt to get my attention, but I keep moving. She needs me. If she's alive, I have to save her. I have to.

"What? Fucking say something!" John snaps.

Gale grinds his jaw. "General, what does this have to do with Briar? She was only a civilian that happened to get caught up in this." He sounds confused but suspicious.

"Briar. Chloe. We used to call her Lethe." Nolan doesn't sound the least bit upset.

Taylor takes a step forward and tilts his head. "What the fuck?"

I freeze, squeezing my vest tightly as I listen.

"Arnold has been in the Dark Forces for over twelve years. He doesn't have a fucking niece. There is no Thornton Farms. No Thornton family that Briar was ever a part of. It's all a hoax. She's Project Lethe. Our forgetful little *non-soldier* soldier."

John stares at him with a disgusted look. "What are you saying? She's a girl from the city. She has a past and memories!" He has tears in his eyes now, too, because it's a really fucked-up reality to believe in.

Nolan shakes his head. "No, she's not. She only knows what we brainwashed her to know. She's never left Seattle until coming here. She has no surviving family members." My blood runs cold hearing him say basically what she's told us. He makes her sound like a robot. Like a tool. "Did she ever tell you where she's been in the last eight months since Callum attempted to terminate her? She's been in 'hiding,' hasn't she? No? It's because she doesn't know. We picked her up in the forest and put her under for surgery. That little prick almost killed her. She's been in our care this entire time. Until Grahm reached out with the ploy of luring her in as an estate attorney."

Our silence is loud. Practically numbing.

Sutherland lured her here? Why?

"How can she not remember any of it? What did you do to her?" Bensen asks, sounding hurt.

"A little serum that we've been using for years now. She's the most susceptible person to it. And look at how she's blossomed." Nolan looks at me. I stare through him. "I knew you'd take a liking to her, Syxx. She's just as broken as you. You're practically magnets for each other. Shame that you didn't keep your promise to her. I was willing to let you keep her if you would disobey a direct order. You know I like seeing how far you'll go."

I force my head the other way and strap on my gear.

"Where are you going?" John asks with a raspy voice.

I don't look at them. I just clutch my helmet tightly. "I'm going to go get my girl."

Bensen and Taylor approach me and set their hands on my helmet.

"Me too," Taylor says definitively.

"Squirt's coming home," Bensen adds.

Gale nods. "No member of the Icarus Squad left behind."

My chest warms, and I look at them. I didn't expect them to do this. For me, of all people. They know I wouldn't do this for them…but maybe I would. I'm not the same man I was before.

We collectively look at John. He flexes his jaw and gives me a slight shake of his head with a pained grin. "Let's go get her."

General Nolan doesn't say anything as we suit up. He doesn't try to stop us. That man's mind is a sea of mystery. I don't know what he's planning to do. I don't know what he anticipates will happen. But I have a sick feeling that this was one of the scenarios he thought of because he doesn't seem a bit surprised.

Hold on, Briar.

Callum stares up at me through hooded eyes as I drag the sharp end of my knife over his throat. His pupils dilate, and his pulse leaps as I lean down and press an empty kiss to the top of his forehead.

"You're terrifying. You know that?" He presses his thumbs into the soft divots of my neck, making my breath stagger.

"Am I?" I ask as I take in his lovely features before nicking his ear. He all but winces, letting the blood drip down his neck without a care.

"Yes," Callum murmurs, pulling me down and kissing me.

I bite his lip and draw blood. I want to scar him in as many ways as he has me.

Grahm kicks the truck we're in the back of and whistles for his crew to hurry up with the shipment. Callum groans and sits up.

He's frustrated that I won't give him the affection I once did.

All I have left is the darkness that was left in the wake of love. Of his. Of Roman's.

I shift out of the truck and shove my hands into the pilot-style jacket Grahm gave me.

We're expecting an important shipment today. I'm not sure what the product is or why it's important enough to deal outside of the underworld, but it is. And to my utter displeasure, of course it's at the bonfire party.

Roman was right about Sub-Rosa using the townspeople for protection. No one would dare give up their positions to out the group. It's diabolical and twisted, but I don't have the will to fight any of it anymore. I'm just here to enjoy what little I can.

Grahm leans against the truck beside me while Callum speaks with one of his grunts. "We have one more stop after this."

I groan. "Seriously? Don't you ever get tired of working?"

He laughs and crosses his arms. "Honestly, Thornton, what do you even have to be in a rush to get back to?"

I lift a brow at him. "Our game of chess. The last episode of that stupid drama show. There's a bowl of chili someone left in the fridge that I plan on eating tonight." I crack a smile, and he laughs.

"Jesus, you're fucking something else." He grins and shakes his head a few times before letting his eyes shift over to Callum. "I want to give you a heads-up, but you need to keep it to yourself, or Callum will lose his shit."

My humor fades, and I nod.

"You're meeting the boss tonight. It's nothing formal, but he's interested in meeting you. So be on your best behavior, okay?" He sounds serious.

"The boss. Like of Sub-Rosa or…more?" I hesitantly glance at Callum to make sure he's still not listening.

Grahm shrugs. "I've never asked. As long as I get paid and I do my job, it doesn't matter. I don't want to get into it any deeper than I already am," he admits.

I bite my lip, debating on asking more. "Did you kill my uncle?"

Grahm's eyes flash, and he shakes his head. "No…but there is something I've been meaning to tell you."

I stare at him expectantly. He clears his throat.

"Hello, Miss Thornton. It's Mr. Holland." His voice is exactly how Mr. Holland's voice sounded over the phone.

"You're Mr. Holland? But…why?" I thought I'd be more upset hearing this, but after being left for dead twice, being lured into a town doesn't exactly top the list.

Grahm sighs. "I knew someone had Chloe's phone. I was tracking its movements, and when I called and you picked up, I knew there was a chance it was you. Callum didn't believe me, so I lured you here myself. Once I verified it was you—" He breaks off.

"You told Callum."

He nods. "Sorry, Thornton, but it sort of worked out, didn't it?" He gives me a weak smile.

I shove his shoulder playfully. "If this is your definition of things working out, then sure."

His expression falters into a frown. "There's one more thing." My expression mimics his. "When we were patching you up earlier this month, we found something."

"What?" Like a growth or something?

"We learned a while ago that all Dark Forces soldiers have trackers in them. It tracks their vitals, location, lots of things. Well, we found one in your neck."

I flinch and go deathly still. What the fuck? Did Roman tag me at some point?

"Yeah, that's kind of what I thought. You had no idea, did you?"

I shake my head and try to understand what he's getting at. "Did Icarus do this?"

He pales and shakes his head. "No, this was done a long time ago, Briar."

"How do you know that?"

"Hey, I need your help with this, come on," Callum interrupts, and Grahm quickly acts like we weren't just having a deep conversation about important shit.

What does it mean if I had a tracker? I smooth my hand around the back of my neck and frown. This was way deeper than I wanted to get. I try to push it to the back of my mind until we can talk more tonight.

"I'll be dancing by the speakers," I say to them both as I trudge up the hill. There's a dusting of snow on the ground and soft flakes that fall aimlessly from the sky. It couldn't be a better night to let the world fall to the back of my mind.

For the briefest of moments, I wonder where Icarus is. Did they end their mission? Did they get what they wanted?

"Stay where I can see you, Briar," Callum calls out as he watches me walk ahead.

I give him a fake smile and nod. He knows I won't do anything to lose my "upstairs" privileges.

I'm not used to the higher elevation and how it fucks with the weather. It's fall, and yet there're already nights dipping below thirty and mild snowstorms.

My eyes focus on my boots as I make it up the hill. It's strange, I don't remember ever being in the forest during the onset of snowy nights, but the scent of pines and the brisk dryness of the air and snow stirs a familiarity within me.

I shake the feeling and focus on just dancing.

The music booms through the crowd. It's warm with all the bodies and the usual bonfire. The sun has already set, and every other person is at least three beers into their night.

I put my hands in the air and rock my hips. Two songs into the evening and someone is already behind me, wrapping their hands with mine in the air. A sensual smile pulls at my lips.

I almost feel bad because they have no idea what kind of shit show they're walking into with me.

Their fingers glide down my wrists, slowly feeling my skin and gently exploring the scars along my arms. It sends chills through my entire body, and butterflies flutter through my stomach.

They dip down and place their lips close to my ear.

"Hey, Squirt." His voice is broken.

A sharp breath tears through my chest, and I abruptly put distance between us. I whirl, glaring at the man standing before me.

Roman.

He looks like a wreck. His eyes are dark, and redness blooms around them like he's been suffering. It's almost enough to make me laugh. How dare he be tortured by his own design.

I don't know what to say to him.

He clearly doesn't know what to say to me either.

We stare at each other as the bodies dance around us and blur until all that's in focus is us.

He firms his lips, and tears brim in his eyes. He opens his mouth a few times to say things he can't give words to.

I don't know how to react. My heart is at war with everything in my head. He left me to die.

"Briar." Roman finally gets the word out as he takes a step toward me and reaches for my hand.

I take a step back, eyes widening with the rush of emotions

that have evaded me for weeks—seeing him breaks something deep inside me. "How dare you touch the scars that you allowed to grow," I say with a shaky breath, drawing my hands to my chest to comfort myself.

Roman's tears build more, and he shakes his head with guilt, biting his lower lip. "Briar, I—"

"You left me!" I shout, startling him and bringing his attention back to my face.

His misery is contagious. "I know," he chokes out, tears streaming down his cheeks and wrenching at my heart.

"You used me and lied to me." I wipe my tears furiously. I don't want him to think these are for him. These tears are for *me*. For what he did to me. "You promised you wouldn't let anything happen to me," I say softer, and my throat constricts.

Roman's hazel eyes narrow, still glazed with tears, and he nods. "I know I did, baby." He closes the distance between us and wraps his arms around me. I fight his embrace and unsheathe my knife. He doesn't react to it, only watches with the same hurt expression.

"Why did you do this to me? Why? Why!" He tries to hug me again, and something snaps in my mind. I don't want him to comfort me. I don't want him to make it better. All I want is to stop hurting.

I plunge my knife into his chest.

Roman makes a pained sound as the tip of my blade skates across the bulletproof mesh covering his heart. It stopped the knife from going farther than a few centimeters into his flesh, but the act itself speaks volumes.

I realize what I've done, and horror ripples through me. I gasp and drop the knife, seeing stars and stumbling backward as I stare at his bleeding chest.

Roman grabs my wrist and pulls me to him, wrapping me in his arms tightly and stroking my head. "It's okay," he murmurs in my ear. "I'm so sorry, Briar. I'm so fucking sorry I lied to you."

His blood warms my chest, seeping into my shirt and making me hyperventilate.

"I love you, Briar. I love you, and I'm not letting you go again. Not ever. No matter what you do to me. I will never let you go." He kisses the top of my head and pulls back enough to see my face. "I'm so sorry."

Tears fall from our chins.

He waits for me to say something. *Anything*.

"I hate you, Roman."

His eyes widen as I shove him back and run into the crowd. I lose him quickly and have to bite back the emotions. I don't stop until I'm back at Callum's truck and find Grahm leaning up against the back.

"There you are—" his expression falters. "Thornton? What's wrong?" He catches me as I collide into his chest. It took everything I had to not let Roman hold me. *Everything*. But he fucking betrayed me just like Callum did. Sure, he didn't try to kill me himself, but he left me with the devil.

Grahm holds me at arm's length and looks me over with concern. "Are you hurt? There's so much blood." He sounds panicked and quickly escorts me into the back of the truck.

"It's not my blood." I manage to get out between shallow breaths. I can't control my breathing, knowing that I stabbed Roman.

He stills and looks over his shoulder. Roman and the Icarus Squad are standing at the top of the slope just before the crowd, staring down at us.

"Shit," Grahm curses and slams the door before getting in the driver's seat and backing out of the parking lot.

I watch the squad break for their motorcycles from the rear window.

"Where's Callum and the others?" I ask, still feeling like a passenger in my own body.

Grahm drives quickly down the dirt road before he turns hard onto the highway and floors it. His truck roars, and we're thrown forward as he speeds in the direction of the lake.

My bones chill. Why are we going to the lake at this hour?

It's pitch-black outside. Wait, is that where we're meeting the boss? My veins go cold, and chills move up my arms.

"They went ahead to meet the boss." He glances in the mirror at me.

My brows are pinched.

Five motorcycles pull out behind us and are catching up fast.

Grahm curses and pulls a gun from his center console. "Looks like this might be the end of the line for us, Thornton."

I look at his somber expression and understand what he's getting at. I quickly buckle my seat belt and grip the door tightly. "Grahm, we can talk to them. Roman tried speaking with me, but I…" Tried stabbing him. My stomach feels sick.

He shakes his head and glances at how close they are in his side mirror. "No, I don't think we can. I'm not letting them get to Callum or you. Tonight is too important."

I don't have time to process his words because Grahm slams his brakes. It feels like my brain is being torn from my skull, and a fraction of a second later a body comes crashing through the back window.

I scream as glass and blood cover me.

"Hold on!" Grahm shouts as he floors the gas again. Gunshots are popping off now and hitting the metal siding.

I hesitantly look at the unmoving person next to me. Who is it? My heart is in my throat as I unbuckle my seat belt and move to check if they are okay.

There's so much blood, but I can hear his labored breaths. I work quickly to take his helmet off, being careful of his neck in case it's injured.

The second I see his blond hair I know it's John. My heart shatters, and tears trickle down my cheeks. His body is so fucking broken. I carefully take his mask off, and he flinches in shock, I think.

When I see the distance in his gaze, I know it won't be long.

I swallow the despair in my heart, and the world becomes so, so quiet. The gunshots fade, the loud roar of engines dissipate, and only the tender draw of each pained breath takes their place.

"I'm here, John," I whisper, holding his hand in mine. A few of his fingers are broken, but I push that idea from my mind.

One of his eyes is bloodshot, and he can't keep his head from bobbing with the damage to his nervous system. My jaw trembles, and I force a smile even though tears drip down them.

"B-B-Briar," he chokes on my name. The word drowns in his blood.

My grip on his hand tightens and I smile wider, pressing my cheek to the back of his hand. "Hi, John. You didn't…need to come back for me," I whisper to hide my sobs.

His eyes are on me, but he keeps going somewhere else before fighting his way back. His lips quiver and he manages to squeeze my hand. It's hot with his blood and my tears.

"I'm…*ngh*…s-s-orry. Please, p-please forgive m-me." Tears rush from his eyes. I trace the fear in his features—he knows, and all I can do is hold his hand and try to comfort him with my useless smile.

"I will always forgive you, always. You hear me?" His eyes soften with relief. I brush his hair back gently and press a kiss to his forehead. His grip on my hand loosens. I pull back and stare down at him. His eyes are dulling, but there's the smallest smile on his lips. One I will never forget. It burns into me, into every icy crevice of my heart. "Goodbye, John."

My shoulders tremble as I let the tears flow with my agonized cry.

"Briar, brace yourself!" Grahm shouts.

But it's too late. I'm holding on to John when the truck tips and the world spins.

CHAPTER 37

ROMAN

aylor's voice tears across the headsets. "Bishop's tracker just shut down."

We all saw how hard he went through the back of that truck. A weight buries itself into my chest, and I force my thoughts to stay clear. This fight is far from over.

"Flip it," I order.

"But Lieutenant, Squirt's still in there." Bensen's voice is torn.

My grip tightens on the handles. "I know, but she'll be okay." I grit my teeth.

Gale's voice comes in. "Taking the shot."

Bang.

The truck swerves a few times before Sutherland loses control of it and the vehicle flips off the road. It turns over three times before it stops upside down.

We surround it quickly.

"Get Sutherland!" I snap before throwing my helmet off and

running to the broken windows. Glass cracks beneath my feet as I crouch and look inside. The back is empty.

My heart hollows. Where is she? I straighten and look around with panic.

A small mound of black clothing catches my eye.

I run to her, falling to my knees when I see all the blood.

John's body is on top of her, and Briar's arms are wrapped around his chest still. My lower lip trembles as I push my comrade's body off her slowly.

Briar's eyes are closed, and she has cuts all over her face and hands from the glass. I watch closely until a breath plumes from her lips into the cold air.

I crumble and gather her into my arms, pressing my forehead to hers. She's limp in my arms, but she's okay. My shoulders shake as I cry with her in my embrace.

John's body lies on the cold ground, and a dusting of snow is already starting to cover him. His eyes are set on us. My jaw wrenches as I let the tears fall.

"Thank you for keeping her safe, Bishop." I lean forward with her in my arms and slowly close his eyes. His blood drenches the few inches of snow around him.

A hand falls on my shoulder and brings me back into the moment.

I look over my shoulder, and Gale's helmet mirrors my reflection. For the first time, I see a man I could someday recognize.

"Sir, we have him."

I absently nod and spare one final look for my sleeping brother before forcing myself to my feet with Briar in my arms.

"I can carry her," Taylor offers, but I shake my head, holding her closer to my chest.

"Where is he?" I say with my hardened officer voice.

Bensen looks up from twenty feet away and signals me over.

Sutherland takes ragged breaths as he lies on his back staring up into the dark, stormy sky. His gaze shifts to me when I stop at his side.

His brown hair is smeared with red, and he looks considerably paler than usual. A lopsided grin spreads over his lips. "Thornton is okay," he says with a weak and relieved voice.

"Where is Callum?" I ask hollowly.

He coughs a few times before looking back at the sky. "The lake… If you were smart…*ngh*…you would just run while you can." He's in a great deal of pain, but I don't feel anything for him. I'm not sure Briar would feel the same way, but John is dead.

"You know I won't."

Grahm lets out a few short laughs. "I figured as much. Hey." He meets my gaze once more. "Don't hurt her again."

I flex my jaw but give him a small nod.

He shuts his eyes. "I'm so f-fucking tired."

I watch him for a few seconds before locking eyes with Bensen. I give him a brief head shake. Sutherland will bleed out on his own in a matter of minutes.

We have Briar, but we need to end this tonight. I don't give a shit if Nolan wants Callum. He can have the goddamn flash drive. I'm not letting this go any further.

"Let's go, Icarus."

My chest feels constricted, almost, not uncomfortably, like I'm strapped to something. Or someone.

Ugh. I wince at the pounding headache and pain that seems to be throughout my bones. It's loud and sounds like I'm on the highway or somewhere windy, but everything is muffled.

I open my eyes and flinch when I realize I'm wearing a helmet. My breaths increase, and before I can panic too much, Roman's lovely voice comes in through the headset.

"You're okay. I've got you, Squirt."

My eyes widen. That's right, the truck flipped… John. My throat knots up, and I can't bring myself to say anything. Where is Grahm? Did he get out okay? I can't bring myself to ask, so I just let my head rest against Roman's shoulder.

"We're heading to the lake to end this once and for all. I'm not letting you get hurt again, and I'm not letting Nolan take you away from me." His words thread through me.

I want to be angry with him. I don't want to feel the way I do for him. But I do. And I can't stop myself from wanting to be close to him again.

"Okay" is the only thing I can seem to get out.

He wraps his hand around mine, and it melts my heart a little more. "I don't deserve you. I don't deserve your forgiveness either, but fuck, I want it more than anything. And I'll do anything to get it," Roman murmurs, his voice raspy from shouting.

Taylor cuts in. "Movement ahead on the satellite map. I think we're going to have company." The heads-up display on the helmet glass shows an aerial view of the mountain coming up, and several little arrows indicate vehicles that aren't us.

"We should go back," I say, grabbing Roman's jacket tighter.

"No can do, Squirt. We'll just be hunted down. It's better if we're outside the town so we can take them out," Bensen chimes in.

"But you couldn't last time," I argue.

"That's because our orders were to take the fucker in alive," Roman retorts.

My heart races. "And now?"

"Fuck the orders. We're taking over. Nolan can reprimand me later." Roman doesn't sound worried about it, but I've never met their general. From what I gather, he's not a good man.

We pull onto the trail leading up to the lake and the snow almost immediately falls thicker. The elevation makes the air colder with each second we climb higher.

"Lieutenant, they're closing in from the rear!" Gale's voice cuts in through the headset.

"Get into formation, Icarus," Roman says tersely as he unstraps the handgun on his chest and hands it to me. His attention is focused straight ahead, but his voice comes in smooth and calm. "Aim for their chests, Squirt."

My breaths are sharp, and the pain in my bones starts to fade as the adrenaline hits my veins. "Okay." This can't be worse than when I shot the man point-blank in the face.

Within seconds I hear trucks and motorcycles trekking up the hill and gaining on us. Roman smacks the front right side of his motorcycle, and a compartment pops out with a pistol, grip facing him. Roman grabs it and keeps it clutched firmly in his hand.

"We'll loop them around the lake trail. Take out as many as you can before we meet in the middle. Hopper and Zeus, take the left side, Viper, you're with us."

"Roger that, Syxx," Taylor says as he and Gale turn off to the left sharply.

"Ten-four." Bensen adjusts his speed so he's lining up to be parallel to us.

I check the clip of ammo before looking over my shoulder and spotting the pursuing vehicles. "Here they come," I say with a knot in my throat.

"We got this, Squirt," Bensen says. His helmet tilts in my direction, and he nods reassuringly. He puts his hand to his waist and unhitches his pistol from its holster.

The small dirt road narrows as it winds around the lake, full of turns and divots. All I can do is hook an arm around Roman's chest and hold on for dear life.

Four bikers catch up to us first; their motorcycles are more like dirt bikes and allow them more control on these roads. The first shot that flies by my head makes me hold my breath.

Bensen lifts his arm and dares a look back as he returns fire.

He hits one of them in the shoulder, and the force of it knocks the man clean off his bike.

I swallow and tighten my grip on Roman's chest before I aim at the next one. He lifts his gun and shoots at us several times before I line up my shot and pull the trigger.

The bullet misses him but hits the fuel line on his bike. It makes a *tink* sound before it erupts into flames.

"Hold on!" Roman shouts as he revs his engine and speeds up as we hit a huge bump in the road. A scream tears out of me, and I wrap my arms around Roman's chest. We have a few seconds of airtime before the wheels are back on the ground.

Bensen lets out a victory sound as his bike lands behind us.

I look over my shoulder and have a manic smile curling my lips as I watch the motorcycle on fire hit the jump, and his bike explodes. Metal and fire scatter across the road and fall into the lake. His comrade crashes into the wreckage and gets sent off his bike, colliding with a tree and making a grotesque sound.

A laugh I don't recognize tears from my throat.

"Fucking Squirt for the kill!" Bensen cheers, and Roman's chuckle comes over the radio, making me more confident.

"Good job, Squirt, but we're not done yet." Roman's shared heads-up display zeros in on movement up ahead. It's Taylor and Gale, and they're still trying to shake one of the trucks.

A bullet whizzes past Bensen and he ducks, throwing his head back and firing off more shots behind us.

These guys are relentless. Two more file in from a fire trail ahead of us. Roman's arm is up before I can even try to get a shot off. He shoots twice and nails them each in the center of their visors.

"Holy shit!" I can't keep the awe from my tone. Who knew he had crazy accuracy like this. I've never even seen him fight.

Bensen laughs. "He's a lieutenant for a reason, Squirt." I don't know how he can talk so casually and drive while evading bullets.

I swallow my adrenaline and focus on shooting our last pursuer. One of us hits his chest, and he loses control of his bike, driving himself straight off the cliff and into the rocks and water below.

"Hopper, we're going to loop back to the front. I think I see them on the lake. Far right corner," Roman says calmly as he slams on his brakes and firmly plants his boot on the ground to pull us into a one-eighty turn. He nearly does a spinout on the gravel, kicking up a ring of dust as we lunge back toward the front of the lake.

"Show-off." Bensen sounds annoyed as he slowly turns around.

Roman laughs. "Keep up, Viper."

I stare off into the lake where Roman said he spotted them, and I can just barely make out the form of a boat.

We blow past the wreckage from the Sub-Rosa men and enter the flat part of the road before it banks around the lip of the lake where the docks are.

I narrow my eyes at something in the dirt ahead, but we're going too fast, and I realize what it is too late.

Roman sees it a moment too late too. He shouts as he banks to the left to evade the mine. "Viper, get off the road!"

Our motorcycle goes flying down the side of the cliff, toward the dark water below. Roman grabs on to me and kicks off his bike as hard as he can with me in his arms so we don't get crushed by it. I cling to Roman tightly and hold in my scream, hoping Bensen hears his warning.

"Wait, where did you go?" Bensen shouts in the headset, and a half second later a huge explosion shakes the sky as we plunge into the water.

"Bensen!" I scream, panicking as I watch the bright fire curl above. But my fear quickly turns to the water that's swallowing us whole. My helmet is filling up fast, and we're sinking.

Roman pulls me up and wraps his arm around my chest as he swims until we're back above water. It's difficult to move my limbs with the clothes weighing me down. Fear pounds louder than my pulse does.

He quickly takes my helmet off, and I sputter in the cold air as it sinks into my lungs. The water is frigid and makes my jaw clatter.

"B-Bensen," I stutter.

Roman's eyes are struck with pain, but he shakes his head. "I don't k-know, Briar. But we have t-to keep going." He's shivering too but drags me to the shore and props me up on a rock before pulling himself up.

My body curls into itself to try and warm up, but I straighten the moment I see a boat approaching us. "Roman!" I point out into the lake.

"*Fuck*, come on." Roman urges me to get up, and I struggle to my feet. "You have to start climbing." He helps me reach the first rock, but they are so spread out and slick. I try to get hold of the next one, but my hand slips.

A scream gets caught in my throat just as a hand extends down and clasps mine tightly. My head jerks back as my arm goes tight and my feet meet the rocks once more. My eyes widen.

"Oh my God, Bensen!" I cry, and tears are already streaming down my cheeks.

His helmet is broken, but other than that he seems fine. The second he pulls me up I throw my arms around his shoulders. "Thank God you're okay!"

He gives me a quick squeeze before letting me go and helping Roman up.

"Thanks to Syxx."

Roman pats his back. "You scared me for a second there, Viper."

Gunshots echo through the valley and snatch our attention back to the lake. The boat is getting closer, and on the road in the distance I see headlights flashing as they race through the trees. It must be Gale and Taylor. *Please let them be okay.*

"Still have that boat?" I throw the idea out there. Bensen and Roman share a look that makes me regret mentioning it.

———

Luckily Roman had the foresight to keep a few handguns stashed on their boat. I lost mine when we fell into the water, and Bensen dropped his when he leaped off his motorcycle.

We stay in the dark cover of bushes along the edge of the lake, waiting for Gale and Taylor. Bensen is the only one with a working helmet, and he's already called out to them a few times now.

Bensen takes it off and shakes his head. "I don't hear them. They aren't responding."

That doesn't make me feel good.

Roman nods. "We can't wait any longer, we need to get moving—" A bullet hits the side of Roman's neck and knocks him clean off the boat.

"Roman!" I scream and dive in after him.

The moon peeks out from the fading snowstorm and lights the water just enough for me to realize how much of Roman's blood I'm trying to see through to find him.

Where is he? Where… My heart drops when I spot him. His eyes are staring up at the moon, and bubbles escape his parted lips.

A rush of air bursts from my mouth as I swim toward him and quickly check his neck. It ricocheted off the bulletproof mesh.

Thank God.

I pull him to the surface where my relief is short-lived as we're met with Callum's crew on a large boat. Taylor, Bensen, and Gale are beaten and bloodied as they kneel at the edge of the boat, assault rifles aimed at the backs of their heads.

Horror hits me as I stare up and meet Callum's eyes. He gives me a timid smile before extending his hand down.

I shake my head and hold on to Roman tighter. I'm fighting with all I have just to keep us afloat and his head above water, and I know Callum won't show him mercy like he did last time.

"Let them think I'm out for the count," Roman murmurs against my ear. It occurs to me that Sub-Rosa doesn't know about Roman having an upper hand when it comes to bullets.

Thank God he's okay.

"Briar, I won't hurt him. Look, he's already half dead. It will only happen faster if you stay in the water." Callum squats at the edge, waiting for me to make a decision.

"Lift him first," I mutter.

Callum smiles as he nods. "I wouldn't dream of leaving the lieutenant out of the fate of his men."

I swallow the dread as Callum lifts Roman up to the boat and then reaches for me. I allow him to help me out and quickly move to Roman's side.

His eyes are shut, and he has the most peaceful expression even though I know he must be in so much pain right now. I want this to end already. Tears brim in my eyes.

I cover Roman's neck to stop the bleeding, even though it didn't hit an artery, and look up at Callum for help. If I can get him close enough, Roman can kill him.

It's so quiet on the boat that I can hear my own heart racing.

"Help him," I beg.

Callum flips his lighter and sparks his cigarette. "Why? So he can keep fucking up my life? Not a chance, babe."

I let my eyes shift to a man I've never seen before. He's dressed in an expensive suit and has a cane that looks like it's from a different time period. An heirloom maybe. My eyes widen when I look up at his face. He's handsome and has the coldest green eyes I've ever seen.

"Nolan's gotten sloppy. His soldiers just get worse as he sends them. Although I'm impressed he found Bane Falls," he says stiffly to Callum as he assesses us.

I wrap Roman in my arms and keep my hand firmly over his neck.

"I'm sorry, sir, this is not how I intended for you to meet Briar."

Wait, this is the boss? Chills spread over my arms, and the shivering gets so bad my teeth start to chatter again.

The man helps me up. I glare at him and shrink closer to Roman. He pauses and watches me closely. "May I check your neck?" he asks.

I nod, unsure if Roman will attack this man or not but prepare for it nonetheless.

He dips down and moves my wet hair enough to inspect the backside of my neck. A small scar is there, from the tracker, according to Grahm.

"Who removed this?" he asks Callum.

Callum lifts a brow. "The tracker? Grahm. He traded secrets with that sleeper agent before we took him out. We gave him the fake locations to the dark cities, and he gave us a box that lets you take those high-grade trackers out. It's how we got that one soldier last year before we left him in the field."

The boss narrows his eyes. "What was the man's name?"

316

"Arnold," I answer.

The man looks down at me, the scar over his eye is intimidating, but I don't find him to have any malice.

He nods and is about to say more when Roman thrusts his knife into Callum's ankle. Callum shrieks in pain, and the other Sub-Rosa men abandon their positions over the squad to help him.

Roman doesn't give Callum time to do anything; he's already on his feet with his fists up, the KA-BAR with the blade facing out in one hand. Callum puts all of his weight on his good leg as he jerks his hand up and fires his pistol. He's not even close to hitting Roman in his panicked state.

Roman takes advantage of that, ducking out of the way of the Sub-Rosa guard swinging his rifle at Roman's neck. They follow through too far and end up smacking one of their comrades in the back of the head and knocking them clean off the boat.

"Let's leave it to them, shall we?" I flinch as the boss speaks to me, grabbing my arm and guiding me to a small paddleboat tied off at the back. "Come, Briar."

He extends his gloved hand, and I hesitantly take it.

CHAPTER 39

ROMAN

Five of them left, including sack-of-shit Callum.

They're very insistent on protecting him, which only makes me that much more eager to kill him. I dodge away from a knife swipe and bury my blade into the man behind me. He chokes and reaches for his chest.

I kick him back and tear my knife out. It's slick with blood, and my grip is already not as tight as it would be. The metal mesh protected my vitals from that bullet, but with the cold air and blood loss, I'm already starting to lose my strength.

Gale manages to stand and shouts something that gets muffled by the gag around his mouth, but I understand what he's getting at. One of the Sub-Rosa guards does too and tries to kick Gale off the boat.

I don't have time to cut him free, so I chuck my knife at the guard. It pierces his neck, downing him, his throat gushing blood. *Jesus, that would've been me if I didn't have the full metal,* I muse.

Gale nods at me and quickly sets to cutting his binds with the part of the blade that's sticking out of the guy's throat.

Three left.

I turn my focus back to Callum a beat too late. His gun is lined up with my forehead, and a wicked smile curls his lips. He doesn't waste his breath saying stupid things like his grand design and his plan for my girl. He just pulls the trigger.

My head is thrown back violently.

I hear the sound of a hundred cries, from people I've killed—their begging and pained looks when they know I'm not letting them go.

Then I hear Briar. "Roman!"

I firmly plant my boot with a step back and catch myself from falling backward, snapping my eyes to the side and spotting her on a small boat with Callum's boss. Blood runs hot into my eye as I tilt my head in her direction.

"*What...* What the fuck?" Callum's voice quivers as he watches me straighten and pop my neck. "What the fuck are you?" he shouts as he lifts his gun once more.

I bring my forearm down on his elbow so hard that it pops out of its socket.

A manic smile spreads over my lips as I catch his gun and bring it to the bottom of his jaw. "I'm bulletproof, bitch."

*B*ang.

Roman shoots Callum beneath his jaw, and blood spurts from the top of his head. My heart pounds so hard that I don't know if the underworld boss says anything. If he does, I don't hear it.

Callum's body falls into the dark water.

My body shakes from shock and the cold.

Gale freed himself with the knife Roman threw into that man's neck and finishes cutting Taylor and Bensen free. The only two remaining Sub-Rosa guards stand at the edge of the boat, looking uncertain about how to proceed now that Callum is dead.

Roman's eyes instantly search for and lock on once he finds me.

The boss laughs. "I guess we'd better get back before he jumps in to come after you." I hesitantly look at him and nod.

It's weird; he doesn't seem bothered at all by this. By his own men being slaughtered. He almost seems more…entertained.

Doesn't he care?

Roman doesn't let his intense gaze lift from us until the boat is touching theirs. I quickly climb up and take his hand. I stare up at his face with my heart in my throat. His forehead has a small gash where the bullet ricocheted off. His face is covered in blood, his own and Callum's.

I choke on my tears. I'm so fucking relieved that he's okay.

Roman's eyes soften, and a weak grin moves over his lips as he sinks to his knees with me in his arms. I wrap my arms around him tightly, intending to never let go.

"I guess we don't have to worry about your ex showing up at the grocery store," Roman says cruelly with a raspy laugh that puts a terrible grin on my lips.

"You're sick." I laugh, bringing my face to his.

He flinches and pulls back. "Briar, I'm covered in blood. I don't want—"

I kiss the words from his lips. "I don't care," I whisper and gently press my hand to his cheek.

Roman's brows knit and he leans in, kissing me softly. "I'm sorry for what I am, Briar. I'm sorry that I let you hurt when you needed me to believe in you." Tears drip from his chin and stain my wrists.

My lower lip trembles with his heartfelt words.

"I don't want to alter any of the scars I get when they're for you." He looks up at me, weariness and hope moving through him like a sickness.

A broken smile that makes me feel whole again.

"I wouldn't dare rewrite our scars," I murmur back.

We share another kiss, and for a moment there's no one else around. It's just us and the quiet lake as the snow falls slowly.

"Jesus fucking Christ, just say you love each other like normal people," Taylor snaps, and it makes us both jolt.

They're all watching us. Gale and Bensen have the Sub-Rosa men tied up, with the exception of the boss who stands at the edge of the boat, staring down at Callum's floating body.

Roman chuckles and slowly stands, helping me up and keeping my body pressed close to his. It makes my cheeks warm knowing that he doesn't want to let go of me either.

"I guess Callum won't be meeting with the general tomorrow," Bensen says smugly. The man with the cane slowly turns and regards all of us.

"Nolan didn't care to meet with Callum. It's me he wanted to speak with, and Nolan always gets his way. He's waiting at the docks," he says as his eyes move to the shore.

I stare into the dark, unable to see anything that far off. *How can he see that far?*

"Who are you?" I ask as I take in his slight limp as he walks over to the steering wheel and adjusts it so we're aiming for the shore.

He grins at me. "The king of the underworld, some say."

Roman narrows his eyes at him distrustfully. "You were… one of us. How else would you know Nolan?"

The man laughs. "Not so surprising, is it? Let's see what Nolan wants so we can be done with this senseless fight. I'm not interested in letting Bane Falls sink just because of that evil old man. It's taken almost a decade to have this town in my grasp."

We sit in silence as the boat moves toward the docks. Gale wraps Roman's neck with some cloth he tears from the guard's shirts and cleans most of the blood from his face.

I stare at each of them, grateful that they're not too hurt. My throat tightens when I think of John, tears brim in my eyes, and I have to rein in my emotions for now. There will be time to grieve John, but I need to know why all of this has happened.

Just as the man said, Nolan is waiting on the dock, dressed in tactical gear with a rifle slung behind his back. He's smoking a cigar and doesn't have any expression when we pull up to the dock.

"Icarus, head to the base," Nolan says without even looking in our direction.

"General, we're not leaving until we get answers," Roman fires back, although it's evident he's exhausted, cold, and weak. I'm sure everyone else is feeling the same way because I sure as hell am.

Nolan looks at him, sparing me a slight look before letting his eyes move back to Roman.

"You will get them, Syxx. Take Briar back and patch yourself up… Pick up Bishop too. I'll return in the morning."

Roman holds his hostile gaze for a few moments before taking a deep breath and resigning. "All right."

The five of us stand around the table where we placed John. We each said our goodbyes, mine shorter than the rest because I didn't know him nearly as well. But my heart hurts all the same.

Gale and Taylor cry over his body. Bensen looks like he's about to pass out from holding in his tears. But Roman stands there and stares down at his friend and squadmate, something deeply altering inside his mind from the loss. I can see it in the way his jaw feathers and his eyes fill with disdain. The darkness inside him craves to be let out. Callum wasn't enough. None of it was.

I head downstairs to shower while the squad wraps John's body in sheets and puts him somewhere cold until he can be properly buried.

I think about that for a long time while I wash the dirt and blood from my skin. I know exactly what it's like to be buried, and the idea of bright, beautiful John being alone in the ground hurts.

Roman returns after a half hour and showers much faster than I did. He doesn't do well when he's left alone with his thoughts, his scar-altering habit is evidence of that. I watch him wrap his neck and put a new dressing on his forehead before he shuts off the lights and crawls into bed behind me.

Light is already seeping in from the windows, morning is nearly here, but I'm so tired even five minutes of rest would do.

Roman pulls me close and buries his face in the back of my head. We don't share any words. We don't have to. His warmth seeps into me and mine into him.

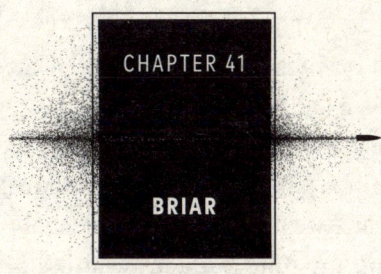

CHAPTER 41

BRIAR

A sharp knock comes at the door, and a very tired looking Taylor pokes his head in.

"The general is back."

Roman groans and props himself up with one arm. "Be out in a sec." Taylor shuts the door, and Roman glances down at me with sleepy eyes. "Ready?" He brushes my hair from my face and presses a kiss to my cheek.

"Nope." I kiss him right back, and he offers a sad smile.

Everyone is waiting in the garage portion of the shop. Gale and Taylor are sitting on the sofa while Bensen leans against the wall beside it. Nolan stands in the center of the room in the same attire he wore last night.

I'm a little shocked to see him so put together. I half expected him to be dead or beat to shit. The guy with the cane looked more than capable.

He regards us with a slight head nod and waits until Roman

returns with two chairs from the meeting room for me and him to sit on.

"Well? Did you get your dark cities like you wanted?" Roman asks in an annoyed tone.

Nolan grins and nods. "Yes, in a way, I did." His voice is cold and smooth, a familiar sound that both makes me shudder and curious. Have we met before? I think about it but come up blank. "Roman, my time as the general has been reaching its expiration date. I'm sure you've noticed, as has Captain Bridger, I'm fucking tired. Too tired to steal the youth from recruits and tired of playing all these senseless games with our corrupt system. The Forces are a young man's campaign."

The general's eyes find me, and they make me still.

"You always reminded me of her, of Private Gallows," Nolan says, sounding nostalgic. It makes me uncomfortable since I have no idea who this Gallows person is. "Your resilience in the face of cruel men and their bad manners. Maybe it's why I chose you to begin with." He lets out a long breath.

What does that mean? Chose me? I don't think I've met this man before. I look at the others and find them all staring at me with knitted brows. They know something that I don't.

"What is he talking about?" I ask Roman.

He squeezes my hand and looks at me tenderly. "You're like me, Briar. You're…" He lets his words trail off and swallows thickly a few times. Pain lingers in his gaze, and he won't look me in the eyes.

"Project Lethe," Nolan answers for him.

Lethe? Why does that word make the back of my neck prickle. It's almost as if my body and subconscious mind know more than I do.

My eyes widen and I shake my head, confused at what this psychopath is getting at. "What does that mean?"

Nolan walks up to me and tilts my jaw with his cold hand until I meet his eyes. "It means that you've been in the Dark Forces' care for many years, Briar. We've fed you stories and fake memories as if they were sweet dreams. A life you never truly had. And yet, you of all the other candidates, remained whole during the process. Your humanity stayed intact, and you always leaned on love. The perfect sleeper."

That…can't be true. My memories aren't artificial, I remember my parents so vividly—my jaw flexes when I try to picture their faces. It's like a hazy photograph of strangers. Faces blurred, and I can't pull any specific features from them.

I look at Roman. "He's lying… That's not true."

Roman's brows pinch, and his eyes linger on my neck. "Tell me where you were when you were on the run from Callum. It was months ago, right? Where did you go after Seattle but before you came here?" He gently rubs his thumb over the back of my hand with empathetic eyes.

I open my mouth to reply but come up blank. I blink a few times. Where did I go… *I was on the move. Wait, no. I was… I was…*

"You don't know, do you? You only remember driving into town." Nolan's voice skates across my nerves, sending chills over my arms and a pit in my stomach.

"But… I remember my father, he passed away." I sound like I'm not sure, because the more I think about it the fuzzier everything is. Is that why I feel nothing when it comes to the death of them? But that would make me…

Lethe. I hear the name clearly in the recesses of my mind.

"And your entire family, too, isn't that right? Do you remember any of them? What job did you have in Seattle before meeting Callum?" the general asks as he walks slowly back to the center of the room.

I'm quiet. So is everyone else.

"Oh my God." I swallow the dread in my throat. Because I can't remember. "Who...am I?" I stare down at my hands, studying the scars in a new light. Many of them I have no recollection of how I got them. My throat tightens, and tears brim in my eyes.

Roman runs his hand through my hair. "You're Briar Thornton."

I blink and look up at him. I don't feel like anyone else except me. Even if my memories are fake, it doesn't rob the warmth of them. The diner with my dad and gardening with my mom... Even if it's fake, like an altered scar, it's a story that let me keep my heart.

"Briar Thornton isn't real," I choke the words out with a teary smile.

Roman offers a gentle smile that warms my soul. "Neither is Roman Syxx."

He pulls me in and wraps his arms around me in a tight embrace. *We really are man-made monsters.*

Nolan pulls five black dog tags with *DF* engraved on them from his pocket and holds them out toward us. "Lieutenant Roman Syxx. I am hereby announcing my retirement from the Dark Forces, and your promotion into the role of the commanding general."

Roman's eyes widen, and he stands abruptly from his chair. The metal clanks loudly against the floor. "What? No, you said we'd get our freedom. Not put me into another position." He doesn't sound angry, more shocked.

"You may walk free, if it's what you truly want. What do I care? I'm done, but Roman, the Dark Forces are evolving—just as the world around us is. With you as the commanding general of the new branch, think of the possibilities."

Bensen pushes off the wall and walks to stand beside Roman. "New branch?"

"A new Under base." Nolan sounds perfectly diabolical.

Roman's eyes widen with realization. "That's why you wanted the gate here? For a new boot camp base?" Roman says scathingly and throws his hands in the air. "We lost two soldiers out here, for what?!" he shouts, and his voice is only amplified by the room.

Nolan keeps his expression flat. "That's right. A new one where I know things will be done differently, under different conditions, and who better to lead it than you?"

Roman freezes. His arms are trembling, and his fists are curled tightly at his sides.

Gale and Taylor stand and join us. "Does Captain Bridger know about this?" Gale asks suspiciously.

"Who do you think gave the operation a go from the moment I started to arrange you boys being sent out here? Arnold was our scout, and he got too close—he wanted the secrets for himself so he could get out. But all he did was prolong the inevitable and get himself killed." Nolan taps his cigar, and a big chunk of ash falls to the cement. "It wasn't easy to convince my old friend to let us use his town. But we came to an agreement: Bane Falls will be our link between worlds. The soldiers here will be trained differently than that of the Under Trials, and you'll work with the underworld rather than against them."

Old friend? He's talking about Callum's boss. How do they know one another? My mind whirls with how deep Nolan is weaved into such sinister things in this world. Work with them? But…they do bad things.

I look at Roman and the squad—I guess they do bad things too.

"Why did you do this? Why didn't you just retire, general? We lost so much…" Taylor asks with a broken voice.

Nolan's eyes don't give even an ounce of pity. "Because I didn't lose a goddamn thing. I got what I wanted: I finally put the Dark Forces' foot in the door of the underworld and put some of my worst regrets to rest."

Roman's jaw flexes with fury, and he steps toward Nolan. "Your legacy will only be your lies, general."

Nolan laughs and hands Roman the dog tags. They each have a skull with *DF* engraved on them. "Your new rankings and clearances have been recorded on these. Captain Bridger will be sending men to help establish the new base in a month's time."

"*Our* new rankings and clearances?" Bensen asks.

"That's right. You can leave the perimeter around Bane Falls freely now," Nolan explains with a wry smirk. "My legacy is all of you. Whether you like it or not. Dead or alive. I crafted *all* of you from the criminals you came to me as. Don't forget what you all are. The heinous things you did to find yourselves down in the dark to begin with. I set up this world for you, and whether or not you take it is up to you. But I know you, Roman, and I know Briar and all of Icarus. You are all made to thrive in the dark."

Roman's eyes are wide, and he's at a loss for words. Nolan pats Roman's arm and looks at each of us before he turns and heads for the exit.

"One of their men is waiting at the burned-down farm when you're ready." Nolan stops at the door and looks back at all of us.

"General Syxx, I wish you a long and successful campaign." He gives Roman a cruel grin and a slight nod.

Then he leaves, and we're left standing in silence.

"What the fuck just happened?" Taylor says as he throws his hat on the ground.

"Give me a second, guys." Roman threads his fingers through mine and pulls me back downstairs and locks the door to his room.

I sit on the edge of his bed and look up at him expectantly.

"Briar… Are you okay?" he asks and kneels in front of me. I know what he's asking me, and honestly I'm not so sure if I am or not.

I'm human, but everything about me and who I am is fake. How many times have they reset me? Can I get my memories back someday? My lips firm, and I stare at the ground. Do I even want them back? There's no telling how that could affect me.

But when I look into Roman's perfect hazel eyes, then to all the scratches and wounds over his face, the bandage over his forehead and neck, the scars he's given himself and the ones he hasn't, I realize something.

We never asked for these things—the pain, the hurt, the trauma—but we still found each other. We're still here. Altered, but maybe that's why we long for each other, why we seem to have an underlying bond.

I'm still me…whatever that really means in the grand scheme of things. Would I have known who I really was even if I didn't have my memories manipulated? Would I know any more about who I am at my core than I already do now?

I know that I love Roman and that he loves me. I'm not sure much else really matters more than that.

Roman lost his humanity when he knew every bit of his haunted past.

I kept my humanity when mine was stolen away.

A wounded smile creeps across my lips, and I cup Roman's face in my hands.

"Yeah, I think I am."

His gaze tells me that he's not sure I'm telling the truth and that he'll be bugging me more about it later, but he nods. "I'm so sorry. I didn't know about any of it until earlier yesterday. I didn't know what Nolan did to you." He bites his lip and shakes his head as if it's his fault this was my fate. "But a sick part of me is happy that we ended up this way. I love you exactly as you are." His smile tugs at my heartstrings.

"The only difference is that you knew what he was making you into and I didn't," I say gently. "You carry a much heavier weight." I wrap my arms around his shoulders and pull him in for a tight hug. "I love you, Roman. I don't want my memories to be anything but you and what we make ourselves from here on out."

He makes a lovely humming sound. "You feed the possessive heart I have for you, Squirt." He holds me close and whispers, "I know this sounds so fucked up, but I think I want this, Briar. I want to be the new general... Maybe I can be better than Nolan ever was." Roman doesn't sound like he wants to do right by anyone.

I pull back and look into his grim eyes. I find anger and hope dancing across his gaze. A malicious mind that only cares about his few comrades and me.

"Better at creating man-made monsters?" I whisper.

There was darkness in Roman from the very first night we met. That darkness always called to me. I see it now, swallowing his conscience whole and tempting him with the same power Nolan had.

Roman's eyes heat at my question, and he leans in to steal a kiss. His answer is concise, pupils dilating for a twisted future he's already picturing for us. "Yes."

What will be left of Bane Falls once our darkness takes root?

READ ON TO
DISCOVER A
SNEAK PEEK OF

LEAVE ME
BEHIND

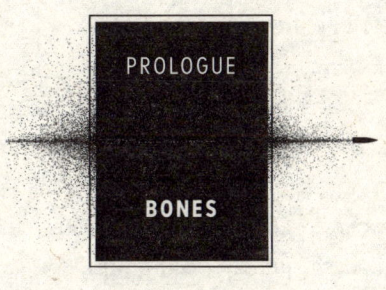

PATAGONIA, TWO YEARS AGO

Abrahm's eyes are blurry with dark blood. I try to wipe the red streams from his cheeks with my sleeve, but it flows relentlessly from the gash on the side of his head. His blond-brown hair that was always so bright is now burgundy and streaked with the call of death. Dirt and rocks cling to the stickiness of his skin. Panic flashes through me; it's through sheer will that I force the planes of my face to remain smooth and emotionless.

"B-Bones."

My chest grows heavy with the weakness that draws out his whiny breaths. The way his fingers tremble as he reaches for me. His black gloves are drowned in blood. I bury my teeth into my lower lip to quell the agony that seeps into my throat.

"I'm here, Abrahm." I shut my eyes to stave off the despair.

"I'm—" He coughs and blood splatters across my mask. I don't blink. "S-scared." His green eyes are murky-yellow with red liquid, waning as death clings to him. I shakily remove my gloves and press my cold palm to his cheek.

Shit. We weren't supposed to be here, not like this. Riøt Squad was supposed to meet us at the checkpoint. Where the fuck were they? I duck as bullets pelt into the dry terrain and kick up dust around us.

Abrahm's chest gapes with a hole right next to his heart, the heat of his flesh quickly fleeing him. *Goddammit.* I lift my head and search through the smoke for the rest of our squad. Only three lifeless hostiles lie motionless in the clearing. I killed them mercilessly, cruelly, like I'd been taught to, but they aren't the ones who shot my second. They aren't responsible for his dwindling life. The bullet went straight through his vest and must be a higher grade.

My fists clench. Why didn't he stay back like I told him to? *Goddammit.*

The rest of my squad is firing back and securing the area, but it will be too late. I've witnessed many men die. I know when there's far too much damage. Abrahm isn't going to make it, and I find myself incapable of leaving his side. There are protocols I need to follow, and the mission isn't complete yet, but it doesn't seem to matter to me like it once did. Not now that he's going to die. I let my eyes fall closed and, with trembling hands, take my mask off slowly.

A face that no one is supposed to know. *I want him to know.*

I open my eyes and look down at him.

Abrahm's eyes widen, brows pinching weakly together with concern. "Bones, you shouldn't—" He tries to reach his hand up to cover my face, but he can't even lift his arm now. I catch his falling hand.

"Bradshaw."

His weary eyes are shutting slowly, but a small grin spreads over his chapped lips.

"My name is Bradshaw." My voice is a mere whisper, but I know he hears it.

Abrahm draws his final breath, and it sounds like a sigh of relief. It doesn't at all sound like the last noise he'll ever make.

His eyes are still on me, hazed over now but seeing straight through me.

The light has gone.

And vengeance is born into my heart.

ABOUT THE AUTHOR

K.M. Moronova is a dark fantasy and romance author. She lives in Montana with her partner, two dogs, and three cats. She loves drinking tea and writing stories with worlds that she can get completely swept into. Her favorite characters are the misunderstood villains.

Website: kmmoronova.com
TikTok: @K.M.Moronova
Facebook: K.M. Moronova
Instagram: @K.M.Moronova
Threads: @K.M.Moronova